Brit

23 July 06

Lights Out! Game Ova!

Let your joy and energy
shock the world to a
higher state of readiness!

J. Matti

www.j-matti.com

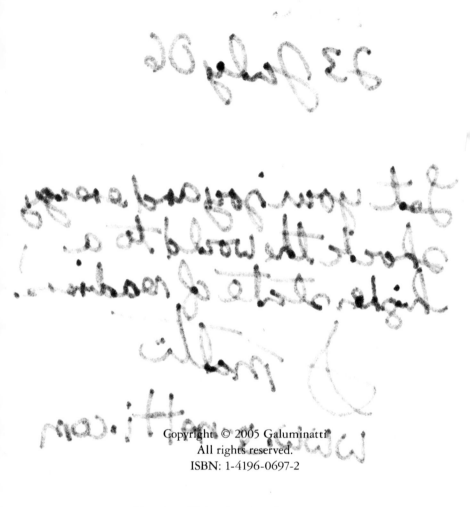

To order additional copies, please contact us.
BookSurge, LLC
www.booksurge.com
1-866-308-6235
orders@booksurge.com

GALUMINATTI

LIGHTS OUT!
GAME OVA!

2005

Lights Out! Game Ova!

I like to dedicate this book to my loved ones whom I have lost recently due to unexpected deaths. I dedicate this book to my grandmother, Minnie B. Fennell, my father, Willie Bear Fennell, and my two aunts, Carolyn and Isabelle Fennell Smith who all seemingly departed before their time. I thank these loved ones for sparking the fire within me to write and to do it to the best of my ability. Your motivation is still alive within me as I set out to deliver to the public the best product my talents will allow. I thank you for your contribution to my life and may God continue to bless you as you have already arrived on the bright side. I thank you and owe my life to you!

CHAPTER 1
Feeling My Way

It was a nice sunny day in Houston, Texas where a brother was trying to just chill out, recover from the headaches of the week, and make a dollar or two to pay some bills. Wow! Friday came so fast.

As a real estate agent at Star Top Reality, I had to bring my "A" game to work everyday, nonstop. Star Top was a very lucrative, busy, and predominantly Caucasian realtor group that definitely cornered the market on real estate sales here in Houston.

On this particular day, I had to show about four houses and do some paperwork in the office then the weekend was mine. Well, to a degree, as I had to show a couple of houses on Saturday and sponsor an open house on Sunday.

The view of the sky was clear on the 249 Beltway headed south past Jersey Village, leaving my pukka, luxury condo in Westfield and headed to Star Top Realty in Magnolia Park. While driving I was trying to decide whether or not to purchase a couple of foreclosed houses as investment property that were located in The Woodlands, which was a very nice suburban subdivision in North Houston. I found myself wrestling with either the idea of paying off all my bills or just jumping right off into investing.

I was feeling real good today after lifting weights and working out on my stationary bike for about 90 minutes on last night. I got my 8.5 hours of sleep and I was ready for the world in the big metropolitan area that was booming in every corner. Two weeks in Texas, after relocating from Ocala, Florida, was starting to pay off for me, as I was fully situated and ready to make that paper.

At twenty-five years old, standing about six feet tall and weighing about two hundred and thirty pounds, this single brother was ready to explore Houston. By no means did I consider myself fat but I was equipped with large thigh, arm, and shoulder muscles and a little too much junk in my trunk as well as a step above having a beer belly. While almond black in complexion with a crisp and shiny baldhead, you would think my skin color seemed more of a liability in these parts of the world. Nevertheless, I was easily forgiven for my looks because I drove a Lexus! *Can I get an Amen on that?*

It was a two-door sports coupe, beige interior and dark black exterior. I could barely afford the car but it complimented my nice Armani and Hugo Boss suits that I wore, which placed my business look on a totally higher plateau than I could afford. *Hey, how could I sell houses if I'm driving a car that needs Pimp My Ride care and dress like I'm a loser? U feel me?*

Besides, in the real estate business, first impressions were not merely lasting impressions but quite frankly could be the only impressions, as those would be buyers might not care to see anything you have to show, if you were improperly attired. I had my BVLGARI watch on, my Robert Lee Morris silver bracelet and my head was freshly shaved, with a diamond stud earring to boot on my left ear. My car was just recently washed and waxed and the Armor All had the tires talking. My car stereo was thumping the sounds of *Styles P and Floetry*, playing the song "I'm Black" over and over again. That was somewhat of an inspirational song for me because it reminded me of the origin of our roots as a people, reminded me of the daily struggle that we faced, thereby ignited my daily fire to stay hungry for success.

I guess in all actuality I was somewhat of a sad case, coming from Florida all banged up by love. Nevertheless, although in the past I had consumed much music that had reminded me of negative times, this song kept me anxious for the daily challenges that life would birth everyday. Despite my past, I had finally reached a point where I had vowed to myself that I would be optimistic and happy. Therefore, on this day I was feeling good, looking good, and I was somewhat ready to get busy.

First up was a 9 am appointment with the Clowers, a young, affluent couple who was interested in buying a house in a nicely gated community known as Brentwood. It was a very choice neighborhood with the best schools, churches, outdoor, and indoor recreation facilities and all the luxuries of finer living. The house was listed at $785K and if I could net a sale, a brother could relax for a minute and enjoy the proceeds of the purchase.

This was another reason why I left Florida to come to Houston, so I could expand my earning potential and gain a lot more experience with the big leagues of the real estate industry. For I was very impressed with the company I worked for and they were letting a brother show some very marquee houses. Back in Florida working for "Leave the Hood If You Could Realty" I would never get the opportunity to show the kinds of houses I was showing in Texas.

My new boss was a very nice Caucasian lady who actually screened my resume and hired me. I think I impressed her after I arrived by how fast I passed the state real estate exam. Then again, who am I kidding? I am nothing but a realtor of this company as a result of affirmative action. For I often had to tell myself to remember that I was a black man.

Regardless, I busted my behind studying for that state exam and thank God I passed it. Texas was very different from Florida when it came to real estate laws. Unfortunately, my life here in Texas had been very secluded with not much of a social life. When I left Florida, I was determined to leave a lot of drama and confusion behind. Once again, I was a single brother who had been an absolute victim of love. Women had hurt my feelings so many times that I was actually afraid of true commitment and love.

Facing that reality, I have buried myself into my job and did not have any desires to get involved with any women, not on a serious level anyway. Now, let me set the record straight! I am not gay, nor am I one of them brothers on the "down low." I was a straight-laced brother with a little charm, so I thought. No! I'm no Denzel Washington, Shermar Moore, nor Morris Chestnut. I was just an average brother with simple thoughts and a normal perspective on life.

When I left Florida I left a whole lot of casual relationships and terminated friendships with lots of people. Right now, my mom was the only one that had my cell phone number, as I had not even gotten a residence number. Mom called every now and then to ask me if she could give my number to some of my old friends, as well as calling to check on me. I constantly told her "no" and that if she did give out my number I would change my number and refuse to give it to her again. I love both my mom and dad, but of course dad was never around. He was always too busy chasing somebody else's dream to where he had deprived his own family of sufficient time to know and love him.

Anyway, back to my first showing today. I pulled up to

the office about 8:50am just in time to meet the Clowers. I did a cameo pass with my boss and she complimented my fragrance. I told her thanks for the compliment and I gave her my itinerary for the day and she in a very subtle manner asked me to check back with her after my last showing of the day. "Yes Ma'am, no problem," I said to her.

"Jamie, don't ever call me Ma'am again. You make me feel so old. Call me Julie and that is my last warning," she said.

Wow, she actually lifted her eyeglasses above her eyelids when she said that. "Okay Julie, got it," I responded.

Now, my boss was a gorgeous brunette who stood about six feet tall in her heels with nice, long hair and very nice features. She was probably about thirty-five years old and seemed to be a very happily married woman. Her husband was a big time businessman who was a corporate regional manager with a local building industry. My boss was built like a sista. She had the thick lips, bootylicious hips, and showcased a nice rack in which her distinct cleavage set her apart from the rest. Her legs were nicely toned with thighs and calves that seemed to be gifts from above. Last but not least, her backyard was as nice as any video hoochie momma on BET.

I liked my boss for several reasons but the most significant one was that she gave me very constructive feedback. For instance, she told me when I arrived that I needed to flatten my belly and that I should wear my contacts instead of my eyeglasses. She said that potential buyers liked good-looking people and if they happen to study the eyes of a real estate agent, they wanted to see and feel nothing but sincerity and honesty. She further showed me how people can be overly sensitive when it came to spending their money. Potential buyers were looking for reasons to buy but they were also prone to detect the smallest sign of discomfort that could discourage them from working with a realtor.

Now, her most important feedback was telling me that I look real sexy in my car with my Oakley shades on and my diamond earring, glowing like a macho lover. *Hello somebody! U feel me?* However, she also told me that I did not have to seek to impress clients with artificiality. Where that came from, I had no clue! *Okay, perhaps I did have a clue.*

"JR, you must bring an authentic personality to the real estate fight," she asseverated.

In addition, she seemed impressed with how I kept my car clean and she also emphasized that as long as I followed her leadership, I would be able to afford my car and more. She had a convincing way of making me believe every word she said and she spoke straight without hesitation. Therefore, I had complied with all her suggestions. Well, the only suggestion that I really did not like was the one where she wanted me to wear white shirts all the time with my suits. I hated wearing white shirts all the time. Initially, I must admit I thought that her pleading was a mere subtle push from the so-called white morality community. The community where they emphasized that white was right and everyone had to conform. *Boy! Was I ever wrong?*

The only other slight irritation that she posed was that she kept calling me by my first name, Jamie, which only my mom normally called me that name. My full name was Jamie Randell Carter. I asked her to call me JR but she kept calling me Jamie. On one note, I wanted to call her Ma'am again just so she would correct me because she did not like me calling her Ma'am. Therefore, I devised a plan in my mind. The next time that she was to correct me about calling her Ma'am, I would remind her to call me JR.

Anyway, I sat down in my office and I immediately got a phone call from Mrs. Clowers. She informed me that they were running thirty minutes late but they still wanted to see the house. Thus, she wanted to know if I would still be available. I assured her that I was here for them and I had hours prior to my next appointment. *Hey! I was no fool. This appointment with them was my barbecue of the day.*

I understand that the Clowers' actually discovered the house via the company's Internet web site and my boss graciously hooked me up with them. Why? I really don't know because I thought the salesman of the year would get all the big jobs but once again, I was new here to this company and this may not have been such a big job. It was just too early to tell right now.

At about 9:30am my desk phone buzzed from the telephone call of the office secretary. Actually, Rosie was the office secretary for most all the realtors. She rang to tell me that Mrs. Clowers had arrived. I grabbed my suite coat and rushed down the hallway to meet the Clowers. As I arrived at the secretary's desk and I looked immediately for the Clowers, I saw what would change my whole perspective on life at a moment's notice.

There, standing at the desk was one stunningly, beautiful, breathtaking woman that literally made me somewhat nervous. I would have never imagined Mrs. Clowers to be a black woman. She had a mahogany colored face with big vibrant eyes, long eyelashes curving up towards the sky, puckered cheeks and black coruscating hair laid like velvet with strands of it falling across the corner of her left eye. Her lips were delicately designed with bright red lipstick and she was like a popular painting that had been brought to life.

"Hi Mrs. Clowers, my name is Jamie Carter but please call me JR."

"Hi JR," she said. "Please call me Veronica."

"Will Mr. Clowers be joining us as well?" I said.

"No JR, my husband was not able to make it today."

In my mind, I said, *DAMN!* You see in the real estate business you always want to show to the breadwinner and the decision maker. In my vast experience, showing a house to one as opposed to both partners meant the possibility of showing the house again to the one with the purse strings. Oftentimes, the purse strings belonged to the man, when showing a house to a couple. But, the decision to buy was often leveraged by the woman.

"Okay Veronica, that's fine! We can head on out to the house if you are ready?"

"JR, can I ride along with you as opposed to driving myself? I have no idea how to get to Brentwood," replied Veronica.

"Sure thing Veronica! I'm parked right out front. Let me gather my clip board and we can press forward."

I went to get my brief case, which contained my clipboard. Hey! *Shortie wanna ride wit me,* I thought to myself. I had no problem whatsoever riding with this marvelous work of art. I returned and Veronica and I got into my car. Like a gentleman, I opened the door for her and boy did her body movements turn me on.

When she sat down, her thighs showcased a great demand for attention and they seemed to be so tasty looking. It was as though they slapped a brotha in the face back and forth. She had on a dark, black mini dress without stockings that really displayed all her curves. She had dark, high heel shoes with a nice, quaint, black Marco Polo purse. Her voice was terribly soft and her perfume was the balm of my car.

The trip to Brentwood was about a thirty-minute drive.

Initially pulling out the parking lot, I focused my attention on driving and I was somewhat distracted by the nice, gray Jaguar that Veronica had driven to the office. She had diamond earrings, diamond necklace, and a big fat diamond wedding ring. Money was written all over her. All I wanted to do was concentrate on the house. In real estate, you will find that buyers can be bigger con artists than the real estate agents. Buyers will flash all their money before you as though they have a lot, but I would never really find myself impressed until the credit check on their account matched the money they flaunted. Believe it or not, but many buyers purchase beyond their means or seek to buy beyond their means. I was rather naïve to this fact until I started working in this business and saw how families would lose their homes to foreclosures or various forms of distressed property acquisitions.

In this business, my loyalty was to the customer and I would show every house to anyone who so desired, regardless of his or her economic status. This was one reason why I answered my cell phone immediately as I would get calls as well as return phone calls of would be buyers right away. I did not demand a pre-approved bank loan like many of my fellow real estate agents demanded. Also, I worked for the seller as well as the buyer in terms of real estate transactions but never during the same transaction. I also returned calls on a same day basis as opposed to waiting 24 to 48 hours like my colleagues did. To me, time was money and money was time. Customers were not wasting my time by calling and asking questions, and that sentiment was a reflection of my positive attitude towards the business. Although I did enforce the client privilege status, I never turned away the questions of a possible customer just because he had another agent.

In addition, I tried not to judge or measure the spending

availability of a customer based on his displayed persona or wealthy profile. For I was the last man to judge anyone, therefore, I showed houses to all on an equal basis. My mom always told me to treat everybody the same and don't show preferential treatment to anyone because of their status.

Anyway, Veronica seemed different than the customers I previously described. She seemed real. She wore the money; the money was not wearing her. Veronica thought my car was nice and I told her not as nice as that Jaguar. Since the drive was somewhat distant, we did engage in fruitful conversation. She basically asked me how long had I been in Houston, where was I from, and did I like the area. She saw one of my business cards on the dashboard and she asked me where I had them made. I told her everything she wanted to know. I did try to impress her but I did not lie to her, at least not at first. I told her I was a young brotha barely making it from bill to bill and all the niceties (leased car, Armani suits, and jewelry) were merely pieces for the stage presence.

Veronica was very attentive and I could tell she was very smart. She told me she was 29 years old and was a forensic scientist. She was married, going on 10 years, to a heart surgeon. I was really surprised that she was sharing all this information with me, as if I really cared. But once again, I don't tend to be totally impressed with obvious money until after their credit check is done. Also, in this business, some people will flat out tell you every lie under the sun just to impress you. More than anything, I was enjoying the conversation. She really captivated my attention by the way she crossed her legs. *Phew! She had the nicest, most delicately carved thighs that a brotha had not seen for dayz.* That was no joke at all.

Finally, we arrived at Brentwood. She asked me a thousand questions, it seemed, about the house. It was truly a nice house with 3800 square feet of mere elegance. Veronica really liked the front yard, back yard, and the cathedral ceilings. The rooms were perfect for her and her husband. The master bedroom was clearly a masterpiece and it was huge with a secluded balcony, a bathroom with a sauna/jacuzzi and the works. Veronica fell in love with the house. She was like a kid in the candy store and she really adored the three-car garage and security entrance and the space for her and her husband. She did quiz me with an honest question too.

"JR, tell me one honest feature that you do not like about this house," Veronica said.

That was a tough question for me but I answered without hesitation. I told her that the front and back yards were too much grass for me to cut and she busted out laughing. I told her that I would love to live in a house like this when I had a family, but as for now it would be too much house for me both in price and size. She took pictures inside and outside the house with her digital camera. She took so many pictures that her camera's battery went dead. We must have spent about 45 minutes to an hour at the house and she seemed very interested and so I was feeling good about the visit overall.

As we were getting ready to depart, she asked me how many houses had I sold since I had been in Houston. Now, this was where realtor showmanship came into play. I told her that I had sold three houses already and that I was likely to sell two of the four I was showing today and that I did not include this house that I was showing her. I lied. I just did not want to tell her that I had not sold any houses. I did not think it would look good. I felt bad about it but I wanted to impress her because I really had nothing to showcase my efforts. Anyway, she told me that I should be more confident in myself and believe that I will sell every house I show. *Yeah right!* I thought to myself of such a Pollyannaish perspective.

"JR, if you don't believe you are going to sell the house, how can you convince a customer to buy? Think about it," she said.

She was right in every respect but I just wanted to sound modest to her. As I finished with the lockbox and got into the car, she asked me if I had time for lunch. *Look here yawl, momma ain't raise no fool.* "Why of course I do, that is if you are treating a brotha?" I paused to see her reaction and then I quickly said, "I'm just kidding Veronica."

"Well JR, I'm the one that asked so I should be treating, fair enough?"

Hey, she ain't got to tell me twice. Besides, she was the one looking to buy almost a million-dollar house not me. If she could afford that, surely she could afford to spend $10 to $15 on a brotha for lunch. What yawl think? Anyway, we stopped at a nearby restaurant on the way back to the office. At the restaurant, I was slightly nervous and she noticed it.

"JR, why are you so nervous?"

"Well, I normally don't have lunch with my customers and if Mr. Clowers walked up, it could make for an uncomfortable position for me."

"JR, you have nothing to worry about. Trust me!"

We continued with lunch and I treated upon my insistence. I really don't know why I did, other than feeling obligated to treat. Heck, I only had about $25 in my wallet. Nevertheless, I did the gentlemanly thing.

As we were leaving, she dropped her lipstick and bent over right in front of me. *WOW!* I thought to myself *TADDOWW!* She had a backyard for dayz that was clearly worth dying for. Her butt was juicy, big, and round. She bent over right in front of me and for a moment I wanted to get ghetto and jump all over that booty. The realtor had lost his mind for a split second. I just wanted to squeeze that nice charmon of hers but I did not. *Yawl would have been proud of a brotha.* I kept my composure and acted as though I did not even notice her traffic stopping booty. Those bad thoughts just raced across my mind.

After she picked up her lipstick we went to the car and proceeded back to my office. As I dropped her off to her car, she got my card and said she would be in touch with me on the house. I told her to let me know if and when Mr. Clowers would like to see the house and that I would be available anytime. I found myself staring at her butt as she walked away but before I knew it, there were my next customers, the Conchettas.

The Conchettas were a Hispanic couple. They, like other customers, were very inquisitive about the house of their interests. I spent about ninety minutes with them and behold I cashed in on my first sale. The profit was not that substantial as I had to share profits with the selling agent, but it started a winning rhythm for me.

My last customer actually called and cancelled but my third customer of the day was really nerve wrecking. He was very prejudice in every respect and did not feel that I was worthy to show him anything.

"So JR, were you raised in the projects, the ghetto, or the hood?" he asked.

That question along with several like it totally rubbed me the wrong way. I showed him the house and I was truly glad when it was over. One thing about the real estate business, like some other businesses, is that it exposes the best and the worst of all folks. I was still floating from the adrenaline of my first sale, so to some degree it was very easy for me to look over the insults of that rude customer.

Finally, at about 5:15pm I went back to the office and met

with the boss. She had already sent the office folks home and she was heavily engaged in paperwork with her pensive look and reading glasses. I walked in and she said, "Jamie, how does it feel to sell your first house in Houston, Texas?"

"Well Ma'am, it feels good and I'm feeling kind of lucky right now."

"What did I tell you about calling me Ma'am?" she said.

I walked forward to her desk and said, "Can we make an agreement? If I call you Julie, will you please call me JR?"

"So, is that why you call me Ma'am?"

"No, I call you that out of respect and sometimes I forget. My mom is the only one that calls me Jamie."

"Alright Jamie, I'll call you JR from now on."

"Thanks Ma'am, I really appreciate that and I will call you Julie from now on."

Afterwards she stood from behind her desk, removed her eyeglasses and asked me if I was interested in pursuing my broker's license? I told her of course but I just wanted to get a feel for the area first before I started school for that type of preparation.

"Okay JR, you got six weeks and I got you scheduled for training at our designated university at the company's expense."

I did not realize it but she was just letting me know that they were going to pay for my brokerage license.

"Wow Julie, thank you very much for that consideration. I really don't know what to say," as I reached out my hand to shake hers.

"Say nothing but just work towards improving your craft so you can be that much of a valuable asset within the company. I know how it is starting out in an area like this. Just handle your business."

I was ecstatic. I got a boss that actually cared about me. I went back to my office to close up and call it a day. I left Julie with her paperwork. As I was getting ready to depart, I shut down my computer and thought to myself, *what will I get myself into tonight?* I needed to celebrate my first house sale and I was determined to do that. Then my desk phone rang.

"What are you doing tonight," asked Julie.

"I don't know but I plan to hit Gold's Gym at 7:30pm and I was going to decide after that. What are you and your husband doing tonight?" I replied.

"I was thinking about coming over to your place," she said.

I paused. I was shocked as to what I had heard and she further said, "Are you there?"

"Yes Ma'am, I'm here. I mean, yes Julie. I'm sorry," I nervously answered.

"I will call you later and let you know if I decide to stop by," Julie gently expressed.

"Okay, Sure!" My voice was confusing even to me as my mind was hard at work as to what her interest might be.

I hung up the phone, got my brief case and left the office right away. I went directly to Gold's gym, changed into my workout clothes and ran on the treadmill for thirty minutes like I was a runaway slave. I thought to myself, *HMMM, I wonder why Julie wants to come over to my place. Am I walking around with that Nelly/Jaheim song, My Place, written on my forehead?"* Anyway, my last workout was on the life cycle machine.

As I finished up, I saw this female fitness trainer that I had been gawking at for about a week now. She was as fine as they came but the problem was she knew it. I went over and asked her about a new fitness regiment and pretended to get her cut on it. She was very difficult to talk to. When I spoke to her, she never even looked into my eyes and she always acted as though she was too busy to talk. Her body language told me she was not interested so I really did not bother to hang around.

Anyway, as I was walking away from her, she spoke to me out of the blue.

"Nice car! You make that kind of money being a realtor?" I turned around and thought to myself, *Wow, perhaps she does notice me.*

"Sure, if you have been doing it as long as I have," I turned and responded. *Dog! I could have made a better reply than that,* was the way I felt.

"Ummm! Okay!" She had such a nonchalant response that clearly conveyed her disinterest.

Then she just walked off. I went and finished my workout and got a quick shower, and left the men's locker room to depart when the supervisor at the desk confronted me.

"JR, you are overdue on your monthly payment."

I responded in shock and anger, "No way Huelio, I just paid yawl last Friday for one month. Get the books right man because I don't owe again until three weeks from today."

"JR, I may be wrong but I'm almost certain you are overdue," said Huelio.

I got stupid, ridiculously upset and just as I began to really express my feelings, the manager came out from the office and said, "JR is not overdue Huelio. You are getting him mixed up with RJ."

"JR, RJ, okay, my bad," said Huelio with a rude snarl on his face.

"The next time you make that mistake I am done with this place, you got that fat boy?" I said with a loud and intimidating voice while pointing my finger at him.

"JR, let me apologize, for you are in good standing with

us and we do appreciate your business, right Huelio?" chimed the manager with a very sincere expression on her face.

"Yeah RJ, I apologize," said Huelio in a very insincere tone.

"JR, not RJ," said the manager to Huelio in a very disappointing expression.

I just turned and walked off from that little faggot. I got in my car and bounced as I was convinced that I would check out Balleys across town to see if they provided better service and appreciation for their customers. I did forget to pick up my suit from the cleaners on today. I wanted to wear my Hugo Boss suit to tomorrow's showing. Then again, I guess I could go by the cleaners very early in the morning and get my suit.

I drove home and took a long bath, just replaying my day in my mind. I thought about the sale today and I thought about Veronica and how lovely she was and then I thought about Julie. I wondered why she wanted to stop by. That really puzzled my mind. Last but not least, I thought about that faggot Huelio and how he pissed me off. Then, I thought to myself, *Hey, I should be excited. I sold my first house today and my boss wants to make me a broker.* Those were positive nuggets to build on.

CHAPTER TWO
My First Night Out

After I finished bathing, I decided I would go out and shake a leg. I got dressed and went to this club called "Groan Folks." I really did not know much about this club other than what I heard on the radio commercials while driving in my car. They made it sound like this was the club to go and get your party on. Supposedly, it was a real nice R and B club that showcased some of the finest women in Houston.

I pulled up to the club and the line was so long but one of the valet attendants walked up to my car and said he would park my car for me. I told him the line was too long for me.

"Of course it is Sir, for no one driving a fine ride like this should be standing in that long line. If you pay thirty dollars you get your car parked and returned to you upon exit and you go straight in on the VIP line," he said.

Now, thirty dollars was a bit steep for me, coming from Florida where you could get into clubs for at least half that price, but the valet attendant made a royal impression upon me. Besides, I needed to enjoy myself after clocking a little dough this week. Hey! I deserved this type of entertainment. I let him take the car and I entered via VIP access and walked straight in.

Of course, there were lots of women on the outside and they were staring.

"You can take me for a ride anytime baby," said some woman from the back of the line.

"I would love to rub that sexy bald head of yours," said another woman closer to the front of the line.

"Is your earring fake or real?" asked another woman near the entryway that I passed. I conveniently ignored them all.

As I went into the club, this elegant looking woman frisked me and she actually grabbed my private part and had the nerve to ask me "What's this?"

"That ain't no gun and by the way that's an act of sexual harassment," I angrily replied as I grabbed and moved her hand.

"Yeah right! You know you like it," was her bold reply while licking her tongue out at me.

"If you do it again, you will be reported," I responded with a very pissed off tone.

Then, I just walked in, paid my money and went into the club. The club was jamming. The honeys were everywhere, wearing all kinds of clothes. I was just scoping left and right, trying to find my comfort zone. Then, I went to the bar and ordered a glass of wine and I took my time and sipped it. I must say that within a half hour's time period, I stepped up my drink and ordered a Hurricane alcoholic drink. The bartender served it nice and strong and it really tasted and felt good. This brother came up and sat beside me and ordered a drink as well.

"What's up playa?" he said to me as though he knew me. I turned and looked around to make certain he was talking to me and not someone else.

"Hey, you got it man. I'm just trying to chill," were my words back to him.

"I heard that," were the words that followed. "These are some fine ass women in here. There are so many hotties that I don't even know where to start," he said as he turned his head watching a woman walk by.

"I feel ya playa. Its tight up in here, but I suggest you start from the beginning," I said in sincerity as I sipped on my drink.

He turned to me with a fake laugh and said, "I see you got jokes, huh?"

I strangely looked at him as to wonder what in the world was he talking about. Oh Well! I did not get that one. We started talking about life in general and he seemed to be a pretty cool dude.

"Hey baby, let me bounce that ounce," he said to this real fine hoochie that was walking by.

She just turned, looked him up and down with a nasty smirk on her face, quickly turned her head and walked off.

Anyway, Loke had relocated to Houston from Austin, Texas and he had just gotten a divorce. Latrell Oliver King, who preferred to be called Loke, was about six feet two, cut and physically ripped and had naturally wavy hair. He was a dentist and could have been a male model for any fashion company. He was a true pecan tan who looked as clean cut as they came.

Some hoochie momma came over and asked him to dance and he did. He was a smooth playa.

I saw this lady that really caught my eye but she was way across the room on the other side. I would hate to walk all the way over to her and ask for a dance just for her to say "no." She had tan like, shoulder length hair and it hung real nicely off her head. She was about 5'9" and had a real nice off white dress that hung on her like a chandelier. She was a caramel tan and had some real nice, upfront luggage. I stared at her for about 15 minutes, trying to muster up the nerve to go over and ask her to dance.

"JR," Loke approached me from behind and tapped me

on the shoulder out of the blue, "my friend's friend told me to come over and get you. We are sitting in a booth over there."

I looked over and saw the two young ladies he was referring to. His friend's friend was tall, dark and banging with a bodacious body. His friend was short, at about five feet tall. His friend's friend had on a very sexy outfit. Stomach out and bearing a ring on her navel, cleavage on strike from a bra, and the blue-laced mini skirt she wore was tightly fitted around her hijacked butt. I went along with Loke to meet them.

"Gina, Debbie, let me introduce you to JR," Loke said. They both spoke and Debbie stood up and said to me "Can you dance or are you the type to stand up and hold up the wall all night?"

"Let's get out there and find out Debbie, don't start nothing and it won't be nothing," was my flirtatious reply.

I grabbed her hand and led her to the dance floor. Debbie definitely knew how to shake up all her assets. Her body had the whole complete package. She looked as though she worked out quite a bit and her hair was cut short in a bob. Her hair was also mixed with some tan highlights, as if that was the hottest style here in Texas, and she had a chest like Queen Latifah before her breast reduction operation. We were jamming to Earth, Wind, and Fire's "Boogie Wonderland." I was dancing very conservatively and I did not stare into Debbie's eyes. She started asking me questions and she could tell I was not originally from Houston. She was very pretty in the face and I really liked the way she danced. I answered all her questions except one.

"So JR, are you married, divorced, or what?"

I just looked at her and smiled. She asked again and I smiled again. Then the DJ changed the song to Chic's "Good Times." I got excited off that song and started dancing more freely. I was doing the Cabbage Patch Kid dance, thinking I was jamming all to realize I was out of date with the dances. Debbie stopped me as if I was embarrassing her and guided me into dancing as she was dancing. Hey, she didn't have nothing on me because all she was doing was a smooth swagger from side to side. Besides, I was really getting ready to turn that mutha out with my Running Roger dance and my Snake dance but Debbie gently reeled me in as to discourage me from making a fool out of myself.

Okay, after making that small transition into dancing as she did, she started to draw in close on me as I was dancing and I covertly backed away. She even turned around and backed that ass up on a brother but I also backed up. Don't misunderstand me! I wanted to thump all over it but I felt the need to be conservative.

Debbie was a social worker and seemed to talk very freely and really did gather my attention. The DJ was jamming. He mixed in McFadden and Whitehead's "Ain't No Stopping Us Now" and Debbie got really excited off that song. She really drew in closer to me again and this time I did not back off.

Her cheeks touched my cheeks as she grabbed my waist. I followed her lead. Then she just wrapped her arms completely around me and I reciprocated. I did not talk to her by mouth but it's like our bodies were talking to each other and they had their own conversation going on.

Then, next up, the DJ mixed in a slow song called "Knocking Dem Boots." As soon as the song came on, Debbie grabbed me tighter and I grabbed her tighter as well. I rubbed my hand slowly and gently down her back and I could tell she liked it because she squeezed me tighter.

Then we started grinding real hard. I gently kissed her on her neck and I could tell she liked that. She put her right hand on my buttocks and I followed suit. I gently let my right hand slowly creep down to her backyard. Man, was she endowed. I gently rubbed her butt with my hand, anticipating pushback. Some sophisticated looking women don't like for you to rub their butt in public. She did not pushback so I got bolder and pawned one side of her buttocks with the palm of my right hand. I grabbed the pinnacle of her buttocks and rubbed it harder and harder but not too hard. Then, feeling her grinding hard and breathing heavier, I placed my left hand and grabbed the other side of her buttocks.

That felt some kind of good, grabbing Debbie's butt and holding it in the palm of my hands. She had on a thong and her backyard felt so thick. The DJ was working with a brother too. He mixed in Prince's sexy song called "Insatiable." I could have paid the DJ right on the spot because my nature was rising and I could tell Debbie felt it because she was maneuvering her pelvic area around it.

Then, after she gently licked me on my ear, I used my left hand and grabbed her upfront luggage. Wow! Her boob felt so good in my hand and it was as big as my head. I had my right hand grabbing her butt, my left hand grabbing her breast, and my nature was centered on her pelvic area. At this time, the DJ was my hero.

The club was dark with dim lights and everybody on the dance floor was about to take their partner down. Loke had picked Gina up and they were kissing and grinding like they were the only ones in the club. The DJ mixed in Usher's "Nice and Slow" and man the heat was rapidly rising and I was totally focused on Debbie.

Her perfume completed the scene and her body was perfect for my body at that moment. The DJ slowly mixed in R Kelly's "Body Calling" and man was that the right song for us. We were both sweating, both excited, and both wanted more of the physical from each other. I played with her large tips and continued to grab and cusp her butt while grinding like I was an electrical appliance. My back was getting a good workout and I was truly enjoying this moment.

Then, out of the blue, the DJ changed back to fast dance music and I responded like I was totally unprepared for that, while grinding to the last tune of R Kelly's song. In other words, the DJ went from a hero to a zero in a matter of minutes, messing up my flow.

Directly following the song, Debbie kissed me gently on my neck. We went back and sat down. Junior was hard as a brick wall and actually did not want things to come to an end.

Both ladies excused themselves to the bathroom and Loke said to me, "What you think man? I think we done ran up on a couple of freaks?"

"I know that's right. I am feeling this sister," I replied with steamy eyes.

"Why don't we invite them back to my crib and make the fun more private?" Loke suggested.

"That's up to you," I replied. "It looks like you and Gina already covered a lot of ground. Hey, don't let us slow yawl down."

"Look here dude; these girls are a tag team. They will not leave separately but together. Trust me on that," he said.

The ladies came back all refreshed and everything. I asked, "Can I get you all drinks?"

They both wanted glasses of White Zinfandel wine and Loke wanted a beer, while I got another Hurricane. When I returned with the drinks, Loke and Gina were dancing again and Debbie was waiting. As soon as I sat down she asked me why I never answered her question. I looked at her again and smiled and then my phone rang.

"JR," I replied.

"Hey JR, where are you?" It was Julie.

"Hi Julie, I'm clubbing right now! What's up?"

"What time will you be home?"

"The club closes around 2 or 3 am. I should be home not long afterwards," I dubiously replied.

Julie seemed disappointed but I really did not know how to respond.

"I'll check with you later JR."

"Thanks Julie! I appreciate the call."

As soon as I hung up, Debbie said, "I guess I see why you smiled when I asked the question."

Now, I really did not want to show my hand so I just continued to smile. I have learned in my short twenty-five years of life that you are damned if you tell the truth in these situations and you are damned if you lie. If I tell women I'm single, they may attempt to get my undivided attention and they may want that prematurely.

My point is I have given of myself way too early in the past just to get my feelings hurt. I refuse to rush down that road again!! Hey, I am single until I get married. I've had experiences in my past where women want to lock you down and put you in hand and ankle cuffs; put you in a chokehold. I'm just not trying to go out like that. When I am shackled down, I am shackled down and I refuse to be prematurely shackled down.

Debbie stared at me and I stared back and then the DJ played Chingy's "One Call Away" and we danced again. This time as soon as we got on the dance floor, Debbie backed it up and I made my lap like a toilette seat ready to catch that backyard of hers. I got firm instantaneously and her backyard was good to my lap. *Oh, her butt felt so good.* I wrapped my hands around her and we were moving with the music. She fed a brother and I was partaking with everything I had.

She remained so permanently stowed in that position and I was not about to let go. The DJ mixed in "Summer Bunnies" by R Kelly and Debbie bent down at a greater angle. Her boobs fell right into both my hands and they felt good. She was tossing that backyard up and I was catching it with every grind.

Now, one thing about women when they see a decent looking brother with an endowed sister, they seem to become more interested in you as opposed to if you were alone. It's as if your stock value rises greatly when you are already with a nice looking woman.

While I was dancing, this other woman kept feeling my butt even while dancing with her friend or husband. She was very bold about it and I looked at her a couple of times and she just stared at me. I got other looks from women on the floor as well as from those that were not dancing. Then again, I could be wrong. Perhaps these women would still stare at me even if I was not with a fine sister. I guess I could only speculate and this could be a total figment of my imagination.

Debbie and I sat down again and Loke and Gina had already returned to their seats and they were sitting real close and Debbie said, "I hope we are not disturbing anything?" She was directing the comment to Gina.

"Nope, not at all," Gina replied. "We were just discussing an after party if yawl are gain."

Debbie quickly blurted out, "JR has to check in because his kitchen pass is expiring!"

They all started laughing and I just smiled and did not

feel a need to comment. Then Loke said, "JR, let me holla at you for a moment."

We excused ourselves to the men's restroom where Loke told me that he wanted to take the party to his house. I was down with that but I knew I had a busy tomorrow and I was also curious as to whether Julie would call again.

I did not want to rush into a sexual relationship with Debbie but I wanted to get to know her first and let things go from there. I liked her company but right now her body was the supreme thought on my mind. How do you tell a woman that you really want to get to know first, that you are afraid that if sex drives the train, it might hinder growth? Don't misunderstand me. I wanted to tear that backyard up but it could threaten a potential relationship.

Then again, why should I care? If she did not care, why should I? Sometimes if you just go ahead and hit it anyway, you preclude a woman from thinking you were trying to fall in love with her as opposed to just getting some booty. My body wanted it badly but I really did not need the hassle. After further review, I decided I would just let it play out because I could be overconfident. Debbie may just be feeding me on the dance floor and that's it.

"JR, are you down or not? Just come along for the ride and see what happens," Loke said to me as we were in the bathroom.

"Okay, but I may not stay too long."

Then, I thought about it and I said to Loke, "Hey man, you can have any woman in this club at your own pace, why such a hurry?"

"Dude, you don't get it. I'm straight out of divorce and I will have every woman in this club before too long."

I laughed out loud and then we both returned to the table

where the ladies were. Loke said, "Okay ladies, let's go." They both got up and we begin to leave. Debbie had driven her car and she was not about to leave it at the club. Gina rode with Loke, and since I drove, we were making a caravan of a trip. Since my car was valet parked, I had to wait up front.

While I was waiting, that same honey that I saw earlier slowly appeared. She was the one who wore the off white dress. She was waiting for her car.

"How's it going?" I said to her. "I wanted to get a dance with you but I was afraid to walk all the way across the room and get turned down."

"All you had to do was ask. Nobody asked me to dance all night long and I wanted to dance," she said in the nicest fashion.

"Really, I do feel bad now," I said to her.

The valet attendant drove up in a red convertible corvette and she was about to leave. I gave her one of my business cards and asked her to give me a call and told her perhaps we could go out dancing and I promised she would get a chance to dance all night. She smiled, took the card and read it.

"Call me tomorrow if you like or call me anytime. The choice is yours but I do relish the opportunity. By the way, my name is JR."

"I might give you a call JR but I won't make you any promises. My name is Juanita, Juanita Coles."

She got in her corvette and drove off. I thought to myself, *Man, she is nice. Houston, Texas is definitely a single man's dream.* It appeared to be that way for me thus far.

The valet attendant pulled up with my car and Loke, Gina, and Debbie were waiting for me near the street exit of he club. I followed them in my Lex.

Now Loke lived in a very nice area on the East side of

Houston. He had all the amenities in his condo complex. He had a nice swimming pool, secure entry, and nice surrounding area with wholesome attractions. We arrived to his crib about twenty-five minutes later. They were all driving fast on the highway and I did as well just to keep up. Loke had a true bachelor's pad. It was spotless, sophisticated looking and had money written all over it.

As soon as we arrived, we all took our shoes off as he had the plushest carpet I had ever seen. I could definitely learn some things from Loke. He was an old school playa and I was just new school, period. I was very impressed with Loke's place. He had this real nice wrap around sofa that actually went all the way around the living room, creating a circle. We sat in the midst of it at first. Loke had a bar with all the wine and alcohol one could dream of. The ladies kept to drinking their White Zinfandel and I had some Hennessey and Coke while Loke was drinking Vodka and cranberry juice.

Loke played some nice slow dance music and that's when it got hot again. Debbie, however, did not want to dance but she wanted to chat. She got real close up on me and we were slowly rubbing each other's hands. All of a sudden I looked up and Loke and Gina were kissing and touching all over each other's body. It's as if Debbie and I were at the movies and they were the movie. I got to admit Gina was thick and she had a lot of real estate to be explored. Debbie was giving me signs that she wanted to get busy. She lifted one of her legs up and placed it near her side while facing towards me.

She had a black thong and her middle area was calling my name. There was this whispering, imaginary sound that said, "JR, JR, here I am JR. Move this thong out my way." My eyes were locked between her legs and I was falling fast. Gina had taken off her dress and Loke was bearing his chest and about to take off his pants. Gina unleashed her bra and down came Mount Pinatubo. I mean, them tah tahs fell out like water balloons, bouncing up and down. I could not help but look. I even think my head was bouncing up and down along with them balloons. Loke was sucking those things like he was a newborn baby, in and out, gently pulling away from them with his lips on her tips.

Then Gina went downtown on him. This was so wild. They could care less that we were watching. Debbie started touching me and rubbing my chest but I was fascinated watching Loke and Gina. I liked the way she was bobbing for apples, licking all around his rocks and crotch area with so much compassion. I was getting turned on just watching her.

Then Debbie unzipped my pants and put her head down into my crotch area and did a lube job. I was still sitting in the chair and she positioned herself in front of me, on her knees. I pulled her dress up and over her head and then I detached her bra strap. Those cantaloupes fell right into my hands and I could not wait to get my lips on them. I never did. She sucked and pulled as if she was determined to move me towards a climax.

Things really got out of control. I was gradually losing all my head and I felt myself entering that zone; the zone of no return. I tried to pull her up so I could ride that back but she was not bulging. Loke and Gina were literally unconscious and totally out of control. Gina was screaming to the top of her lungs and he was bouncing her all over the living room until she fell into a paralyzed like state from climaxing which was a prelude to her falling asleep.

Debbie was going long and strong and I was about to lose it. I pulled her hair from the excitement. Then, all of a sudden she put all of my private parts down her throat. I mean everything; a whole 6.5 inch went down her ocean of a mouth. I thought I was about to explode in every way possible. Then, something happened that I could have never predicted.

Can you believe Loke came out of nowhere and bum rushed Debbie's backside, while she was still baptizing my handlebar with her mouth? I actually thought she was going to stop him but she didn't. He had a razor blade and sliced her thong to where it severed and then he deposited his account. She seemed to enjoy it as though it was the nicest thang since slice bread. I uncontrollably came with a loud sigh, as she lost no focus on my nature, although Loke was banging her backside like she was a naughty girl. Debbie continued to bob for apples even after my deposit between her mandibles. The fluids were streaming out of her mouth and she started screaming from Loke pounding her from the rear.

My nature became numb as I had come already and she was still sucking a brother dry. I was somewhat confused, somewhat in a daze as I saw Loke knocking Debbie like she was a first class hoe. Then, out of the blue, my phone rang.

Can you believe I answered it? It was like a nervous reaction where I did not think. It was Julie. I ran into Loke's nearby bathroom because Debbie was screaming louder and louder, almost as if she was intending to be heard. I could not believe I answered the darn phone. That was clearly a mistake on my part.

"JR," I said.

"JR, where are you?"

I'm trying to cover up the speaker to the phone because Debbie sounded like she was coming and she was getting way too loud.

"Ahhhhmmmmm, I'm at a friend's house."

Julie paused and it seemed as though her pause was forever.

"Perhaps I should let you go. You sound busy," she replied.

I was so embarrassed and Debbie was screaming so loud and saying stuff like "Give it to me baby! Get this booty baby. Get all this ass baby! It's yours if you want it baby!"

"I will call you back or can you call me back later on today?" I foolishly said to Julie.

Darn, why did I ask her a question when all I wanted to do was quickly get off the phone because Debbie was making it sound more and more like a screw fest, which I guess it really was.

Nevertheless, I did not want my boss having this lewd impression of me. I felt so screwed and I was starting to get mad with both Loke and Debbie.

"Sure JR, I'll call you later when you are not so busy." Julie seemed to take forever to respond and then she hung up.

"Phew! Darn! I felt so bad. What will my boss think of me now? I wonder why she called me so late or so early in the morning anyway. What does she want? Is she checking up on me or what?"

I got my clothes on and I left Loke's house for my house. You think Debbie noticed? Heck no, she was too busy with her head in Loke's crotch, cleaning up the entire residue exiting his little soldier. Wow, Julie called me at 3:15am and I really don't know for what reason she called? She is still a mystery to me. I really wonder if she is just checking up on me. This was not covered in my hiring interview and as far as I am concerned, I am not doing anything illegal or outside of company policy. I am on my own personal time and her company cannot dictate my off duty activity as long as I am not doing anything illegal.

Hell, all of a sudden I felt like I needed to get an attorney, but why should I feel thist way?

Oh well! I am certain of at least one thing. I made a bad impression on her with my nighttime antics. I don't know how I'm going to face her when Monday morning comes around. I should have never gone out tonight. I guess that was a bad call on my part.

CHAPTER THREE
THE AFTER MATH

At about 7:40am, the phone rang and woke me up. I was having a deep, deep dream. I answered the phone while being half way conscious, lifting the phone to my ear with my left hand while beating my chest with my right hand. "The Mighty J to the R," I said as though I was chanting a cheer.

"Hello! I'm sorry. I must have the wrong number," responded the other voice on the line.

Those words knocked me straight into consciousness.

"Ah-Hello, this is JR."

"Hi JR," sounded a very excited voice, "I want the house! This is Veronica. Is the house still available?"

"For sure Veronica, the house is still available. Let me see, ahhmm, could I meet with you and Mr. Clowers around 4pm today and we can do all the paperwork then."

"Okay JR, I apologize for waking you up. I left three messages on your voice mail at work but I called your cell to make sure the house was still available. I am so excited about this house."

"I'm excited for yawl Veronica. I think you both will be pleased with your decision. I'll see you at 4pm today, okay?"

"Okay JR, have a nice day."

That was good news. Looks like I sold another house. Cha Ching! Cha Ching! Wow, that was good news today for me.

***

Around 9:40am the phone rang again. I answered "JR."

"What's going on playa?"

It was Loke on the phone. "Why did you leave under such haste this morning?" he inquired.

"No special reason Loke, I just needed to get home and rest up some. I got a phone call from my boss and I thought she was checking up on me and so I felt somewhat insecure and bounced."

"What? Why would your boss be calling you up so early in the morning? Were you working on a project with her or was she expecting you to call and give her some information about something?"

"Not at all! She just said she would call me sometime later on in the evening and that was it."

"Okay playa, I just wanted to make certain you were okay. That is kind of weird of your boss. Hey man, the girls were somewhat puzzled by your quiet departure and I just wanted to make certain you were not misunderstanding my actions."

"Loke, what was there to misunderstand? We basically picked up a couple of loose women and had a bootyfest? What's there to misunderstand about that?"

"Exactly playa! I'm glad you see things the way I do. I have had friends in the past that may have gotten upset because I hit what they would call their stuff. My point is that they were both dangling their butts all over the place and that either one of us could have screwed both women. You feel me?"

I really did not share Loke's perspective on what happened but I did not want to come across as though my feelings were hurt. Besides, those women were obviously itching between the thighs and they just wanted to get laid. Nevertheless, I was not about to let Loke know about my true feelings regarding last night.

"I feel ya Loke. It's not like either one of us had been trying to develop a relationship with either one of them. It was all about one thing, knocking dem boots!"

"That's what I'm talking about playa. Man, I must admit it's good to finally hook up with a brotha that views thangs my way," Loke said with much excitement.

"By the way, Debbie was surprised you left so suddenly but she thought either you had to run home to your woman or perhaps you got jealous of me banging her out."

"Hey man, don't believe the hype. It was all good by me. Besides, with her head crash down between your legs, I'm surprised she even had time to notice me leaving."

Loke started laughing real loud as a sigh of relief and then he replied, "Now JR, I must admit that them women love going down on a brother. That alone will cause them to be playmates for our pleasure for sometime. You feel me?"

"I hear ya man! That is definitely one of their strengths, taking the initiative to go down and then performing to such detail. They both seemed to really crave bobbing for apples."

"That's an understatement playa. Those women were off the hook. By the way, Debbie wanted you to call her when you got a chance."

Loke gave me Debbie's number and I just might call her but I got to get up, put on my business face and show some houses this morning.

"Loke, I'll call Debbie later today."

"Got it JR! Hey, let's you and I get together later on this evening if you get some time. I got a few patients to see and then I'm calling it a day. Also, I want to buy a house. Can you hook a brotha up?"

"I sure can Loke. Just let me know what you have in mind and I will try getting you the best house for the least expensive price. You can quote me on that."

"All right playa, I will call you later on and we can further discuss the house at a later time. Right now, we need to focus on hooking up with some more honeys and giving them what they need. You feel me?"

"I feel you Loke. I'll call you later on."

Okay, I was not down with trying to hook up with some mo loose butt women tonight. Shoooot! I really did not enjoy last night as much as Loke did. Debbie had some nerve, going to give it up to him while she call herself trying to hook up with me. It's not like I was trying to knock the britches off Gina. Debbie will be lucky to ever get a phone call from me. She crossed the wrong brotha. Besides, she won't all that anyway!

Loke was really okay by me even though he caught me off guard with that stunt he pulled on last night. He went from Gina to Debbie like he knew they were down with the program. That's the kind of vision I don't have and could possibly learn from him. Then again, who am I kidding? I'm still slightly unnerved by that free for all activity.

Oh well, time to get up and meet some customers. I got to make that grip today!!

***

Later in the afternoon, I met four customers and showed them all houses. I think two of them could contact me again but I can't hang my hat on anything. I was anxious for Julie to call so I could tell her about the big sale but I've yet to hear from her.

Well, I'm done with showing houses today, so now I can concentrate on the Clowers. I went to the office and got all the paperwork squared away. Julie will be proud, I think, depending on how she responded to my late night activity on last night.

At about 4pm, Veronica showed up right on time but once again she was by herself. Man! She looked some kind of good. I stared her down from the moment she got out of her car until she opened the door to the office. I did wonder why her husband was not with her.

"Hi Veronica! How are you?" I said to her as she walked in to the building.

"JR, I am so excited about buying this house. I just cannot explain to you my joy in doing this," she said.

"You should be excited. This is a big deal. Will Mr. Clowers be joining us as well? I have all the paperwork setup for both signatures."

She seemed a little despondent with the question and quickly responded, "Actually JR, I'm going to purchase this house by myself so please prepare the paperwork accordingly."

I was surprised by that information and somewhat concerned. Nevertheless, I did not convey my concern and I prepared the paperwork as she requested and we pressed ahead with business. Another point of note about this business is when you here questionable information from your customers, you got to learn to wear a straight face and not overreact because it could result in losing a sale.

I was really anxious to do the credit check to see if this deal could fly. We discussed all the details and I congratulated her on her purchase. Veronica was very cordial and she signed everything with pure delight.

Afterwards, she said to me with excitement, "JR, we need to celebrate. You have done a good job selling me the house and I am so happy to be able to purchase it."

She had such a gleam in her eyes and her personality was as vibrant as ever. I looked at her and she looked at me as if she knew what I was about to say.

She said, before I could speak, "JR, its okay! Trust me. What are you doing about 7pm tonight?"

"Absolutely nothing! What do you have in mind and where would you like to celebrate?" I said.

"What about Roasters on 7th and Vitters?"

"Then Roasters it is," I happily expressed.

"We can do dinner and have a drink or two if you got the time," she interjected.

"Veronica, my time is all your time tonight."

I said that with business in mind but the way it came out might have implied other interests and I was somewhat remotely embarrassed. The words left my lips before I could shape them to say what I really meant. Regardless, her reply made me feel as though I was on point with my words.

"JR, you read my mind. I'll see you at 7pm."

When she left, I just thought to myself, *what in the world is going on? Wow! I can't believe it.* I watched her nice butt bounce up and down until she got to her car and drove off. I quickly closed up and rushed off to get a workout in at Gold's Gym before meeting Veronica for dinner.

Honestly, I was more excited about the sale than I was about meeting her. I knew she was married and I did not want to cause or walk into any drama. This was clearly the finality of a great business venture. However, before I left the office, I had to do a credit check to make sure I was not celebrating for nothing.

***

I left Gold's Gym at about 5:45pm with another good

workout. I'm feeling great about now. I just need to drink more water and fewer drinks to get that stomach down. I checked on Veronica's credit check and her record was immaculate, as she maxed out on the highest possible score she could attain. Home girl had no issues in that department. I guess she was pretty well off, financially speaking. Well, let me do the math: a forensic scientist and a heart surgeon should equal a lot of dough.

I have yet to hear from Julie and I was starting to get worried. I couldn't wait to tell her about the sale. Matter of fact, let me call her and see if I can get her feedback. I had to dial her number about three times as I was nervous and I kept dialing the wrong number, but finally I got through.

"Hello," she said answering the phone.

"Hi Julie, this is JR. How are you doing boss?"

"Perhaps I should be asking you JR, how are you doing?"

I guess I should have expected that but I really did not know by that tone whether or not she was going to be rude to me or talk nicely like she normally did. I thought I would play that off by telling her about the sale of the house.

"Julie, I am really doing great now that I sold the Brentwood house."

"Come again JR."

"Julie, I sold the house in Brentwood."

"Really JR? Congratulations! I knew you could do it. I am really not surprised. I got about five more bigger houses for you on next week."

"Really Julie! Are you serious?" I said with an orgasmic like bundle of joy.

"That's right JR! I am rapidly making you the show pony of the company. I think you can handle the challenge. How is that stomach coming along?"

She liked joking with me about my stomach but that just confirmed to me that she was not upset with me for whatever reason regarding my late night activity.

"Well Julie, I think it's getting there. I plan to start drinking more water and less sugary substances. By the way, I left all the paperwork regarding the sale of the house on Margot's desk and hopefully there were no errors with it."

"JR, your paperwork is one of your true hallmarks. Keep up the good work. I need to run now but congrats once again and I'll call you later."

"Sure thing Julie! Thanks for your bode of confidence too."

We both hung up the phone. Wow, that was a great conversation for me. It was so nice to have a boss that pushed you like Julie did. I felt so great knowing that she approved of my work and that she did not attack me for my late night indiscretions. Now, I was really ready for Veronica. Julie just made my day!

***

On Saturday about 6:45pm my cell phone rang and my caller ID said it was Debbie. I was in the car on my way to meet Veronica. I did not tell Loke to give that nymph my cell phone number. I'm really going to need to chat with him about that. I really had nothing to say to Debbie. I mean really, what can I say? Ask her if she enjoyed Loke's pipe? Anyway, I reluctantly answered the phone.

"Hello JR, how are you today," she said in a very nervous like tone.

"I'm doing okay Debbie. Life is good."

She paused and I could hear her heavy breathing, confirming the fact that she was nervous. "JR, are you mad with me?" she said.

I had to fake it like nothing bothered me. Besides, she's just a straight up hoe.

"By all means no Debbie, and why would I be mad?"

I said that with jubilant joy as to be somewhat sarcastic but to confuse her as to whether or not I was serious.

"Well, I just noticed you rushed off from Loke's house last night and I was not certain as to why? Did you get in trouble?"

Now, I had to make a decision. Do I imply that I did get into trouble to keep her at bay or will telling the truth give her the impression she can do a full court press? NOT! I'm talking about a woman I met on the first night and she gave it up to me and another stranger too easily so perhaps I should treat her like a hoe. That's the way she acted and I should keep her on that level.

"Well Debbie, I did get into some trouble on last night so I can't repeat that mistake again." *God! I felt so funny lying like that.*

"I'm sorry JR! I guess we kept you out way too late. Please don't let me wear out my welcome okay. Call me when you can get away."

I listened, I studied and I replied, "I sure will Debbie. I had a great time with you and I will call you real soon. I have to handle some thangs but I'll get back with you perhaps next week sometime."

Darn, why did I say that? I know I probably won't stay away that long, or will I? Then again, I really don't know when I plan to call either.

She replied somewhat downtrodden and with a pitiful voice, "Okay JR! I'll be here. Do keep in touch."

Now, back to the issue at hand. I'm about five minutes out from Roasters. I got my dark blue linen suit on, a matching

Versace shirt with the Pat Riley collar and some black leather boots. I arrived at Roasters about ten minutes early. This establishment was like a club restaurant that was slightly above the norm of a regular restaurant. I got Veronica and I a nice table and a bottle of champagne. I waited patiently for her.

At 7:10pm, Veronica came through the door. When I saw her, it was as if she was walking in slow motion. Her 5'9" frame was bouncing all over. She wore a turquoise blue dress suit that appeared to be like cashmere.

"Hi Veronica, how the heck are you, you new homeowner?" I said.

"I'm doing well JR. I'm still excited about the house."

She was very upbeat and positive. I was happy too and I popped open a bottle of champagne. Veronica went to make a special request to the DJ. Afterwards, he played a Brian McKnight song entitled: "Keep It On The Down Low." I did not think much of it until the DJ kept playing that song over and over again.

"JR, have you ever really listened to the words of that song?"

"Not really but I certainly will listen to the words now," I quickly conveyed.

Veronica seemed real relaxed. I listened to the words. Wow! Veronica was 5'9" and the song talked about a woman who was that height and the song had a definite message. The song spoke of a woman who was not happy with her man so she apparently got involved with another man to make up for what she was not getting at home.

It was really blowing my mind as to the subtle message she was sending. Nevertheless, I would not broach that conversation. We ordered dinner and afterwards she asked if I wanted to dance. She was in some high heel shoes so she stood as tall as I was. I was truly sliding into a serious state of infatuation with her. We danced for quite awhile. She moved very graciously and everything on her body shook when she danced. I was feeling this woman from head to toe. The DJ finally changed the music. I had a couple of drinks and I finally got the nerve to ask what I thought was a difficult question. "Veronica, what's your story?"

She sipped her glass of champagne and said, "Can you be more specific?"

I looked at her and sensed that she did not want to go where I wanted to go. I really was not even sure that I wanted to go where I seemed to be going. I took her hint and backed off.

"Where were you born and how did you become a forensic scientist?" I uttered.

She was very pretty and intense with her thoughts. She gave me her life story and I was very impressed. She also told me how she met her husband. He was one of the surgical doctors that performed numerous medical studies on corpses that her office had processed. Not that he killed a lot of people but she said oftentimes that they were already dying and he would get the late night call, just as he continued to get now.

In the conversation, I was more like the interviewer, asking all the questions. She was very cooperative and had no hesitation whatsoever with answering my questions. I was ready to stop while I was ahead. Then came the stunning mouth opener.

"JR, my husband and I have been separated for one year. I will be officially divorced on Tuesday as I sign the divorce papers with my attorney. I really cannot wait."

"Wow! You have got to be kidding me," I replied as my eyes stretched open as wide as they could.

"I am truly sorry to hear that. That's why you purchased the house by yourself?"

She smiled and quickly replied, "I have wanted to purchase my own house for quite sometime. I live in a stuffy apartment now. I moved out and refused to get anything that my husband and I owned together. I just want to start all over afresh."

I was very attentive and I wanted Veronica to feel my support as a friend, not as someone who could remotely be interested in her and not as someone who was being nosy.

"Wow, breakups/divorce can be so tough," I said.

She sipped some champagne and said, "No, not always. I was married to my husband one year and he started cheating on me with his head nurse. I knew it for a long time but I pretended not to know. I can tell you their hotels of choice, vacation getaways, as well as dining restaurants. I can tell you about the numerous late night phone calls he would get as though he was going to surgery, but was really going to perform a sexual surgical operation on his lover, if you will. It's been going on for nearly eight years."

Veronica was talking about her death bound marriage as though she enjoyed sharing with me the disappointing news. I wanted to add some humor to her conversation, as she seemed quite intrigued with the conversation.

"Veronica, when you say head nurse, are you referring to a real nurse who was in charge or just a regular woman who was taking care of his small head?"

She looked at me and started laughing and replied, "That's a good one JR but actually she was the nurse in charge okay. By the way, where is your head right now? I mean your big head?"

I laughed along with her. Nevertheless, I sat in my seat totally shocked. I mean, Veronica could have any man she so desired and to know that a brother would treat her this way was so unbelievable for me.

"Dang Veronica, you stood by him that long and was still faithful too?"

She laughed again with a very animated look on her face. "I haven't said anything about being faithful. I was faithful for about five years and then I said the hell with it. The problem with cheating for me was that the men I cheated with would get too involved and wanted to marry and get all serious with me. I just needed a distraction, time to grow in my job, and time to get my own money."

I was very impressed with Veronica. She had to have a lot of patience and courage to tolerate all that cheating from her husband.

"So Veronica, you let your husband have a lot of rope. A lot of women can't handle that messing around stuff."

"Well, I thought some of it was a cultural endeavor. My husband is Caucasian by the way." I almost choked on the wine I was sipping. I dropped my lower chin as in slow motion. To say that I was shocked was immensely an understatement. I was in a complete state of shock two times over.

"'You have got to be kidding me."

She boldly responded, "Nope, I kid you not."

My mouth was further wide open. "I should have known better. I don't think any sista would tolerate that from a brotha; especially these new generation sistas."

She laughed louder than she did the first time and then replied, "Ain't no brotha gonna pay me for tolerating his mess like my husband did. Don't misunderstand me. I'm not out for money but my soon to be ex-husband agreed to my settlement after I told him about my knowledge over the years of his infidelity. We didn't even need attorneys to divide the spoils. I wanted a 55-45 split and he agreed to a 60-40 split. I took the other houses we had but refused the mini-mansion he has here. I wanted to start all over with my own house here locally."

I wanted to be nosy and ask Veronica exactly how many houses did they have but I figured I would just allow her to volunteer that kind of information. Besides, I really don't want her to think I'm all up in her business anyway, although I was listening to every drop of word flowing from her mouth.

Now, I would have never thought Veronica had all this going on in her life, as she seemed to be so content with everything. As time quickly went by, I begin to feel as though I knew her in spirit and truth. I sipped on some more champagne and then my cell phone rang.

"What's up playa," said Loke on the other end.

"Hey Loke, what's going down man?"

He replied in such a salacious way "Not a whole lot dude! What are you doing tonight? You sound a little lit."

I conservatively responded to Loke. "I am actually busy right now but I'll holla back in a little while." He sounded somewhat inebriated and replied, "Okay dude! We need to make some decisions on tonight. Gina and Debbie want to hook up. I got some other options as well. GETATYABOY."

I quietly but quickly replied, "Got it Loke! I'll call back later."

Besides, perhaps those two sluts want to hook up with Loke alone. I mean they hit off so well the other night that I would imagine they would continue what they started. Veronica had captured my world, although I really did not sense that she was interested in me, as opposed to being just happy with her life developments. That's okay. She's too much money for me anyhow. *Stop it JR! There you go again disqualifying yourself.*

"How is your lobster?" she asked.

"Pretty good! The steak isn't half bad either. How is your shrimp and veal?"

She smiled, showcasing her nice big pearly whites. "This is too good. I always eat too much when I come here."

"Well Veronica, you sure do keep a tight figure, so it's okay to pig out every now and then. You must have a fitness trainer or have a regimented workout program?"

She illuminated with an obvious flash of her big pretty eyes. "I try to eat a lot of negative calorie foods and I do work out about five times a week when I get the chance. I had a trainer but he spent more time trying to get up my skirt than helping me stay fit. I had to fire him. Thanks for the compliment. You look like you workout as well?"

"I'm just trying to get the belly down and stay toned. I want to look good for the business as well," I timidly responded.

My phone rang again and I answered, "JR."

"Hi JR, do you remember Juanita?"

I almost fell to the floor. I could not believe Juanita had actually called my number. I responded in a low tone voice as I turned my head away from Veronica.

"Juanita, nice to hear from you. Can I call you back in a little while?"

She responded with high energy and excitement, "Sure JR, do you have a pen to write my number down with?"

"My phone has your number. It automatically stores your name and number. I'll call back okay. I'm glad you called."

"Okay JR, give me a call later, bye bye."

Veronica chimed in with a look of concern, "JR, I hope I'm not keeping you too long."

I quickly replied, "Veronica, the pleasure is all mine. I am enjoying myself beyond expectation. You are too cool."

She laughed and said, "Really! And I thought you were just being nice to me because I bought the house?"

I smirked and responded, "Oh No! Make no mistake

about it. That is first and foremost why I am having a good time." I stared at her as her facial expression changed from the acknowledgement of my comment. Her facial expression was transformed from a smile to a pout and I quickly corrected my statement. "I'm just joking Veronica, Ahahahahah! I can separate business from pleasure. My enjoyment of your company has nothing to do with your purchase of the house."

Now Lord, please don't strike me down. A brotha had to say what a brotha had to say. Please forgive me now, as I will be in church on Sunday. She looked into my eyes and stared as though I was supposed to say more. I could tell that the champagne was loosening her up quite a bit.

I thought the evening had gone great and I was wondering how to make an exit because when it's this good, it could only get worse.

"JR, have you ever been on the river side? It is really nice at night."

I had no idea what she was talking about. However, something about the tone in which she asked me, the glitter in her eyes, and my overwhelming anxiety truly aroused my curiosity.

"What is the river side? I can say that I have never been there before." She looked somewhat puzzled by my words.

"Really, I am surprised. It's a very popular attraction here in Houston. It's a place where you just go and you just can't describe it. I would have to take you there. I sometimes go walking out there for my exercise. It is full of complete serenity and it's truly a nice getaway from the fast Houston lanes. Do you know what I mean?"

"Veronica, feel free to show me the river anytime. I mean, the river side." Man, I guess the champagne was trying to make its presence known as I found myself flirting with Veronica on a higher level.

Heck, the way I was feeling her, she could take me to the river and baptize me right now if she wanted to and I would have no problem with that.

"Veronica, let me know if you need a walking partner. I could join you sometimes if you don't mind the company." She smiled, leaned forward towards me, stared and seemed slightly interested in my proposition.

"Okay, let's go walking on tomorrow evening around 6 pm. I'm serious JR. I would walk more often but I always get stopped or interrupted and then when it begins to get dark, I don't like being out there by myself although it is a well lit area."

I was elated by her invite but I pulled out my blackberry as if to check my schedule, knowing that I was more than available for tomorrow evening.

"Let's see! I got church at 10 am, a house showing at 2pm and then I should be free by 6pm."

She looked down at my blackberry and smiled.

"Are you putting me down just for Sunday? How about Monday, Tuesday, and Wednesday too?"

She laughed rather loudly. "I'm just joking JR."

"Yeah right! That's why men be trying to lock a sista like you down."

Although she said she was joking, the thought really crossed my mind as to whether or not she was really sincere. Then again, I had to be careful with her because Veronica could just be nice and flirtatious like that. Some women will flirt you down to the ground, all to tell you that they were just joking and not serious. I must also remember that she kicked guys to the curve who tried to marry her. Anyway, the bell saved me as my phone rang again.

"JR," I said.

"Hi there! What are you doing tonight?"

It was Julie and she sure sounded sexy, much sexier than she ever has.

"How are you? Can I call you back?" I said.

I realize I did not answer her question but I did not want to talk in codes to my boss right there before this phenomenal beauty. She knew I was not alone by the way I sounded.

"No JR, I will call you again later on. Will you be available?" *Ouch! How do I answer that?* "Of course I will, check back okay," I said.

Phew! Julie was starting to really arouse my curiosity. What is the deal? Veronica got another bottle of champagne while I was on the phone. I mean she voluntarily gave a brotha some privacy. Those are skills that a brotha just can't teach. She was really beginning to let her hair down.

"JR, I have another friend who is also looking for a house."

"Really, what type of house is she looking for?"

"My friend is a he not a she."

"No problem, here is an extra card for him. Please tell him to just give me a call or you could also give me his number and I will call him. He is also more than welcome to stop by the Open House showing on tomorrow. I can give you the details on directions before we depart."

"Sounds good! I'll pass on the information about the Open House and yawl can hook up from there."

It was rapidly approaching 10pm. Wow, how time flies when you are having so much fun. I still wanted to call Loke and Juanita too but I was not about to rush Veronica off. She told me she would probably not drive home from being slightly tipsy and I told her I would gladly do the honors. Initially, she declined my offer but after about thirty minutes later she changed her mind. I guess the alcohol was taking effect. The only catch was that she wanted me to drive her car, as she did not want to leave her car here. I had no problem with that. I secured my Lex and proceeded to take her home in her Bentley looking Jaguar. I did ask her how to get to her place and she responded to my surprise, "Oh No, I'll be going to your place if it's not a bother."

Heavens to Betsy! She wanted to come to my place. Let me think. Is my place clean, are my underwear all over the place and how fast can I clean it up? I graciously replied to her question, "Of course not Veronica, no bother at all."

CHAPTER 4
Is A Gentleman In The House?

As Soon as I started driving to my place, Veronica fell asleep. I knew she was somewhat tipsy but perhaps she was a little more wasted than I realized. She had this real nice split in her dress and you could see the side of her upper thigh. All I thought to myself was that she was overcome by alcohol and not aware of all of her faculties.

I was determined to be a true gentleman. Then again, is that what Veronica really wanted or did she want me to just be a normal man and go for the end zone. I must admit that her pretty face, nice chest, and nearly perfect, voluptuous body were all calling my name. I was anxious, somewhat scared, but yet very excited.

When I detected that she was asleep, I took out my cell phone to call Juanita back.

"Hello," she replied but sounded as though she was asleep.

"Hi Juanita, this is JR. I hope I did not call you too late."

"Hi JR, glad you could return the call but I am about to doze off. What are you up to?"

"I'm headed home after a nice evening out. I can buzz you sometime tomorrow. I realize it is about 1130pm."

I really wanted to just return the call and get off the phone because I really did not want to be talking around Veronica.

"Please do JR! I have an early church service in the morning but call me sometime tomorrow evening."

"Okay Juanita, you have a good night's rest and we will hook up on tomorrow."

That actually worked out well as Veronica was out cold. I also decided to call Loke.

"Hey man, how are you?" I said to Loke.

"Look dude, I thought you were gonna call me back earlier." He replied.

I could tell Loke was doing his normal workout with some lady. The voice in the background sounded like Debbie but I did not want to go there.

"Loke, I was gonna call back earlier but I was busy. It sounds like I should let you go because you sound busy."

"You right playa! I gots to handle mine."

I hung up the phone knowing that Loke was screwing Debbie but for some reason it really did not bother me. I kept thinking as to why Julie did not call me back. I arrived at my condo and parked Veronica's Jag in my designated parking spot. I stared at her beautiful body before waking her up. She was oh so fine! I went around and gently lifted her from the seat and she woke up but she was still high but not drunk. I held her in my arms and she laid her head on my chest. I took her straight to my bedroom and I did not turn on any lights as my nightlights lit the path to my bedroom.

When I laid her down, I took off her shoes first and I got my big redskins jersey out for her. I removed her outfit and put my jersey on her, as she lay clad with bra and thong. I rubbed her hair and gently placed the sheets and bedspread over her body. I kissed her on the cheeks and wanted badly to caress her breasts but I refused to go there even though I sensed that she would have expected it. *I mean you do the math with me. She emphasized that her biggest problem with seeing other guys when she was married was that they would get too serious and expect more from the relationship. That tells me that she is down with a bump and grind kind of relationship as long as the quest for more (like serious relationship) was not prevalent.*

I was a true gentleman. After I tucked her in, I went outside and got my mail and turned on the sports channel in my living room. I looked at sports and news for about 45 minutes and then I turned to the 24-hour realty channel, just looking at houses. I took a shower and went to bed.

As I lay down next to Veronica, she was calling the cows home as she was snoring like a drunken sailor but I was not at all complaining. I fell asleep right next to Veronica. She actually rolled over right into my arms. I held her like she was mine. I was tempted to explore her body but I was not about to violate her in any way. My cell phone rang but I left it in the living room and I did not elect to retrieve it.

Then, at the spur of the moment, while curious as to whom was calling I made a diving effort to retrieve it before it stopped ringing. By the time I got to the phone, it had stopped ringing but left Julie's caller ID on the phone. Wow! Julie called again about 1240 am on a Sunday morning. Is she checking on me since she heard strange voices on the first late night call? I was really beginning to get concerned with my boss checking on me during late at night activities. I mean, what in the world is the point? Okay, she busted me on the first late night call but does that justify her checking up on me every night? *Come on man! This is just another way in which the man is trying to keep the brother man down.* I was getting furious just thinking about it and I explored everything in my mind from quitting the job to challenging her work practices.

***

At 7:45am on Sunday morning, I woke up and Veronica

was still asleep. I stroked her hair and kissed her on the cheek. I got up and cooked breakfast for her, figuring I would display my excellent culinary skills. I made some buttermilk pancakes, cooked some turkey bacon and eggs, and prepared some freshly squeezed orange juice. I took it to her in the bedroom on one of my nicest food trays and I woke her up.

"Roni." I called her that name about five times. It just came so natural for me to say and she eventually woke up.

"JR, you are too sweet. Good morning to you. I hope I did not snore too loud."

Now she did snore extremely loud but I won't about to bust her out on that. Then again, why not have some fun with her? She has a great sense of humor and I really think she can handle it.

"Girl, let me tell you. I was up all night long. You slept so hard like you haven't slept in years. At first I thought there was somebody else in here.... naw, naw...I'm just messing with you. You were okay. I didn't mind."

She stared at me in a very thoughtful kind of way like I had committed a crime. For a moment, I was wondering if my jesting was entirely a bad move.

"So JR, you put me to bed, clothed me, and you are feeding me too?"

She was eating them pancakes like she had not eaten for days.

"UMM! These pancakes are so good. Did you make these or did you have some gourmet cook make them? Don't lie now JR?"

"Oh yeah Veronica, I had this other woman stop by while you were sleeping and she cooked for both you and I," I sarcastically replied.

She seemed to easily tell that I was just kidding as she

moved on from the food to the jersey she was feeling and wearing.

"JR, what's up with this Redskins jersey? Don't you know you are in Texas now? I'm a Cowboys fan and we hate the Redskins."

I laughed and pretty much knew in general that most Cowboy fans clash with Redskins' fans.

"Whatever hata, how are your bacon and eggs?" I replied.

"I am too impressed. What are you trying to do JR, get inside of a sista? This food is good. I am glad you cooked for me because a sista show nuff woke up starving. I could get used to this."

"Oh no you can't because I would be expecting it from you," I jokingly responded.

She smiled and kept on chopping as though she really liked the food. I poured her some more orange juice and started to walk out the room.

"Look Veronica dear, I need to take a quick shower and get you to drop me off at my car so I can attend church this morning. You are more than welcome to come along with me."

"Child puhlease! I don't have any clothes to wear because I sure won't wear last night's outfit. I will get up, take a shower and then we both can leave to go and get your car, and then I'll see you at 6pm. You can pick me up or I can pick you up. On second thought, I will pick you up."

"Okay Roni, I got to roll."

I took a shower and got dressed right away in my guest bathroom. She used my bathroom and I noticed she did not close any doors at all. She obviously did not recognize the security mirrors I had all over my place. The mirrors were designed to detect perpetrators if the security system failed.

I accidentally looked in my bedroom mirror near the ceiling and I saw her in all her glory. I wanted to bounce on her so badly but I did not want to scare her off. Then again, she left all the doors open and did not act as though she was trying to hide anything from me. I don't know how many men she was seeing nor sleeping with and I definitely did not want her to think I was trying to marry her. My intentions might send the wrong message. *Hell, I was anxious to let her know that marriage was the last thang on my mind. I just wanted to rotate them tires.*

Anyway, the ride to my car was very pleasant. I drove her car once again and I caught her staring at me quite often. I actually could read her thoughts. She was wondering to herself what I was up to. Picture this, I practically got her nearly drunk, took her home with me and slept in the same bed with her and clothed and fed her without making a move on her. Can you imagine how puzzled she was by all that?

She dropped me off and I kissed her on her cheek and said, "I had a great time."

"Me too, I'll pick you up at 6pm today. You look real nice in that suit by the way."

"Oh thanks Veronica! I'm just trying to be presentable for church. I'll talk with you later."

When I sat in my car, I noticed a brochure underneath the windshield wiper and I grabbed it to throw it away. I noticed there was a note, name, and number on the brochure and it read: "Call me when you get this note...Valerie."

I had no idea who Valerie was so I put the note in the glove compartment and pressed to get to church. I arrived at the church about fifteen minutes later and the choir was singing. The service was great and the minister preached about resisting temptation. It was a message I needed to hear.

Afterwards, I greeted several folks and a couple of people

asked me for a card and said they were going to buy a house. I get that quite often and sometimes I wonder if it's legit. Nevertheless, I always give a business card to potential buyers. I left the service feeling energized and went to my office to gather some goods for the open house.

I arrived at the house thirty minutes early and got everything prepared. Loke called and left a message during the church service. Debbie called as well and so did Julie. The open house was a success in that I think I might have another buyer. About five couples expressed interest and seemed like they were ready to go forward but a realtor never knows who is really serious when dealing with open house customers.

I got home around 4:30pm and called Juanita after I got somewhat comfortable. She wanted to meet me for coffee and I was definitely curious about her interests.

I rushed off and met her. She looked just as sexy as she did the night I met her at the club. She had on some tight white pants that showcased all her curves, a black V-neck top that stopped just short of her navel. She also wore some dark black shoes that matched her top.

We talked for a while and I literally lost sight of time. My phone rang and it was Veronica.

"JR, are you still working?" She asked.

"Not exactly but I am running a little late."

She sounded relieved. "That's fine because I am too. How late will you be?"

"Can you give me another ninety minutes and I should be at home ready to go?"

"Okay, that should work for me as well but if not, I will call and let you know," she said.

Veronica sounded like she was really running late but I was also so I could not complain about that. Juanita was intense, available, and ready to start something up. I told her I was involved but not engaged and she thanked me for being honest. *Why did I tell her that?* Well, I just did not want to make the same mistakes as I did in Florida. I did not want any woman to feel that I would be committed to them or that I was ready for commitment because I truly was not ready for that. I wanted to just date and check out sistas to see what I really wanted in a woman. I don't want any woman trying to take me to the altar right now and that was one reason why Veronica's value had really catapulted to the top.

I don't think a woman fresh out of marriage or about to be fresh out of marriage is gonna want to get right into a serious relationship. Although, I am very well attracted to Veronica, Juanita, and Debbie. Well, the jury is still out on Debbie. I mean, I would have to know that she is really into me and not just into the obvious.

Moreover, I could be totally misreading Juanita. She could have been asking just to make conversation. Besides, she has not given me any reason to believe that she was racing me to the altar anyway. Also, she did not sound disappointed when I replied like I did to her question.

Thus, I left Juanita with a happy spirit felt by both. I got home and called Loke. He told me about his evening on last night. He told me that Gina came over and he made out with her all around his apartment. He reluctantly told me that Debbie was looking for me. She came over to Loke's place after Gina left and he said he also serviced her jets all night long and he really enjoyed it. My feelings were not even hurt and I really felt like a friend of Loke's because he seemed honest. He did also tell me that Gina did not know that Debbie came over later and that Debbie asked him not to tell me about their sexual rendezvous. I was really appreciative of his honesty.

I was not mad at him at all. He just allowed me to make a necessary cut and that was to leave Debbie alone. I talked to Loke until Veronica came to pick me up. She was looking some kind of fine and very irresistible I might add.

She wore this red, mini tennis skirt and a red, white, and blue top with white sneakers. Her hair was pinned up and she had on some nice perfume. She drove to riverside and it was a real nice park with the river trail fit for both romance and walking.

We walked four miles and talked about everything in life. She told me she was not seriously seeing anyone and that she was not engaged sexually with anyone. Although I did not comprehend what serious meant to her, I still found myself in a neutral corner.

I told her I was involved but nothing serious as well. Once again, I told her that because I wanted to let her know I was not trying to get serious with her which really fulfilled two objectives: first of all, it keeps her from thinking that I am trying to get serious with her and secondly it keeps me free to do as I had planned, date around until I feel it for a sista.

At one point, I thought she was going to kick a brotha to the curve but she seemed to let what I say go in one ear and out the other. At least she gave the impression that she did not care. Besides, she was still a married woman technically. She did however drop me off and say that she would be in touch. I did not kiss her on the cheek or anything like that. I just said I had a great day and enjoyed the time with her. She responded by saying: "Likewise."

I went to my pad to just chill and get ready for work on Monday. After taking a nice bath and chilling at home, I got a phone call from Debbie.

"Hey JR, how are you?"

"Doing well Debbie, how are you?"

She sounded real sexy on the phone and I was very alert as to what she would say next.

"I'm doing fine but missing you. Can you get away? I just want to see you."

Yeah right, I thought. I'm sure she was missing me after kicking it with Loke all last night. She really did have some nerve. I guess Debbie is what you would call a stupid hoe. Nevertheless, my rule is never saying anything to hurt a woman if you can, even if she is a stupid hoe. Besides, you never know when you might need some luvin on a rainy day.

"I'm kind of in for the night but perhaps another night would be better," I said.

"What night is better JR? I wanna go down on you so bad."

Oh Lord! She is playing dirty on a brotha. Heaven knows she does know how to bob for apples and that statement alone got me to thinking. I got to admit the sound of that really did get me a little excited.

Nevertheless, I had to hold my guns. Besides, I don't know how long I can continue to go behind Loke. Then again, I thought to myself, why not just go ahead and bounce that trick and then call it a day. Besides, I didn't hit it the other night because she would not come up from bobbing for apples before Loke got greedy.

"What's your address? I might can get out the house for a moment," I said.

I can't lie to myself. I am very much attracted to Debbie's body. I cannot deny that. I really don't care if Loke is wearing it out. I just want to go ahead and get some too. Why should I feel bad about it? I am single and this seems to be all Debbie wants. For the moment, I'm down for that.

CHAPTER 5
Becoming A Boss Playa

It took me twenty minutes to get to Debbie's house. She had a nice, small, and very quaint like apartment. It was just a step up from a residence in a public housing area and it perfectly fitted her world. I pulled up to her door and knocked twice and she opened the door immediately. Debbie greeted me with all smiles while wearing a baby blue colored robe that you could see through.

As soon as I walked in and she shut the door, I turned and grabbed her and started kissing her. It came so natural too as I got an instant hard on as soon as I saw her.

She was desperately trying to take off my clothes. I took that robe off and stuffed her boobs in my mouth like I never tasted them before, which I actually never have tasted Debbie's boobs. She was banging like a drummer. Beneath the robe was nothing but her naked body and I grabbed that inner tube tire like butt of hers and pawned it with both my hands like I was holding a basketball, one in each hand.

I started bobbing for apples, going up and down sucking them juicy tips of hers. Then I picked her up and found the bedroom. I laid her on the bed and then kissed her juicy lips like a thirsty man had found water. I was lying on top of her and it all seemed so natural. She grabbed junior and rubbed it with her hand, and then she rolled me over and started sucking like that was feeding her every passionate move.

She put all of it in her mouth and then consistently went up and down my shaft. Then, she started licking and sucking the tip of junior very succulently, making loud eating sounds. Afterwards, she went to town with her tongue licking my private anchor in the most stimulating way. I could not take it as she could tell I was about to lose my fluids. She put each side of my scrotum sack in her mouth and circled it with her tongue. She repositioned her mouth to where she could receive all my deposits. She tore off the rubber with her teeth and put the center of her mouth on my rod.

She must have gone up and down sucking over 50 times it seemed. Next thing I knew, my volcano had erupted and all I could do is express a loud sigh of relief but she started sucking harder and was licking every drop of my milk as though it was some sweet ole fashioned, country lemonade.

As soon as I came, I was ready to go. It was something about coming that forced me to have guilt beyond my imagination. Its as though I'm fine up until the time I come and then I must depart the scene and do it right away. She still kept sucking after I came but her pressure was much lighter as I was much more sensitive in that area.

Before you know it, I was hard all over again. As soon as my nature stood straight up, she attempted to sit on me but I put another rubber on first and then allowed her to proceed. Debbie screamed real loud as I knocked her stuff way into next week. She must have come about two or three times and I think her climax started as she was bobbing for apples on me.

I left Debbie sleeping after some crazy sex. We both fell asleep but I woke up earlier than she did. She was sleeping so well that I did not want to interrupt her. I hopped in the ride and headed home in time for about six good hours of sleep. On the way home, I was thumping Ice Cube's song entitled "Today Was A Good Day."

***

I woke up fresh and crisp Monday morning, feeling very good. Nothing like getting your batteries charged to elongate the service life of your body. I slept like a baby in a crib. As soon as I got to work, Julie wanted to see me. I had also gotten messages on my cell phone from Debbie, Juanita, Loke, and Veronica but I had not returned any calls yet.

Julie was quick to tell me that the couple I showed the house to on Sunday had called to inquire about the current availability. Basically, they wanted to purchase the house. Julie also hooked me up with about ten other high price houses to show in prestigious neighborhoods. Last but not least, she asked me how was my weekend and wanted to know why was I so busy?

"JR, I know you can't be showing houses late at night?"

She smiled and I replied, "No Julie, but I am trying very diligently to move every piece of real estate I need to sale."

"Well, I can tell when I call you that there is a lot of movement going on in the background and I can't attest to it being real estate. Then again, perhaps it is personal, body real estate."

I could not believe she went there. I must have had a very pissed look on my face because she quickly expressed that she was joking, patted me on the shoulders and quickly turned around to say, "But on a serious note, you are doing a great job. Keep up the work effort."

Okay, those words made me feel better. I thought for a moment I would have to give Julie a piece of my mind. Boy, am I glad that I did not jump to speak as quickly as I could have. Her final words relieved me a great deal. I went to check my other appointments and I already had a busy day to include company orientation.

The Gordans were persistent in buying the house I had showed them on Sunday. Money was rolling well. I'm selling houses, getting commission, and exercising my body as well. Bottom line, I'm getting paid, getting sex, and getting ripped. Who could ask for any more? I also started investing my money. Life was good.

Orientation was truly boring. I had several ideas on how to make it better. I was informed that the guy in charge did not like it. No other realtor seemed interested in the program but I was.

After work, I went to the South Side Gym to play some ball with the boys down in the hood. I would like to go there about twice a week if time would permit. I love to talk some junk and play some serious ball with the young bloods.

I was a superstar basketball player in high school, at least by my own account, until I hurt my back and became a normal Joe Blow. I still got game but not as good as I once had. Nevertheless, it was enough to compete with the best guys that came to hoop there.

After playing four basketball games, I did call Debbie back and she was ranting and raving about last night. She wanted to know if I wanted some more on tonight. I got to admit I was truly tempted to go right back over there tonight. I mean that girl got it going on. I left the South Side and went home to bathe in the tub. Before I could get out of the tub, Juanita called and asked if I would like to come over.

Okay, I got a bird in the hand and one on the ledge, which way should I go? I was no fool. I called Debbie back and told her if I made it over, it would be late that night. She replied, "I understand JR! I just want you to know that my stuff is always on 24/7 alert for you baby."

Wow! I got to admit that Debbie really knew how to spike a brother's interest. Her comments were so compelling. Nevertheless, I did call Juanita and I got her address and proceeded to her place.

Juanita had a real nice place on the West side of town in Bunker Hill Village. Upon arrival to her crib, I was checking out her outfit. She had on a red laced short set that was revealing all of her assets. I came in and we talked for a while. She did tell me that her friend might stop by, and of course it went in one ear and out the other.

Juanita was as fine a stallion a brother could find. I was really feeling her. I had a glass of wine with her and then out of the blue, the doorbell rang. *Oh my God! Houston, there is a problem!* I cannot believe that Houston is so full of fine women. Penelope was about 5'10" with nice facial features, long hair, nice long legs, and her light skinned complexion was the perfect fit with tan hair.

"Hi JR, how are you," she said.

"I'm good Penelope, nice to meet you."

Penelope looked at what we were drinking and said to Juanita, "Girl, you know you need to get out the Hennessey and Coke for me, bump that wine stuff."

Juanita laughed out loud but complied immediately. Penelope asked me a thousand questions. She's one of those types of women that have a question for every minute of the hour. It was almost as if Penelope was checking me out for Juanita.

Before long, I felt like a complete spectacle and I begin to come up with an excuse to leave.

"Hey Juanita, I'd really love to stay longer but I got some houses I need to check out for tomorrow's appointments."

I stood up and Penelope said with a serious voice of confidence, "JR, sit yo ass down. You ain't getting off this easy nigga."

I was somewhat startled by her commanding tone but I sat right back down right away. Juanita giggled and said, "JR, do what you got to do. Penelope is just being a pain."

I sat there and Penelope stood straight in front of me. She had on bright red satin pants and a tight red top with cross-stitched laces that were blue. She bent over and put her butt right in my face. Now, get a load of this. Penelope was a big time sales manager with the hottest computer firm in town. She had a real round butt but I won't biting by any stretch of the imagination. I was still trying to find out what the bottom line was here.

Juanita seemed to be getting a little high and Penelope by all counts seemed to have arrived just a tad bit tipsy so she was not too far away from being high as well. I was completely sober as all I consumed was wine. Penelope continued to back up and then she sat in my lap. Juanita was just watching as though she wanted to see how I would act. I had this very surprising look on my face. I thought to myself that this mess was getting ridiculous and that I would not participate in this toying activity that was going on. I was determined to bring things to a sudden halt because hommie don't play dat!

Then again, as Penelope sat in my lap she started moving her butt as though she was trying to feel my love parts. She started rubbing my chest and she put my hand on her titties. I was not high but I was getting slightly turned on. Penelope was really a nice woman with a lot of class but I understand her ex-husband hurt her about six months ago.

She caught him in bed with another woman and she left him and never looked back. She told me that story herself before she started getting too lit. Her story now is that she falls in love with noone.

"Ahhhh! That feels good JR. Now take it out and suck it real delicately."

I was rubbing her titties when she commanded me to go further. I was directly following Penelope's orders.

"Take the other one out JR and stop acting shy because yo horny ass is about to screw both of us."

Say it isn't so! Not I! Juanita was quiet and then it just seemed that hormones started flying. Juanita took out her breasts as well and fed them to me. Man, I went back and forth from titty to titty.

Then, Penelope started taking off her clothes.

"Let's take him into the bedroom and JR you better screw us good or you won't get this chance again," said Penelope.

She grabbed my collar and I had both my hands down each one of their panties as we walked in sync. They wanted a threesome and I was given an order to screw them so I had to do this. A threesome would be my first ever.

I was rushed off into Juanita's bedroom like a patient being rushed off to the hospital for surgery. I must admit that I was somewhat overwhelmed as I was treading upon ground that I had never entered on before. They threw me on the bed and one went downstairs while the other one was working upstairs feeding my face with their coochie. Penelope turned her back towards me and moved them hips all over creation. Juanita almost sat directly on my face and they did switch up.

I came with them, took a break and went back at it. Juanita got the short end at first but after the break I wore that ass out. I had to make sure I was an equal opportunity employer. I fell asleep and woke up about 2am. I had Penelope to my left and Juanita to my right. *Damn! What a Kodak moment? If momma could see me now?* Oopps, I really did not mean that at all.

I started licking Penelope's titties at the tips and she started moving her lips and tongue. I got on top of her, put junior inside, and screwed her like the joy of a handy man in a tool house. She was good, pushing them hips off the bed as I thrusted back and forth. Her ass bounced back like a springboard and I came like thunder. We both rolled over and our activity of course woke up Juanita.

As I rolled over, Juanita said, "JR, I want some mo too. What about me?"

Her voice was so sexy and low with a moaning sound. You know that sound that a woman makes when she really needs to be stroked all over.

"Give me fifteen minutes and you can come and get yours too baby," I said to Juanita. She didn't wait until then. She just jumped down below and started sucking junior and all the deposits that had settled around it.

She actually got me rock solid in about five minutes and then she got on top of me and rode me hard like a runaway horse. We went at it hard like ships in the night engaged in naval warfare, and we both rolled over. I fell asleep again.

I woke up about 6am to Penelope sucking on junior. Juanita was licking my nipples. As soon as I got hard again they jumped on me like I was strictly there for their pleasure. We all had to go to work and they both wanted to leave on a sexual high.

I rushed home just in time to get ready for work. Wow! Houston is out of this world. I went from being dumped by women in Florida to being the man in Houston. I went from being a shy, insecure no namer to being a boss playa.

***

I arrived at the office just in time for orientation. Julie saw me and said, "JR, be home tonight around 10 pm."

"Okay Julie, what's up? I got your messages. Is everything okay? I'm starting to get concerned."

"JR, everything is fine. We will talk. I'll see you then," she said.

She actually whispered when she said that. I took it as marching orders. I sold two more houses today after surviving orientation. I did meet another sister today who taught the budget review block in orientation. Her name was Jewel. I didn't even know she was a member of the company. She was another hottie.

Man, this place was full of beautiful women. I went from hating women in Florida to wanting to screw every fine woman walking in Houston, Texas. The more hoochies with coochies I got seemed to make me want more hoochies with coochies. This was scary to me somewhat. I went from coochie hell to coochie heaven and I must admit I'm enjoying it. The more I got, the more I seemed to want and won't nobody trying to pin me down for total commitment. Whoever thought that a man can get all of this stuff for free?

***

I had a good workout at Gold's Gym. I was headed home in my car when my phone rang."

"Hi JR, guess what? I am a free woman now," said Veronica.

"Congrats Veronica! I know you are glad it's finally over."

"I am so free in every respect now. By the way, can you help me move my cars when I move into my new house?" She inquired.

"Of course I will Veronica, just let me know when you are ready."

"By the way JR, what are you doing tonight? Do you want to meet for dinner or what?"

She seemed excited over the phone. "Okay Veronica, just tell me where you want to meet."

"How about Logans?" She said.

"Logans it is!" I replied without hesitation.

***

I met Veronica around 7pm. She was looking extremely sexy once again. While I was there, Debbie and Loke called. Julie also called to remind me to be home at 10pm. I clearly forgot about that until I heard her mention it on my voice message.

I called Juanita to let her know I had a great time. I told Debbie I would hook up with her later in the week, and I told Loke I'd go with him to the Rockets/Lakers game later in the week.

Veronica was extremely happy and ready to get lit. I started drinking with her and she insisted that dinner and drinks were on her. I thought to myself, *you ain't got to tell me twice.* Logans was one of the more expensive restaurants in Houston and I was not about to argue over that decision. Veronica was so different tonight.

"JR, I'm taking tomorrow off! Can you?" She asked.

I did not know how to take that but I was not about to say "no" to Veronica. However, I did have some hard appointments but I knew I could report later without missing the entire day. I told Veronica I had to plan the entire day thing in more advance notice.

"I can go in late but not take off all day. Also, I did have plans later on with a friend."

"Oh, is this the lady you are seeing but not that serious with?" She replied.

"No, actually this was a late business engagement with my boss."

"JR, tell your boss not tonight. We got plans!"

I looked on with complete consternation. "We do," I said with the naïveté' of a virgin. I was finally getting some "let's screw" vibes from Veronica. I know that Julie really wanted to come meet with me about something. I will try and see if I can push it off until tomorrow, as Veronica would not be denied tonight.

"I will see if I can postpone our business meeting until tomorrow night."

"Good decision JR. Let's eat and go to my place," she replied.

"Oh boy! You mean I get to go to your crib tonight?"

"Yes, since I'm legally divorced now."

I saw Veronica staring into my eyes like she was horny. Oh yes, I think I can tell when a woman has that horny look. I called Julie on her cell phone to cancel our appointment on tonight. I was really somewhat nervous because I did not want to continue delaying my boss from what I think is a business venture, although I sometimes wonder if she is just keeping me in check.

"Hello," she said.

"Hey Julie, this is JR. Hey, I need to postpone until tomorrow and you can name the time, if that is okay?"

Julie blew on the phone as though she was disgusted.

"Certainly JR, I'll let you know tomorrow at work. Is everything okay?"

"Oh yeah, all is well. Tomorrow, I'll be much better prepared. I'll see you in the morning, okay," I said.

"Bye JR." I felt relieved to get that out the way.

I followed Veronica to her house. It was a nice, expensive

condo from the outside to the inside located near Magnolia Gardens. I was somewhat confused as to why she was buying another house but she told me that she wanted to start anew and own real estate under her divorced state as opposed to her married state. She further explained to me how she wanted to escape the memories of her husband and invest in more real estate on her own as opposed to under his watch.

I really liked her master remote system. It opened one of her car garages, opened the house door, turned on the lights, deactivated the security alarm system, turned on music and automatically played her telephone answering machine out loud. It was also equipped with a light charging system that lit up the place to your choosing. Also, her bar automatically opened and the drinks rose from an elevated counter to the top counter.

While I was checking all this out, Roni showed up in some white panties and bra. I immediately started undressing but she would not let me finish. She threw her arms around me and we started kissing as I was feeling her body all over. Within minutes we were butt naked and in the middle of the living room floor on this huge bear like rug that was as comfortable as any bed I had ever slept on. The music was R Kelly's "Get Up On A Room." It was some beautiful lovemaking going on, not screwing, at least that was what I thought.

You see lovemaking progresses a relationship from outside to within and vice versa. You feel the other person's emotions, passion, tenderness, and almost become spiritually entwined as one. Your movements become synchronized and the feeling is so mutual as though you have been craving one another for years. That was lovemaking.

Stop It JR! Remember, this was the lady who was not looking for a serious relationship but just some companionship. Don't make the mistake of going there too soon. Okay, so I need to focus more on screwing the heck out of her and calling it a day.

Anyway, her avalanche fell on my face and I sucked them inner tubes, licked them nipples as though they were full of tasteful cotton candy on every inch of their surface.

I licked and kissed all the way down to her navel and on down to her private passageway. She turned around and before long her head was buried down between my legs and so was my head buried down between hers, as she was on top. I could tell that she had not been stroked in quite awhile as she delicately kissed and licked my twin balls like they were coated with candy.

I rubbed my hands in her hair and then I pulled her back up so I could stab between her legs with junior. Her mid section was so tight and it had a firm grip around the head of my nature. I plunged deeper and deeper and she was moaning and groaning my name. "Oh JR! Oh JR! " She moaned. I got in a rhythm where I was bouncing my butt off the floor and thrusting real hard into her pleasure spot, as she laid on top of me. "Oh…Oh…Oh…" She cried out with greater and greater intensity. Then, I rolled her over and got on top of her. I tried to ram my six point five by three point five inch all the way up her belly and she was screaming as she grabbed my butt. I also started hitting it at various angles while changing the thrust speed from slow to quick, quick to slow and that really drove her crazy. I was bouncing my butt that was driving my nature as though I had hydraulics moving my thrusting endeavors.

I moved my nature in where it was barely moving and brought it out like that as well. She was dripping like rapidly melting ice spikes from off a house after the sunlight exposure. I was thrusting from the hips while one hand was on her left titty and my mouth secured the other titty. Then I put my hands underneath that juicy butt of hers and thrusted harder and harder, faster and faster. I must admit that the strength training with my hips proved highly valuable; as my thrusts would rock her forward all to let her rock back so I could hit it on perfect timing.

She must have come about two times already but the J to the R was not finished. I helped her get on her knees and I went doggy style. I first grabbed her shoulders and pushed my nature back and forth in that gold mine and she was screaming uncontrollably. "PAT, PAT, PAT, PAT, PAT" was the sound that was loudly heard as I was banging that backyard of hers. Then came the grand finale. I grabbed her hips and thrusted as hard as I could and she came all over the place. "OH JR! OH JR! LORD HAVE MERCY! OH THIS MUST BE LIKE HEAVEN BABY! LORD HAVE MERCY! I hit that coochie so good that I came so hard that it seemed like it took a whole three minutes for deposits to shoot out of me as my body shook like the highest Richter scale earthquake.

I woke up around 7am and I was feeling great. Veronica was still out cold. I laid back down and brought her over into my arms and she moved over as though it was expected. I rubbed her body again and she was ready to get some more loving all over again and so was I. I could tell she was still sleepy but I could also tell that she was anxious to give me what I so much wanted again, and I was not shy about what I wanted.

We carried on for a good hour and both fell asleep all over again. I woke up again around 9:30am. I had to rush off to get to work. I kissed Veronica and explained to her I had to run to work so I took off. I had to call to cancel a few appointments but I did arrive in time for orientation.

Jewel was leading the orientation and she truly was the

life of the entire day. She seemed to notice that I was mentally out of sorts and she commented on that.

"JR, you seem a little fragmented today."

"Excuse me Jewel! I did not comprehend the comment."

"JR, you just seem somewhat distracted, like a lot was on your mind."

"Oh, I'm okay. Just thinking about all that I have to do."

"Oh, I understand! You must be extremely busy then?"

"Yep, I'm getting real busy here of late. I'm just trying to keep up with the schedule."

Then, she stared at me with curiosity. "JR, I been here for about a month. Can you slow your schedule down enough to show a sister around?"

Dang, what in the world is going on? I'm starting to feel like every which way I go, some woman is trying to hit on me. I got to talk to my mom about this. Its like something is going on. All of a sudden I'm beginning to wonder if this ain't the devil.

"Sure Jewel, when do you want me to show you around?"

"Well JR, how about this upcoming weekend. Here is my number."

She gave me a card with her home number on the back. "Ok Jewel, I'll get back with you."

I always said in Florida that a man couldn't have too many women, especially a single man. However, here in Houston, I'm starting to feel like I could be getting in over my head. Perhaps I need a committed lady who can regulate for me. I don't know if I got the will power to turn down all these gorgeous, fine ass women. Besides, I'm just a country ole Florida boy gone to the big city.

I left orientation and went to my office. Julie left a note and said to call her when I got in. I called Julie and she said, "JR, we can get together about 8pm. Will that work?"

"Most definitely boss, do I need anything?"

"No, I'll call you with the location where we will meet."

"Okay Julie, looking forward to it."

Now, I'm beginning to believe that Julie has a special business project for me. Guess I was wrong thinking that she was just being nosy and checking out my late night activities. Oh well, I'm very much relieved a great deal anyway. I still sold a couple of houses today. I was selling houses just like I seemed to be attracting women. That was somewhat scary.

I left work about 5:30pm. I called Veronica from the car to let her know I was thinking about her. She was glad to hear from me and wanted me to stop by later. I reminded her of my appointment with my boss and she understood. Debbie called while I was talking to Veronica. I called her back and she wanted to know when I could get away again. I said perhaps later in the week. She was not a happy camper but such is life. I called Juanita to say hello and she also told me that Penelope was asking about me and wanted to know when we could all hook up again. I guess we will always be a trio when it came to those women. She also told me that Penelope wanted my number and I told Juanita that was her decision. I refuse to come between two women who want to screw and not fall in love. This seemed to be the norm here in Houston.

I called Loke and he was still at his office, about to see another patient. He still wanted to make sure I was going with him to see the Lakers and the Rockets. I was not going to miss out on that. I was going to tell Loke about Juanita and Penelope but heck a guy like him would probably take both of them away from me, so I left well enough alone.

I started to call my mom but I elected not to. I'm not ready to hear any stressful news and therefore I think I will pass for now. I went to Gold's Gym and got in a good workout and the fitness trainer, the fine hottie who never gave me the time of day came over.

"JR, you looking more fit than ever."

"Really! Thanks a million! By the way, what is your name again?"

"I'm not going to tell you. If you don't remember, you don't deserve to know." She walked away after that, as usual.

I finished my workout and booked. I got bigger fish to fry anyway. While leaving Gold's, Julie called and said, "JR, meet me at the Lakes, house number 1175 at 8pm. I will let you come in from the secure gate, so just ring buzzer at the gate."

"Okay Julie, I will be there at 8pm sharp."

Wow! Julie got plans for me to do some real estate business in Hollywood Heights with the rich folks. The Lakes are nice and all the houses have a view of a beautiful lake. It's about a forty-minute drive so I had to rush home, change clothes, and head out.

I stopped off the highway to get some gas. Before I could even get out my car, this classy looking white woman pulled up in a white convertible BMW. While I was pumping gas, she spoke to me. "Wow! Can you wash and wax my car to where it looks half as good as yours?"

"Sure, I'm certain the same folks that did mine can do yours as well," I replied.

"Really, I sure would like that," she said.

She got out to refuel her car and she kept staring at me and finally said, "It's a beautiful day, isn't it? I mean the weather has been great today."

"Yep, it has been really nice the past couple of days," I said.

I went to pay for my gas and as I returned to the car, she got my attention. "Hey, you can't just leave without giving me the number to get my car done."

"Oh, I don't know it right off the top of my head but I get my car done at Adam's Car Mart on the corner of Biscayne and Turkle."

"Wrong answer dude, call me soon and we can both wash each other's car."

Okay, call me slow one more time. She was interested in more than I imagined. I got her card and I uttered the least of words. "I got it Cindy."

The name on the card was Cindy Taylor, Attorney At Law. "I will call you later this week perhaps," I said.

"You call me tomorrow after 6pm and don't you forget that," she said.

She was trying to look serious but a smile was coming through her sincere voice.

"Yes Ma'am," and I snapped a salute as though I was in the military.

"Your name soldier is what," she said.

"Call me JR, but I'm not a soldier." I gave her a card. "Realtor huh? I might need a new house real soon," she said.

"I might need an attorney," I said. She laughed and I got in my car and headed out. Five minutes later my cell phone rang and it was she. She said she was checking to see if my number was correct and she also wanted to partake in heavy conversation but I told her I did not like long conversations on the freeway but she kept on talking.

Cindy was cute but a bit too bossy and too bold for me and not to mention very discursive in her conversation. I talked with her for a few moments and then I told her I would call her later in the week. Finally, she got off the phone. I really don't think I would be calling her anytime soon unless she really wanted to buy a house.

CHAPTER 6
World Phenomena-Julie

I arrived at the Lakes' around 7:58pm after speeding down the highway. I rang the buzzer and what appeared to be a French maiden answered the doorbell.

"Hi JR, come on in. I'm Erica and Julie will be right down in a moment."

I spoke to the maid and proceeded into what was a masterpiece of a house. This house had the true marble floors, sturdy walls with the very expensive chandeliers hanging throughout and the classic cathedral ceilings. This house was clearly a mansion or min-mansion should I say. It had nothing but space on top of space. It had enormous rooms, solid marble walls with very expensive pristine like structures. I was in awe of the house alone. Little did I know but what happened next would be monumental changes to my present world as is.

Julie had on a white robe as she came rushing down the turnpike stairwell.

"Hey JR, come on in and make yourself at home."

After she said that she walked ahead of me and slipped her robe off. Wow! She had on a bikini (blue silk) two-piece with a thong bottom. Her butt cheeks stood out as though they busted out of jail as she walked away from me. To say this white woman was built like a sista was clearly an understatement.

My eyes focused on her backyard like I was hypnotized. Then, she turned and said to me, "JR, join me in the Jacuzzi out back."

"OKay Julie, but I don't have any swim trunks with me," was my hesitant reply.

"Don't worry! Your birthday suit is fine."

I was like in a dream or something and it all seemed wrong because this was my boss. What was I supposed to do next?

I really felt reluctant because I had no clue where this was going. Perhaps Julie was just open and care free like this and there was nothing about to happen, but I knew that the obvious signs would indicate a sexual endeavor and I knew that a relationship like that with the boss could be fatal.

Nevertheless, I slowly walked forward to view the stage of the selected scene. I walked all the way to the center of the house where there was a Jacuzzi with a window view to this perfectly manicured lawn and the most gorgeous landscaping my eyes had ever set view upon, all showcased by this outdoor swimming pool that was the size of a public pool.

Julie hopped in the Jacuzzi and said, "Come on JR, you can lose the suit on the table over there. I won't bite."

I stared with much curiosity and I started to undress. While I was undressing, the French maid came through to check the temperature of the water in the Jacuzzi and I refrained from undressing and just stared.

"JR, Erica works here at the house and she is a trusted soul, okay?" It was as if Julie could read the concerns and expressions painted on my face. Erica proceeded as though she was a normal fixture within the scene. I pleaded to Julie, "Is this the right thing for us to do?"

Julie got out of the Jacuzzi, walked over to me and let her bra strap down and her full size, voluptuous breasts busted out of incarceration and looked at me from the standing alone position. I mean, those bazookas were standing at perfect attention and they were purely natural.

"Get over here! Don't play that shy stuff with me," Julie said.

She lifted her left breast and put it right towards my mouth. I hesitated and said, "But Julie! This is all wrong. What about your husband? What about our superior and subordinate relationship?"

I'm not going to lie. I was in way too deep over my head. I literally went buck wild on her. Before long, she was in my lap inside the Jacuzzi with my nature firmly inside her forbidden fruit and her titties were all over my face. She leaned over the Jacuzzi and bent over for me to do a doggy style show. I was pounding and pounding like a field slave turned loose on the white wife of the house owner.

Afterwards, we went upstairs to the bedroom and just kissed up a storm. Her body was perfect for me and I craved every inch of her. Then, we went to sleep for a moment. She woke me up by sucking on junior. I mean she stayed down there like there was no tomorrow. She clearly went on for hours it seemed. It was so soothing that I almost fell asleep again.

Then, we reloaded for a second round. It was truly a night of passion. Finally, after we were done, she fed me shrimp, steak, and caviar. Erica was the in house chef of course. She brought it up to the room. Julie trusted her and I guess I had to trust Julie. Erica wore a French, sexy outfit. She looked at me like I was the lucky one. I just returned her look and smiled. Julie seemed so relieved and then she told me that she was interested in seeing me once a week as long as I could keep my feelings away from the job. She also hinted that she had greater things in store for me and that she knew I would be able to handle much greater responsibility.

I had no idea where she was going with this other than more houses to sale. I did ask her what about her husband and she told me their marriage died years ago and that they were strictly business partners. She emphatically disclosed that she was not interested in falling in love but that she just wanted some good sex about once a week. I told her about my special significant other that I really did not have.

"JR, you don't have a special significant other. You just tell your other women that so you can keep them from having false hopes. You don't have to worry about keeping me at bay. My interest is strictly sexual and when you deem it necessary for us to stop, I will easily oblige. Now, if my intelligence about you having a significant other is wrong, then you should let me know right now."

I was stunned in every which way you could not imagine. I said nothing about a significant other to her again because I sensed that she knew the truth. How? Well, it would not surprise me that a woman of her power probably had a detective checking up on me.

In essence, she wanted to give me some loving weekly, increase my responsibilities, work around my schedule and deliver sexually, unless I cry foul due to a significant other, of which she knew I did not have.

Man! I love Houston, Texas. I can definitely handle this proposition that Julie offered. I did have my doubts however.

"Julie, isn't this pretty dangerous to be sleeping with your boss?"

"How do you figure that?" She was wrapping a towel around her head. "Let me put it this way, the better you screw me, the better your professional job will become. Trust me on that. Look at all the perks you have now and that was before we even started screwing," she said.

Well, that told me a lot but it also placed a lot of questions in my head. Questions I chose not to pose just yet. I was confused over this engagement however. *Am I using Julie or is Julie using me?* Let's see! Let me review the bidding. She wants the sex and I can really do without that because I do seem to be getting a lot of sex in my life but Julie was definitely a good partner in the bed. I think it's just her seemingly, voracious sexual desire and she definitely has skills.

Then again, is she any better than the rest or is it the black/white, forbidden fruit thang where I'm making her all that because she is white, the historically untouchable for my race. I do think I need the professional perks, or do I?

Well, once again, my momma ain't raise no fool.

"Julie, I'm down with that but I do emphasize that the client/boss relationship could make this very dangerous."

She came closer to me on the bed and rubbed my chest.

"JR, the only danger that could possibly exist is that of discovery where reputations are at stake. Besides that, there is not much danger. You can even get married for all I care but just remember the better you take care of me on a weekly basis, the better your progression in the business world will be. I'm sure you can handle it but if for some reason you can't, just let me know. By the way, remind me of eight more clients I have for you. They want the big, luxurious houses." I listened and looked and she started kissing me again and I returned her kisses.

I finally left Julie and I must admit I was somewhat confused. I got back home after midnight and I started doing a lot of thinking to myself. I asked myself while looking in the mirror *Am I a hoe?* I always felt that women who slept with a lot of different men were in fact hoes. I even began to rationalize by saying that women are hoes because they cannot resist men but that I can definitely resist women? I'm just engaging in a lot of sex now so I can put the damaging feelings of my past behind me.

These women that I was currently seeing were nothing more than mere distractions. Matter of fact, they were practically therapy for me. Yeah, that sounds better. This is all pure therapy. God, please understand. This is all therapeutic for my mind, soul, and body. *Now that sounded justifiable and a lot better.*

Besides, it's my time to shine and to be the one that all the women wanted. I had been beat up by love way too much and now, it's my turn as Diana Ross proclaimed in one of her songs years ago. The other significant factor is that I am not initiating anything but these women are coming after me. Hey, as Malcolm X said, "we didn't land on Plymouth Rock, Plymouth Rock landed on us."

***

I woke up the next morning feeling some kind of good, almost like I had another tune up. Wow! If I could only describe the feelings I was experiencing. Nevertheless, I went into work and my desk was full of appointments to show houses. It appeared that Julie had already loaded a brother up. Besides that, my phone was ringing like crazy. I had sold six houses by the end of the day. I would have sold more if there were enough time but some appointments I had to move into tomorrow.

I was literally worn out. I went home at the end of the day and went straight to the bathtub and almost fell asleep in the tub. I put my phone on silent mode and I refused to answer any more calls. I was getting calls from folks interested in houses up until about 9:30pm. It was then that I decided I need to go ahead and have a private number in the house and use my cell phone and work number as my business phone or an additional means of communication when I'm away from the house.

With caller ID on my cell phone, I can screen calls first as opposed to talking to customers all the time. I must admit, I never thought I would ever reach this point but now I see why folks separate work calls from office and personal time. It could literally burn you out. Still, I can't believe that I would ever reach a point where I was tired of customers.

Julie really did have the hookup. I got to make sure I take real good care of that stuff. Anyway, tonight I'm not even looking at my phone. I plan to just crash and reload on tomorrow.

***

I woke up very early Friday morning and had the energy to check all my messages. I had forty-nine messages and thirty-seven of them were from customers interested in buying houses. Julie left a very sexy message and said, "JR, thanks so very much for the other night. I needed that very badly. I am so glad to have you as my lover and I promise to take care of you as I'm sure you will take care of me."

Veronica, Juanita, Debbie, and even Penelope called and Cindy too. As I got out the shower, Loke called.

"JR, what's up playa? What you been up to?"

"Hey man, I just been working real hard lately. Business is picking up."

"You still going to the game tonight," he replied.

"Fo Sheezie Maneezie man! I'm definitely hitting the game."

"Look here JR! Meet me at my crib no later than 6:45pm and then we will have a few hooks (drinks) and then hit the game. Afterwards, we will be attending a private party thrown by one of the NBA ballplayers."

I got excited, as I have never been to a party like that.

"Really Loke! That will be great man! I'm excited about that!"

"You should dude because ain't nothing but the finest honeys in Houston going to be there. We will have much to choose from," he said.

"Well, actually Loke I just wanted to meet some NBA ball players. I think I got enough women in my life right now."

Loke quickly replied, "JR, are you out yo mind? You can never have too many honeys. Stop thinking about a wife dude and treat these women like they want to be treated, like hoes. Is there too much sand on the beach? Are there too many fish in the sea? Is there too much money in yo bank account? The answer to all them questions is hell no!"

"I hear ya playa. I'm just saying my plate is full right now but I'm gain," I said.

He started laughing. "JR, you get a little piece from Debbie and your plate is full. Come on playa! Don't let me take your playa card from you."

"Okay Loke, you got a point," I quickly replied.

I did not want to tell Loke about Veronica, Julie, Juanita, and Penelope. Besides, he might try to move in on my action with his good looks and ole school, new school charm. Therefore, I was keeping my mouth shut. I got all dressed for work and Julie called.

"JR, I would like for you to accompany me to a very important staff meeting. Be in my office at 4pm for a 5pm meeting."

"Sure Julie, I just need to cancel another appointment."

"JR, stop scheduling late appointments on Fridays. Learn to coast from 1pm on," she said.

"Well, I would Julie but my boss keeps me busy, but I'm definitely not complaining."

She gently smiled before expressing, "I'll see you in my office at 4pm." I got calls from other folks as well. Now, how can I fit in everybody over the weekend? Debbie left a long message along with Veronica, Juanita, and Penelope. Julie called me again later on around 1030am to cancel the 4pm meeting since the staff meeting got canceled. I sold another four houses today and of course I got to credit Julie. She has sent me nothing but ready now buyers.

Nevertheless, there were a few customers whom I had showed houses to a couple of weeks ago, that had bad credit and thus were turned down for loans. I got to admit, that was a daily occurrence in Ocala but not at all the case here in Houston. It was clearly opposite in all respects when it came to the acquisition of real estate. Then again, I really thought that it's the exclusive customer base that Julie's company attracts. I firmly believe that's really the bottom line.

CHAPTER 7
Another Wild Weekend

On Friday, Jewel and I had lunch together. This was the first time I had actually gone to lunch since I went with Veronica. Jewel was pretty cool. She wanted me to start showing her around on tomorrow but I had too many appointments to show houses. I told her about the NBA game tonight and she wanted to come along but I did not invite her.

I knew that Loke and I had plans to attend an after party and meet some NBA stars and I did not want Jewel to feel upstaged. Besides, as far as I knew, Loke only had two tickets. I told Jewel I would get with her on Saturday and she also wanted me to take her to church on Sunday. I agreed.

I arrived at home and showered. While getting ready to attend the basketball game, I got a phone call from Veronica. She wanted to know if I was for certain that I was not in a serious relationship because she thought it was very difficult to catch up with me. I did not give her any response to that comment, but I told her I would see her real soon.

Veronica was really nice and I did not want to upset her by any means. I was really reaching a point where I had to start making a schedule as to when I could check all my ladies. I was listening to Krazy Bone and Ice Cube's "Get Your Mind Right" as I was headed to Loke's place. Loke was a very interesting fellow. Not only was he a very good dentist but he was also a social butterfly.

Although he was recently divorced, he was taking good care of his kids and he was a very giving person. Loke loved women a lot more than I did. I showed up at his place just as planned at about 7pm. We knocked down some hooks and proceeded to the game. My drink only consisted of Jack Daniels and coke but Loke was drinking straight 150 proof rum.

Loke's popularity was profusely huge. The valet parking attendants parked his car in the VIP section and they seemed glad to see him. Even as we walked into the arena there were several folks that spoke to Loke; most spoke to him by shouting out Dr. King.

The seats that we had were clearly off the hook. We sat in the midcourt area about five rows back from the players. I'd say we had the best seats in the house. The game was a thriller and Houston won in the last four seconds of the game. Steve Francis hit a three pointer and it was lights out, game ova. I was quietly routing for the Lakers. Shaq and Kobe had a terrific game. Nevertheless, they lost.

Afterwards, we went to the party. Loke and I showed up and it was truly a celebration of many sorts. The superstars showed up later. Loke introduced me to several players on the Rockets' team. The place was full of the finest sisters I have ever seen in my life. Loke was truly on point when he made that description as to what the party would be like.

A few honeys thought I was a celebrity on television and I told them I was one in the making and not on television just yet. Women were so plenteous there and they merely created reasons to talk to you because they knew that if you were at this party, you were someone special.

Loke went down early. He was passing his card out to everyone and it seemed like a very distinct business move so I clearly followed suit. Matter of fact, I passed out all my cards to various folks, trying to get some business. I had to get away from Loke however, because the Dr. conversations clearly upstaged the realtor's conversations. Women clearly displayed much more interest in a Dr. as opposed to a realtor.

Then again, Loke's charisma would also open doors for him. After I made my way back around to Loke about an hour and a half later, he had fixated on this really fine sister and I could tell he was going after her. This woman did not seem to bulge at the lines at which Loke was throwing. However, she did have a friend who was really all up in my face and she was the bomb!

Thomasina was very intelligent and highly sophisticated. We talked for quite awhile and she told me her friend, Sasha was not feeling Loke. Keep in mind, most of the men at this party were top businessmen, professional athletes of other sports or men who were close friends or relatives to the professional basketball players.

The women were mainly groupies who were highly attractive and fine but gold diggers and hoochie mommas deep down within. That was the case for most of the women but definitely not the case for all of them. Thomasina and Sasha to our surprise were in the small class of women with their own bank.

Loke acted like he was in love and I really could not figure out why. Both these women were on average just as fine as the rest of the ladies but to me, nothing seemed to separate them from the pack until I engaged in deep conversation with them. As I observed Loke talking to Sasha, there were other women that came over to make their interest known to Loke and he had to gently brush them off.

Sasha was the type that was not impressed with the Dr. status and seemed turned off by the mere fact that a lot of the women seemed to know his profession. I did manage to talk Thomasina into getting Sasha to consider leaving to Loke's place. Hey, Loke's a nice guy and I really did like him. I wanted to help as best I could even though I really was not interested in Thomasina.

Thomasina really worked on Sasha and finally she was gain. The ladies followed Loke and I to his place. Sasha drove a pretty, gold and black Mercedes Utility vehicle. I mean that ride was tight. Loke was talking about her like he was in love and I was very surprised to say the least. Thomasina was nice but I definitely won't trying to take her home to mom.

"Loke, why are you going on like you are in love with Sasha?"

"JR, you got to understand how the game is played. She's got money, class, time, and she's a nice trophy to sport around the town. I need a lady for cover. I definitely am not trying to marry again no time soon. Sasha would be good for politics. A good dentist needs to have a fine, classy woman for cover. As you get older you will see where I am coming from."

Actually, I totally understood where Loke was coming from.

"Also JR, Sasha's rejection of me is a reminder of all the rejections I've ever gotten in my life from women. Last but not least, but she also reminds me of my wife but a little younger and more arrogant. Trust me JR, I'm going to break her down to her knees. You will see. Also, she's got plenty of money and that's good because I ain't trying to spend my kids' money on some woman."

I listened to Loke just as though he was the boss playa that he was. We arrived at Loke's pad and it was some kind of immaculate. I did not realize it but Loke had a maid that takes care of his place. He informed me that she came through while we were at the game. I thought we would go into his place with his underwear and socks all over the place like it was before we left but that was not the case.

These women were not impressed with Loke's high fly dollar because they were every bit of big money. We all gathered in Loke's den and Loke got out the drinks. The ladies wanted to shoot some pool and that we did for a while. Now, the most intriguing phenomena about these women were that they were both married and I did not realize that until we arrived at Loke's place. I saw the wedding bands on both hands of each woman but I also know how my sisters wear wedding bands even though they have already been divorced.

That realization made me put the brakes on fast. Upon that discovery, I made up my mind that I was just going to be a good gentleman and call it a night. Besides, that was my plan all along because I thought there was no way these classy women were going to do anything else but have drinks, flirt, and then leave.

However, Loke as usual did not share my perspective. He thought that I knew all along and he felt that their status clearly simplified our effort, whatever our effort was?

"JR, that's why Sasha is not overly interested in me. You should have gathered that information at the party."

Loke spoke to me as the ladies went to talk their pool strategy, whispering in the corner of the room. Perhaps his explanation was clear as to why Sasha was very reluctant but it did not explain why Thomasina was deeply interested as she was married too. It also did not support his logic of being able to have Sasha for cover because her married status would definitely not allow her to go flossing all over town with Loke. Thus, I was somewhat confused as to where he was coming from.

In addition, as we played pool, they both claimed that they have never had an affair and I must admit they sounded very truthful and believable. I later told Loke I did not believe that but he insisted it was not important either way. Thomasina did a lot more drinking than Sasha. We shot a lot of pool and finally played teams against one another.

Thomasina wanted to play strip pool. I had never heard of this before in my life. The rule was every time a team knocked a ball in the pocket, the other team had to take a shot of vodka and then take off a clothing item. After the clothing items were expended, then you would just take a shot of vodka and then perform a sexual favor on the other two competitors.

Loke had a sigh of relief as Thomasina uttered the rules. He had a look as though he knew the outcome of this game. I was slightly uncomfortable and nervous, as I was not a pool shooter at all. The ladies went first. Thomasina started the game off and knocked in two balls on the break, which was pure luck. Thus, Loke and I took two shots of vodka and took off two clothing items that the ladies chose.

Initially, they wanted us to take off our suite coats and tie and so we did. I knocked a ball in next after Thomasina missed the next shot and I told them to take off their shoes and they both did so without reservation, after they took their shot of vodka. I missed the next shot and then Sasha knocked in two more balls. She had Loke and I take off our shirt and pants, after we took our two more shots of vodka. Then Loke knocked in a tough shot and had the ladies take off their dresses after they took their vodka. They both had like camisoles or slips underneath their dresses. That's one difference between a sophisticated lady and a hoochie momma. A hoochie momma would have had nothing on underneath or just a thong. Then again, some sophisticated women do go without anything underneath when they really want to dress loosely, so I'm told. Loke knocked in another shot and had the ladies remove their camisoles. Both their bodies looked nice and tasty.

I was beginning to focus more on their bodies but I was also noticing how the alcohol was definitely affecting them. Loke could drink all day long but I was not a heavy drinker. I could handle it better than either of the women, although they acted real tough. Sasha seemed like a pool shark. I could tell by the way she held the pool stick and by the way she executed her shot.

Anyway, Loke made another tough shot and he went where I knew he would not go. He had both of them take their liquor shots and then take off their bras. They both removed them right away and you could tell that both women were getting inebriated. Now, I was looking at both their chests and Loke was too. He missed an easy shot from staring so hard. Thomasina missed the next shot and I missed directly after she did.

Sasha was going down fast. She started slurring as she spoke but she was still as sexy as ever. Nevertheless, she knocked in the next ball and said, "Okay boys, drop dem draws." Wow, I could not believe she went for the jugular. We still had on tee shirts, but they wanted us to let the underwear drop. After taking our Vodka shots, we released the hounds.

They both acted like it was no big deal but they stared at both of us without shame. Sasha missed the next shot and almost stumbled after the shot from the alcohol. Loke hit the next pool shot and had the ladies pull down their panties. They took their liquor shots and proceeded. They were both very hairy and they both had butts that were perfect for one of those videos on BET. They both had on stockings up to their thighs and they looked ripe for the eating.

I asked the question what next since we were all naked and Sasha said, "now its time for the sexual favors." The ladies won the first game because I knocked in the eight ball but I also scratched as the cue ball trickled into the side pocket. They added to the rule that the team that won would get an extended version of a sexual favor.

The two women huddled up and came up with a sexual favor. Before they did however, Thomasina told Loke, "You need to settle down big boy." He stared at her real hard while holding his armor in his hand and gently rubbing it. "I don't know what you got on your mind but you got the wrong one here," she said as she gently pushed Loke away. Then, she started laughing. Loke was rock solid hard and protruding up without any doubt whatsoever. I was nowhere near hard as I was somewhat uncomfortable.

They demanded that each one got their titties sucked by both of us at the same time for 15 minutes each. They wanted both men on one woman at a time. We started with Sasha because she said she came up with the favor. Thus Loke and I begin sucking her titties and Thomasina was the timekeeper as she was looking on intensely. I had the left titty and Loke had the right one and we started sucking and licking at the same time.

Sasha had some small titties with pointy nipples. I tried to put every bit of her titty in my mouth. Nice brown titties with nice dark brown spots and nipples that clearly stood out as she got turned on. Sasha was looking towards the sky as she sat on a bar stool and started breathing real heavy and before I knew it she was rubbing junior. Her touch was so welcoming and perfect for the moment. She also grabbed Loke's junior with her other hand. I gradually started licking her tips in a vertical way, up and down, up and down. I gradually started sucking harder and even gently gripped her nipple with my front teeth and rolled it from side to side.

Sasha was making sounds of pleasure and so was Thomasina. Thomasina was leaning back on the pool table while Sasha caressed both my junior as well as Loke's in her hands. Then, as Loke was getting ready to go down on her, Thomasina yelled "Times Up."

"Are you sure Sina," Sasha said as her pleasures came to a seemingly abrupt end.

"Yes child, your fifteen minutes are up. Its my turn," said Thomasina.

Thomasina positioned herself on the other side of the pool table. Her boobs were also pretty. Matter of fact, to me all breasts are pretty whether big or small. I believe in cherishing titties just like the bible says a man should. *Lord, you don't have to tell me twice.*

Thomasina had some nice, medium sized, Halloween pumpkin breasts, and I went after them thangs like a lion about to devour dear when he was real hungry, but in a much gentler way. Rather than ripping with my teeth, I was using my tongue and I sucked real loud as to mess with Thomasina. I really wanted to make her laugh and she did for a moment. Thomasina couldn't wait to grab both our juniors as Loke was sucking her other titty.

"Thomasina, you are cheating! You are not supposed to handle those until the last three minutes," Sasha said.

"Girl please! You weren't even supposed to touch them but you did. Let me handle my business and you handle yours," said Thomasina.

"OOOHHH! That feels good," Thomasina uttered.

Then, before you knew it, Sasha got down on her knees between Loke and I and started gently licking our private parts.

"Sasha, you cheating with yo horny ass," Thomasina said. Sasha did not say a word but boy did her tongue feel good licking the lower edges of my scrotum sack. It felt so good. She went back and forth from me to Loke. Then, Thomasina started grabbing the back of my head as to guide my tongue while licking her titties.

Then, I saw Loke putting his finger between Sasha's legs as she sucked his junior. Sasha started to pull Loke away and as she did I put my fingers up in Thomasina's gold mine. As soon as I did I felt the moisture of her stuff and she begin to moan. I got more bolder and started kissing her in her mouth. My tongue was boldly touching her tongue and guiding it into my mouth.

I gently put a nice suction on her tongue while kissing her. My left hand had three fingers stroking her hairy, juicy stuff while my right hand was squeezing her right titty and my tongue was sliding back and forth across her tongue and with a nice suction from my mouth. She began to pull my head tighter with both her hands and then I eased up on her. I tilted her body on the pool table where I positioned junior to stroke by and over her coochie. At this time, I positioned both my hands on that ass of hers. It felt like a balloon full of water. Then, she got louder and louder with her moans and groans. She quickly grabbed junior and quickly stuffed it into her coochie.

"Fuck me JR!! Fuck me baby! OOOH, fuck me JR."

I started stabbing junior in and out to get a firm hold on that coochie. I went slow and gentle at first. Then, I started going strong and hard and I was pushing my junior back and forth at a fast motion. Powered by the gravity of my round ass I pushed harder and harder with the momentum of my body.

"OH JR! YES! YES BABY! YES BABY! Then I slowed

down and laid the whirlwind motion on her. I would swing my ass around nice and slow so junior would penetrate all parts of her coochie in a circular motion.

For some reason, this was driving her crazy. I slowed down my movement and she really acted more turned on than ever. I gently pushed her further back on the pool table, got on top of her and pawned her ass with my hands. I thrusted as hard as I could and she moved about uncontrollably, while shouting: "YES BABY! YES! YES! OH-OH-OH-YES JR! Fuck me harder! I'm coming baby." She kept on going at that pace, repeating the same words for about two minutes.

Then, all of a sudden her body went into an arrested orgasmic lockdown as I delivered the lumber to the fire.

"Oh Yes! Oh Yes!" She cried out as I moved my hips quickly and powerfully. She fell back in a relaxed mode and said to me, "Okay baby, how you want this stuff? Just tell me how you want me to position myself because you have earned my coochie," as her body moved spastically and uncontrollably.

I guided her to her knees and then I stood at the end of the pool table and tow that ass up from the doggy style position, my position of strength. I yelled out, "Gimmie dat big ass! Gimmie all dat big ass!"

I thrusted my junior hard and fast from the doggy stance position. She responded to my call by saying, "Get it baby! Get all dis ass baby! It's yours baby! Its yours."

Then, before I knew it the greatest sensation overcame me as I shot fluids straight up into my raincoat.

We both seemed to collapse at the same time in the most pleasurable way. I fell over and laid beside her across the pool table. Thomasina was trained right. She got on her knees and gently removed my raincoat and started sucking junior. It felt so good. Unfortunately, I could not get an erection right away but her lips and tongue sucking my junior made me so at peace that I fell right asleep.

About forty-five minutes later I woke up to a cold wet mouth on my junior. As I opened my eyes and came to my senses I realized what was going on. I heard Thomasina moaning and groaning but not to my fondling. My junior got so hard to that wet and somewhat coarse mouth. Next thing I know, Sasha got up on top of me. Then, it all became clear to me. Sasha was doing me while Thomasina was doing Loke in the other room, the reverse of what Thomasina and I were doing earlier where Loke and Sasha went in the room together.

I was barely coherent but all I know was that tight coochie rode junior like I was a racehorse. I grabbed her hips and lifted my ass like it was a trampoline, back and forth hitting that coochie. Her tender pit was so tight and it choked every drop of fluid out of me. Sasha screamed real loud which was such a turn on that it shot me straight into an orgasm right along with her.

She placed my head underneath a pillow as I realized we were lying on sheets and a quilt. Loke was still screwing Thomasina in the other room. She was loud just as she was with me.

"Damn, that felt so good," I said to Sasha. "Don't yawl have to get home to your hubbies?"

"Yeah, but we're okay. They know we always go out to eat breakfast after clubbing all night," she responded.

I thought to myself, *what just happened? Am I supposed to be with Thomasina or Sasha or does it even matter?* I thought Loke was so heads over heals with Sasha?

Anyway, Sasha gave me a long tongue kiss before she got up. I reciprocated while holding them nice titties in my hand. Loke was still banging on Thomasina. She was still moaning and he was still screwing her as I heard the consistent sound of swish, swish, swish, as his skin was clashing up against hers, as though they were straight up doggy style.

Sasha and I, for some reason, took a shower together and I was so thrilled with her body. I bathed every inch of her body and she really enjoyed it. We winded up screwing again in the shower. It was a quickie but it sure felt good. As we got out the shower in Loke's guest bedroom, Loke and Thomasina were still screwing. Wow! This was nothing but a screw fest. I can honestly say I enjoyed it although I had no business going there.

***

"JR." I answered my cell phone as I stepped into the car to leave Loke's place.

"Jamie Randell, where the hell have you been?" My mom yelled through the phone.

"Nowhere Mom, how are you doing?"

"I'm doing fine son and how are you? What's been going on with you?" She replied.

"Not much mom! Just working real hard and enjoying Houston," I said.

"Now son, please don't be so quick to fall in love. Take your time and wait on the girl of your dreams."

Mom knew me real well; too well in fact. She knew that I have been hurt in my last few relationships and she thought I fall too quickly for certain women.

Man, if she could only see me now.

"Mom, I am not falling in love with noone. I am having a good time, working hard, and enjoying life."

"Alright son, how is the job?"

"Its going well mom. I am selling a lot of houses and I got a real good boss who favors me quite well."

I wanted to tell her more but I did not want to say anything to my mom that would lead to her being suspicious of my current mode of operations here in Texas. Besides, mom was just checking on me. I was tempted to talk with her about my new lady friends but based on lessons learned in Florida, I was determined not to put her in my relationship again. Mom just gave me her love and scolded me for taking such awhile to call her and check in basically. Afterwards, she got off the phone with the normal "I love you" and I of course reciprocated.

CHAPTER 8
The Jewel Bond

I checked my messages and I got calls from Debbie, Veronica, Penelope, Juanita, and Jewel. I called Veronica back and left a message on her machine.

Jewel called again around 7:40am Saturday morning and said, "JR, can I get my tour today?"

"Sure Jewel, I got to make that paper first and I'll be free later on. Now, if you would like to accompany me as I show some houses, you are more than welcome?"

"I would love that JR. Are you going to pick me up or should I meet you somewhere?"

"Its 7:42am now, I will pick you up about 11am."

I wanted to go back to sleep, relax, catch a few Z's and then hook up with Jewel just prior to my noon appointment.

"Okay JR! I look forward to learning a few tips from the hottest realtor in Houston."

"Well Jewel, I don't know about all that but I'm trying to bring everything to the table, leaving nothing on the shelf."

"Alright JR, pick me up at 11am and I'll see you then."

Jewel was an interesting person. She was very adamant about me showing her Houston, like I had a clue about this place. She was another one that had migrated to the Southwest.

When I picked Jewel up, she was dressed like a typical female realtor. Her nice dark black pant suit was very conservative and business like. Jewel was about five feet seven inches and as light as any bright, high yellow sister. She had nice long hair, a nice backyard like a sister should and softball size breasts. She had some nicely carved legs, complimented with a very nice and sexy voice. She had to be about twenty-four years old. She also had some very pretty white teeth. She was a novice in every respect in terms of the realty business but she was definitely a very strong manager and aggressive businesswoman. She was engaged to this high profile attorney in upstate New York. Her rock could literally blind you if you stared at it for a long time.

"Jewel, that's' a nice ring on your finger," I said.

"Thanks JR! My man gave it to me the night prior to leaving New York. I guess he wanted to make sure I knew that we would really marry after dating for eight years."

"Wow, that's a long time. Were you guys high school sweethearts?"

"No, we met in college." Jewel is a graduate of Harvard Law School and her fiancée graduated from there as well. She had a very radiant personality and was very loyal to her man. Why she never pursued law, I will inquire about later.

Jewel and I showed about six houses and sold four of them. I was starting to rise on the company charts as far as selling houses. The more houses you sold, the more business flowed your way. But, make no mistake about it, Julie was my biggest supporter. Jewel and I traveled all over Houston and I actually discovered some new places. She was fun to be with and we were developing a straight up plutonic relationship. Jewel was rapidly becoming like a blood-sister image upon me. In many respects we were like siblings of the same household.

On Sunday, the preacher talked about the value of telling the truth. After church, Jewel and I went to supper and then she joined me again for a house showing. The house sold once again.

Now, one thing interesting about church was that Debbie showed up. She assumed that Jewel was my main squeeze. Debbie was looking good. When she walked away, I casually looked at her and I thought to myself that I really wanted to see her real soon. She was looking that good. It was almost as if she strategically placed herself in my view just so I could get a most recent, full view of the merchandise.

As fate would have it, Debbie called my cell around 10pm just as I showed up to her house. I did not answer but instead knocked on her door and she opened the door and we tore each other apart and did not talk in regular conversation until both of us came.

CHAPTER 9
Booming Business - Got Swole

J R, I sold another house."

"You go girl! Cha Ching!" I said, responding to Jewel's call as I was traveling home from work.

"I really appreciate you looking out for a sista! I owe you a lot JR."

"Oh no you don't! It's actually quite the opposite Jewel. I'll call you later okay," I replied.

"Alright JR! I'll talk with you later."

Jewel rapidly became my jack-of-all-trades. Here's the deal! I was 15 months into Houston, Texas. I had blown up like Wesley Snipes did in the movie New Jack City. I had made over four hundred and fifty thousand dollars and I did it by starting my own business on the side. I owed Julie big and here's why. She pushed me into starting my own business when I became a licensed broker; again an accomplishment she pushed me towards. Julie informed me that she had this plan all along the first day she met me. I felt like the title of one of Keith Sweat's old songs, "I Didn't See It Coming."

I got so busy selling houses that I had to take Jewel under my wing. Without me, it was obvious that she was struggling but once again Julie had told me early on to make sure I take care of Jewel. It was almost as though Julie knew that Jewel would have a difficult time working with her staff. I could not totally put my finger as to why but it was fairly apparent as I begin to work more with Jewel.

Now, I still sold houses but I utilized Jewel to do my legwork and I finalized the deals as the broker but I still sold for Julie and Star Top Realty. I told Jewel that I would take her up the ladder as far as I go and Julie has launched me to a high spiral. I also thank God first and foremost and I make sure I pay my tithes. I am also not only a broker but also the company Orientation Coordinator and I have made that project one of the company's finest. The manager is, guess who? That's right, my girl Jewel.

After winning salesman of the month for six consecutive months, Julie informed me that I needed to work through someone like Jewel to disguise the social relationship that Julie and I had strongly developed. I fell for that bone like a starving dog. Now, I knew in fact who buttered my bread and I knew that Julie controlled who won such awards because all huge contract sales flowed through her but now also through me as an assistant broker.

Julie was not greedy at all but her motive for raising me to the top was due to her lack of trust in the rest of her staff. We clearly do have some racist white men who clearly seem interested in taking Julie's job. Little did they know, she was not just the executive leader but the owner as well. Julie says they are also male chauvinists who she hired as a favor to her extremely close friends. I have also learned that Julie is a lot richer than I ever realized and she keeps it so quiet that most of the staff don't even know. More than anything, Julie has taught me well about the business. I was becoming more attractive to Julie but I kept it under wraps. I enjoyed sleeping with her on a weekly basis and it was not because of how well she was taking care of me in the business. *Look, I can't front however. Money does make the pole swole a lot quicker.* I can't even lie about that.

Remember the place I started out meeting Julie, called

the Lakes. Well, as a gift and for her appreciation of my service she sold that place to me for only 75 percent of the overall market value. It took me by surprise but I was totally thankful for her generosity. Julie actually purchased the place at a very inexpensive price as foreclosure property, at least that's what she told me.

According to her, she profited greatly for selling it to me for 75 percent of the value but I also know for fact she could have really made out by selling this place for its overall market value. Now, having said all of that, I was not mad at my boss.

I relocated after selling my condo for a ninety thousand dollar profit. Guess whom I sold it to? You go that right, my girl Jewel. I would have held on to it as the property in that area was appreciating annually at about fifteen percent. All I did was lower a hand to Jewel because Julie lowered a hand to me.

My house in The Lakes was the bomb. It was fairly brand new and had about twenty-four rooms of which seven were bedrooms, inclusive of an outdoor swimming pool, tennis court, and inside basketball court. Julie said it was designed by an NBA great who had financial troubles and the bank later had to foreclose on the property. I also sold a house to Loke who lives nearby and Veronica's friend, who was a retired marketing director of some large company. I guess I need two more cars to fill up my three-car garage but of course I'm in no hurry for that.

Since I can't make it out to the hood to play basketball due to my busy schedule, I thought I would bring the hood to my house every Saturday around 9am until about noon. I hired two security guards who drive a school bus and picked up about fifteen ballplayers, and sometimes twenty ballplayers. We played some good competitive basketball and my security guards made sure that the players were legit. Of course, in time, fifteen quickly became about thirty-five within about three months. Of course I diverted from this weekly plan when I was either out of town or just too tired to compete. All my old financial bills were paid off but more money created new bills which I had serious control over. I was determined not to create any long-term bills. I was only creating bills that could be paid off to preclude any high interest debt. Julie had really taught me well. Since I got my bills in order and I was establishing myself more as a shrewd professional businessman, all else was falling in place. Well, my spiritual and love life could be at question. Then again, I'm doing all right. Besides, God is blessing me and that must mean something!

CHAPTER 10
The Good Life!!

JR, I got something for you."
I had just finished making crazy love to Julie and now she was anxious to share something with me.
"Julie, please don't feel obligated to do anything else for me. I owe you big already."
She handed me some papers and said, "I got a proposition for you. You have a chance to be a minority owner of these properties over time, but for now I just need you to oversee and manage the subdivision development. I am basically making you the CEO for these properties."
I read what appeared to be deeds to land property. It was 500 acres of land in Austin, Texas, 300 acres in Stockbridge, Georgia and 700 acres in Burke, Virginia.
"JR, I want you to be my chief Project Manager of this land and I'll tell you why in a few minutes."
All I could say to myself was *wow.* Then Julie proceeded to explain to me her history.
"First off, all the areas are nearly fully developed and ready to be strategically carved into subdivisions. The area in Virginia is about 50 percent complete and that of course is the wealthiest of the three areas with the highest annual appreciation rate and greatest land mass. I'm giving you the opportunity to be a minority owner underneath me and we can further discuss how you can make payments to me to acquire that status. Keep in

mind JR, these properties are worth close to over half a billion dollars. In time, as you develop the subdivisions, they will be worth at least five times that much."

I was shocked and in complete awe.

"Julie, I can't afford to be a minority owner. How much do I have to pay to become an owner?"

"JR, its not as difficult as you think it is. You are making good money as an owner of your own company and manager within my company. I will also pay you an additional $375K annually, to oversee development of these properties. All it takes are payments to me to purchase say ten percent ownership and then more over time as you can afford it."

I quickly said, "but Julie, ten percent of half a billion is—-," she quickly interrupted me. "JR, I understand the math but once again don't focus on that. This is an investment that you cannot afford to turn down. Now, if you don't care to join me on this, let me know and I can forget I ever mentioned it to you. It's really a no brainer and I am not in need of a minority owner. This is just another opportunity that I am extending to you."

Having feeling like a stupid idiot, I quickly told Julie, "I guess I just never imagined trying to buy that type of property for that type of money. If you tell me I can do this, then I guess I can."

"Oh yes you can do this JR. You will earn every bit of your portion and as the Project Lead you will be responsible for seeing this barren land into luxurious subdivisions. I have all faith in you and mainly God, of course."

I was looking out into the midair as though I just saw a ghost or something.

"Julie, I sure hope I don't let you down. You sure do have a lot of confidence in me. Can I include Jewel on the management and leadership aspect as well?"

She stared and said, "of course JR; you can include whomever you deem necessary to get the job done. I'm relying on you to hire all essential personnel to get the project completely accomplished. This project will probably run over a 5 to 10 year span if we move reasonably fast."

My level of shock was equivalent to a bank thief being arrested by an old lady.

"JR, I got to tell you a secret that only you and I will share."

I was getting scared. I knew what was next to come. I'm thinking that my lovemaking was so good to her that she wanted to leave her husband for me. I can't do that. I can't take this.

"Julie, I can't let this go on——," I frantically exclaimed.

"JR, please shut up and listen."

She sat down right in front of me.

"My mother got pregnant twice by a black man that she loved and she gave birth to myself and my brother, named Corey. Just before my mother died, she told me that my father was black. She also told me that she knew that once my grandfather found out who he was, he would make him somehow disappear. Anyway, my father gave this land to my mom. He had it in her name and asked her to take care of it. All I knew was that my father and my brother disappeared. My mom knew that my grandfather had something to do with them both leaving the country. I did not know this until I was twenty years old when my mom died of cancer."

"Wow Julie, I'm sorry to hear that about your mom," I lamented.

"Thanks JR but here me out. My mother made me promise that I would at least sell portions of this land to another black man that I would find myself fond of. My mom taught me to never be prejudice and that returning this land back to a smart black man would exonerate the evils of my grandfather. Now, here is the most treacherous part of the story. My father was given that land in exchange for oil he discovered while searching for crude oil. He did not want to exchange the land for the bottomless pit of oil he discovered, but certain people took away that choice and forced him to take, what was then, very underdeveloped land in these three geographic locations. Thus, they literally ripped my dad off."

I was so stuck on her words that I couldn't even imagine anything but what her father went through during that time.

"JR, I don't know of anyone as innocently kind and giving as you are. Sex has nothing to do with this."

Julie really rocked my world with this information. She convinced me how her grandfather and family had so much more land and oil.

"My grandfather was a very powerful man. He once owned nearly thirty percent of Houston. Currently, I own thirty three percent of Houston and his hatred and prejudice made me always want to exceed his endeavors. JR, noone else knows this but you and a small few. If you need anything in Houston, most roads flow through me. I also have influence in other states and internationally but my power stems from this secret."

Julie continued to tell me more. She told me that most people thought she was rich from her husband's money but it was just the opposite. Julie was definitely a multi-millionaire and probable billionaire and not many people knew it because she kept it private. She owned Star Top Realty and numerous other business ventures in and out of the state of Texas. She also owned a professional sports team but would not tell me which team or sport it was. Most importantly, she told me not to advertise my soon to be newfound wealth because as a black man, you become a quick target.

She asseverated that I refrain from being flashy and flamboyant with money but to be conservative, quiet, and very private. Her words that really sounded in my ear were, "Be wealthy for generations before you ever wear or advertise your money." She also liked the fact that I did not do drugs nor did I waste a lot of money on alcohol or gambling.

"JR, buy your mom a nice house and car and let that money harvest throughout your family's lifetime. Don't waste it on women, friends, and most definitely strangers. Trust me on that."

I did not know what to say. I was lost for words.

"Julie, why me?"

"JR, you are a good man. I wanted to fulfill my promise to my mom and you seemed to be the right guy. I studied you for a while. You are a hard worker and very trustworthy and I know you will allow this land to bless another generation of black folks. I hope to someday see my dad and Corey too again but until I do, all I have are the pictures that my mom hid from my grandfather. Those pictures show me being held by my dad when I was about three years old. He would play with me a lot and stare into my eyes. I remember when I was six years old when my mom would sneak away and allow us all to be together. My dad was so much fun and I really do miss him."

Julie's eyes started watering and I wiped the tears that were dropping from her face as I caressed her and brought her closer to me.

"My grandfather was very prejudice and most of our wealth derived from slave ownership over the years. My husband was also very prejudice but I did not realize it until I married him. He hid it oh so well."

"Julie, is that why you cheat on him?"

She looked down to the floor and her eyes got real watery again. I felt bad and told her, "Julie, I'm sorry. I did not mean it like that."

"JR, don't apologize. I love the race that is within me. I love black people but he hates working with them, hiring them and dealing with them. Before I even knew that my father was black I was always attracted to black people. It was always like a fire that burned within me like candlelight. My husband knew my father was black. Nevertheless, he still treated my dominant race of people badly, even before my eyes. To answer your question, my husband's hatred does make me want to enjoy making love to you that much more but I have always been heavily attracted to black men, probably due to my true blood that lies within me. At least, that is what I have always figured it to be."

She rubbed my head as I laid next to her.

"JR, I must admit that I am very floored by your lovemaking. However JR, if for some reason you want to stop now or any other day, just let me know."

I tell you what, this woman has just about made me a millionaire and gave me good loving and romance too and I'm about to give this up? I don't think so! Once again, my momma didn't raise no fool.

"JR, my husband and I have been divorced about three years now but we paid the attorney a lot of money to keep it quiet."

I responded with my mouth wide open like I just got a knockout blow. What the hell is going on here in Houston where couples are getting divorced and pretending to the main populace that they were still married. This was quite different than it was in Florida. Hell, before you even think married couples were having problems, you somehow knew that they were getting a divorce. The gossip network is stronger than the Paparazzi.

"Julie, why pretend? I asked.

"He thought that if we went public, his business would collapse which it would. I am the life of his business. His being married to me is what put him on the map. Our relationship is strictly business. He does what he does and I do what I do. I had thought about leaving for good after my son and daughter leave home."

I interjected, "but Julie, you are so young with such a long life ahead of you."

"Thanks JR but I don't think 42 is that young. I may be a little well off but I work just to keep from staying home all the time. My goal now is to help others make money. I don't have to work another day in my life but I want to because I get bored easily. As long as I have enough money for my kids for generations to come, I am pretty much contente. You have been a great source of my motivation lately."

"Wow Julie! You have been a great mentor and lover to me. I love making love to you. I really thank you for everything. I have got to pay you back if it takes the rest of my life," I interrupted.

We kissed and made passionate love one more time before we departed. This time it meant so much more to both of us.

CHAPTER 11
Downtime

J R," I answered the phone on a Saturday morning.
"Hi stranger. What's going on?"
Veronica sounded so sweet on the phone. I saw her about four days ago at her house. She had her place looking as extravagant as ever.

"Hey Roni! How are you doing with yo fine self?"

"I was just laying here thinking about the hardest working realtor in Houston with the most not so serious relationship."

I busted out laughing like I was listening to Redd Fox or Richard Pryor. Veronica is always throwing that statement back at me. I was sore and tired after sleeping with Juanita and Penelope all last night. It was Juanita's birthday and I was the gift, all wrapped up underneath a big cake. It was nothing but a freak show.

My cell phone rang and it was Jewel.

"Hey girl."

"Hey JR, did you want me to book those tickets for your flight to Austin, Georgia, and Virginia?"

"Sure thang Jewel! We both need to go. Book the hotel reservations for two nights at each location and a rental car as well."

"JR, you want me to come along?"

"Right Jewel! I am on another line but I can call you back to discuss."

"Do call back JR, bye."

I got back on my regular line to Veronica.

"Hello, I'm sorry."

"So, is Jewel that significant other JR? You can tell me for I am fresh out of a divorce and I am not trying to lock down anytime soon."

"Roni, I keep telling you Jewel was a business partner but if you are thinking that we got something going on and it keeps you in check with your feelings, believe what you choose."

What? I can't believe I had the gall to say that. What in God's name was I thinking? Those words just rushed out of my mouth and I wish I could just pull them back.

"Now that is funny Mr. Realtor boy. Are you coming to the house today?"

"I'm not for sure. I got a lot of business work but I will call and let you know."

"Ok JR, I'll talk with you later."

"Bye, Bye," I said.

I got off the phone with Veronica and I did appreciate the fact that she was not at all pressuring me into a relationship. God, I love this house. I can't believe that I would ever enjoy a house this big all by myself.

Julie really hooked me up and I tend to follow every bit of guidance she has given me. I really do understand what she means about keeping a low profile and keeping my wealth on the down low. Even the fellows I play ball with that came over thought that I was keeping this house for some millionaire.

That does not bother me at all. I guess because I really feel deep down inside that I did not earn it but it was practically almost given to me. Nevertheless, I'm going to apply that lesson to my life. Julie's example of keeping your wealth private was great for me to emulate. Not that I will ever have her kind of riches nor does that matter to me in my life but I will learn to keep quiet about what I do have.

The cell phone rang.

"JR."

"JR, are you still on another line?"

"Negative Jewel—we can talk now; before I forget, please add on the Stockbridge, Georgia visit a trip for me to go downtown Atlanta to meet with my tailors at New York Fashions, okay?"

"JR, can we discuss this trip? I mean, should I really be going with you? What do I tell my fiancé' Sidney?"

Wow, I did not think that her going with me would present a problem by any stretch of the imagination but I could tell it was bothering her.

"Jewel, its strictly a business trip. If you really feel uncomfortable about going, then perhaps you should not go. I really don't want to send any false messages to your fiancé. This is all about business."

I had not clued Jewel in on all the property Julie had hired me to develop into subdivisions. I have not told a soul and I was going to keep it quiet. However, I was just going to take her and I was entertaining the idea of putting her in charge of one of the developments. I was considering the Virginia property, which would put her closer to her fiancé, but I needed to get her feelings on everything. Right now, I got Jewel practically doing everything and I probably need to consider hiring another manager.

Julie's number one nugget next to paying tithes and keeping God first was always surround yourself with people that have a heart like you along with superior talent. I still needed to consult Julie about this ownership stuff again. I'm a great worker but I am a novice at ownership.

"JR, perhaps we need to sit down face to face and discuss everything."

"Sure Jewel, you want to come over today or what?"

"JR, you mean I finally get a chance to come and see that mansion you have been keeping?"

That question alone spoke volumes to me. Am I sure I want Jewel to come over now and will she continue to believe that I am keeping this house for a wealthy friend?

Then I thought to myself, *well, Jewel is very trustworthy and I'm sure she will be smart enough to figure it out and to maintain my secret.*

"JR, wow, I must be gaining ground on the food chain list?"

"Jewel, you are funny but you must know that you are my number one confidant and you will be the first of my women friends to come to this house since I been maintaining it for my friend, other than the house managers."

"Okay JR, I'll be there around noon because I got an appointment at the office around 3pm. But JR, don't be referring to me as one of your women friends okay. People could definitely get the wrong idea about us."

I laughed in somewhat of a surprised state. I mean, what does Jewel know about me? Not a thang but what I told her and I haven't told her much. Anyway, I went on to ignore that comment by Jewel.

"Jewel, what did I tell you about working on the weekends? We got a crew of personnel that can handle those jobs now."

"I know JR but do you remember how you were? Trust me, I need to keep busy."

"Okay Jewel, I'll keep that in mind."

I was laughing with her very loudly. I knew where she was

coming from. We got off the phone and Jewel would arrive about the time I would be playing ball in the gym. That's fine. She would learn a lot about me this weekend.

CHAPTER 12
The Man Child - Ricky Lyles

Wow! Ricky Lyles! I got to remember that name. That boy will go pro and he may not even go to college with his skills. Ricky tore my five-man team apart. He dunked about eight times and scored about forty points and snagged about twenty rebounds, what we call boards. The shocker was that he was a freshman who just newly arrived in time for the high school basketball season.

His family relocated here from Dallas, Texas. That boy could start on any varsity team in the nation right now. He's only fourteen years old and stands six feet tall. The only drawback I here from the few that have dealt with him is that he hated school and his family, supposedly his dad, was strung out on drugs. He and his mom left Dallas to get away from him.

After he practically dismantled my five-man squad and before he got on the bus to leave, I spoke with him.

"Ricky, I'd like to meet with you and your mom sometime. Can you come for dinner at my place tomorrow or perhaps we could meet somewhere for dinner?"

"Sure JR, I'll check with my mom."

"Here is my card and please call back sometime today to confirm."

Ricky got on the bus after taking down some strawberry juice drink.

"Wow, JR, who are you keeping this place for? This is the largest house on the estate in the subdivision. Five acres and double layers of security, who are you working for, please tell me so I can kick you to the curve and work for them?"

Jewel made her arrival known with plenty of junk talk as she came in the gym with security.

"I got her Jackson, thanks."

I told my security guard that Jewel was under my custody now and Jackson walked off.

"You are too funny Jewel. Look, I need to catch a shower and make myself more presentable. Why don't I have Lydia give you a tour and I'll pick up after I'm out the shower."

Lydia was my chief house attendant who did practically everything in the house from cleaning up to cooking and laundry. Jewel responded as though I had hit her upside the head with that informative piece of conversation.

"JR, who is Lydia?"

I took Jewel to the living room area and I called out "play Confessions" and my computer music stereo system immediately played Usher's "Confessions." Jewel stopped and almost fainted. I called out Lydia and less than one minute Lydia, my house attendant not maid showed up in her French maid outfit. I introduced her to Jewel and told her to give her a tour of the place.

Jewel's mouth was wide open.

"Jewel, give me about twenty-five minutes to take a shower," I said.

One lovely feature in the house was the voice-activating computer. It responded to my voice only and it did just about everything I needed as far as communications. I can call out any song and it came on instantly. When the phone rings, my operator knows if I don't say JR within three rings, she would answer the phone for me. All I say is JR and I'm connected with the caller via my global, remote speakers throughout the house. I can be in the shower and yell out a television channel and the sound system comes in and the wall television in the bathroom automatically shows within thirty seconds. It was an awesome setup.

I took a shower and threw on dishabille to talk with Jewel while planning on going to Veronica's house later on today, after I stop by Loke's place. Jewel was waiting on me in one of my nice sitting rooms with a conference table towards the back.

"Hi Jewel, I hope you saw everything."

"JR, I am so flabbergasted. I thought I was your closest pal and you hid this mini mansion from me. Can you please give me the rest of the tour?"

"Jewel, I've got your best interests at heart."

The phone rings.

"JR."

"Hey JR, this is Ricky, the guy you met today at the house." I interrupted, "I don't need no introduction from you ball player; your skills gave me all the introduction I need. Did you talk with your mom?"

"I sure did JR and actually she is standing right here and would like to speak with you."

"Okay partna, put her on the phone."

Jewel is looking with much surprise as I sat down at the conference table and talked with no phone in sight.

"Hello," she said.

"Hello Mrs. Lyles how are you? My name is JR Carter."

She quickly replied with a snap in her voice.

"My name ain't no Mrs. Lyles but Miss Lyles; I ain't marry

my baby's daddy, he just stole my virginity. Anyway, call me Evelyn."

"I'm very sorry Evelyn. I won't make that mistake again. But look here, I was wondering if you and Ricky would be interested in joining me for dinner on tomorrow?"

"Now I ain't about to turn down no free meal but I don't plan to be going to your house and Ricky is under punishment for going without my permission. How I know you ain't some drug dealer or hustler anyway?"

"I can definitely appreciate your concern Evelyn and I do value your caution."

She interjected, "Anyway, what you want to meet with us for? I ain't got no time for no mess!"

"I can also appreciate that too Evelyn but I have a proposition for you and Ricky. I just need to make sure I'm on track with my assessment."

"A what? Look, this ain't no reality television show now. What the hell are you trying to say?"

"Well, I was wondering if Ricky had already started school yet and I was interested in tutoring him and another group of kids and I also wanted to put him in my Big Brother Program."

She said reluctantly, "Okay, well we have yet to get into a school because we just got here and I'm still searching for the right school for Ricky. We have only been here about two days. Ricky is pretty much an honor roll student so he don't need no tutor. I refuse to allow him to attend this school over here near the projects. I am just trying to find a nice private school for him. Ricky has attended nothing but private schools and I plan to keep it that way."

Wow, a superstar athlete and honor roll student as well. I guess the street rumor was nothing but that.

"I understand Evelyn, can we discuss in great detail on tomorrow. Why don't I pick you and Ricky up around 5pm, is that okay?" I chimed in.

"Okay! But let me emphasize that I am not interested in nothing but what you just talked about. I got no time for no hanky panky mess, you understand Mr. JR?"

Wow, she was so insulting that she almost made me laugh and she almost made me reconsider and just leave well enough alone but nope, I wanted to make certain that this kid got the opportunity that other kids sometimes fell to get. I grew up with kids that were great ballplayers but they never got off the block because they became victim to alcohol and drugs while refusing any form of education.

"I understand Evelyn! I promise to be in my best behavior."

She quickly uttered, "You got no choice! I don't care whose house you watching. I ain't impressed by no dollar signs. U feel me?"

"Gotcha Evelyn! I'll see you at 5pm; bye, bye!"

As soon as I got off the phone with Evelyn, I barely had enough time to pick my ego off the floor before Jewel went on an attack.

"JR, what the hell are you doing?"

The phone rings again.

"JR," I said.

"Hey JR, this is Evelyn. You need our address?"

She had shot me down so badly that I clearly forgot all about getting the address.

"Right Evelyn! What is it?" I replied.

"Its 1508 Lennox Projects, just off Dickens Avenue."

I may not have known much about Houston but I did know that Lennox Projects was one of the most criminally, drug infested hoods in all of Texas.

Wow, that stark realization definitely produced a dose of doubt altogether in my mind.

"Got it Evelyn! I'll see you at 5pm on tomorrow."

"Okay JR, and by the way, if you are as much as five minutes late, we will not be going. You got that?"

"I got that Evelyn and thanks for forewarning me."

Evelyn greeted me and then I hung up. Jewel, who seemed to be in a state of shock, bombarded me with questions.

"JR, what is going on? I mean, what is that all about? We need to talk!"

"Jewel, you want to talk and walk so I can show you the place," I said.

Jewel and I talked for quite awhile. She loved my new house and thought she was living large when she bought my old place but now realized that she was just biting the crumb of a big cake. Jewel was glad to know that I was starting a tutoring college to help underprivileged and uneducated kids. However, she did not approve of me meeting with Evelyn and Ricky without her being present for the first meeting.

Actually, she did not know it but I had wanted her to come along anyway. She informed me that business was going well and she received about four phone calls from her agents who were glad to tell her that they sold some houses.

Once again, Julie inspired me to open up my own realty business and I named it, "On Time Realty." I started out with about four employees but after six months, we were standing strong with twelve employees. Jewel and I still worked for "Star Top Realty" but she was about to resign and Julie already knew the story.

Matter of fact, Julie envisioned it well ahead of my ever thinking of the idea. As lead broker of my company and associate broker of Star Top, I was heavily inundated with paperwork along with starting up some new projects such as the Big Brother's Program of which an offshoot of that will be the Tutorial Program while attempting to manage property in those other three states.

Jewel would be a huge part of these endeavors if I could spike her interest.

"Jewel, I understand you and Sidney plan to marry but have you set a date yet? I'm asking because I got a lot of plans with you being a big part but if you plan to leave soon, I need to come up with other options."

"JR, I plan to be here for a while. Sidney knows that. I tell him all the time that there is plenty of work here for corporate law."

There's a thought. I will need a corporate attorney within our business. Sidney could really make a killing working with me. I attend about fourteen closings per week and he could make out real big here. However, I don't know his work ethic. Jewel was awesome but I did not know Sidney.

Jewel nagged me jokingly about having a key to my place so she could come and swim at will. I informed her that she could do that anyway because the hired help was always here and I could just inform them to allow her entry whenever. I mean, this house was way too big for me. If it was not for the five people that worked here, I would be so lonely up in this monster size abode. Too bad I don't have any relatives living nearby who could come and help occupy the place with me. I'm not going to lie. This place was a bit lonesome for me.

Anyway, to say Jewel was overly impressed with the swimming pool would have been a major understatement. She wanted to know what I would do with such a big place if I had ever owned such and I told her I had my ideas. Its funny how she focused right on the very issue that overwhelmed me most.

I explained to her about the phone communication system. I even had most rooms built where you could talk on the phone and not be heard outside the room. I had this capability in my bedroom, bathroom, and a few other rooms near the kitchen, as well as my office.

Jewel was so impressed with this house. She thought that my place was the perfect location for her and Sidney to get married. She had all types of ideas. Also, I gave Jewel a strategic business plan. I told her that I expected her to run "On Time Realty" and I told her that before she resigned with Star Top she had to get her Broker's License.

Also, I wanted to go ahead and finalize her salary contract.

"Jewel, let's discuss your salary."

"Okay JR, what's your offer?"

"Is $135K per year okay for starters with quarterly pay raise options pertinent to overall company sales?"

"JR, you can afford to pay me that much?"

"Okay Jewel, how bout 150K then and please don't be upset. That's just for starters."

"JR, do I look upset? I only got 125K in New York and you think I'm upset? I just want to make sure I'm not ripping you off."

"Jewel, trust me, you are not and you will earn every penny of it. Now, I'm about to blowup and I'm taking you with me but you got to promise me that my ownership and wealth is our secret. If you can't live up to that, then you are not fit for the job."

"JR, you don't have anything to worry about."

"Jewel, I am really in dire need of a house manager as well. What do you think about that?"

She dubiously glared at me.

"JR, I don't know how I would be able to be the house manager and your business manager too. That would be unrealistic for me to even attempt because a house manager's position can be 24-7 and I won't be here during the greater portion of the day. I can definitely be on the lookout for one however."

Jewel's logic made all the sense in the world, although it did not currently solve my problem.

"JR, how have you managed thus far? I mean, you are the current house manager, correct?"

I was not ready to tell Jewel that I owned the place and so I did not.

"I have barely managed Jewel but I need someone who can run this place as I am not here most of the time. I guess we can be on the lookout for a highly qualified person."

Jewel smiled and said, "So JR, let me make certain I comprehend. You are the house manager but you need someone else to really do the job because you are too busy. I know for fact that you are way too busy but I'm just surprised you elected to do the job."

I just chuckled along with her.

"Jewel, I just agreed to do it because the owner is a close friend of my father and I just thought it would be great staying here as I continued to get on my own feet."

Anyway, Jewel and I had no answers for the house manager position so I returned back to discussing her salary and benefits.

"Oh yeah, a nice percentage of the houses that you sell to include those on the internet and all the additional things you do to make money is all your money in addition to the salary I pay you. Now Jewel, that could be a lot of money but please do me a favor and get out of working on the weekends. I used to do it but now we got people who can share our work ethic and get out there and do that kind of work."

Jewel was quick to inform me, "JR, for me, this is not about money but about being able to do quality work that makes a difference. I am not stuck on the dollars at all."

"Okay Jewel, I got that. Now, let's change the subject for a moment. I know we need a secretary and I think Evelyn could be a good secretary for the company and the house on Jensen that I like could be good for her and her boy. I'll talk more about that."

"JR, how do you know she would make a good secretary? You barely even know this woman, much less her son and why are you talking about a house for them?"

"Jewel, I could be wrong but I just got a feeling that she could be a great employee."

"I guess you like how rude she was to you on the phone right, with her country self?"

I smiled and looked at Jewel and said, "She is quite country, isn't she? However, she sounds very structured and rigid and I like that for a secretary. Jewel, you do the hiring okay! I could be wrong but look hard at her on tomorrow. It's her job to lose or turn down."

Jewel stared at me and smirked, "Okay Boss, but if I'm doing the hiring, let me do the hiring. You know nothing about this woman. She could be a thief. Didn't you say her boy's daddy was a drug addict so what kind of gold are you expecting out of her? I'll take care of that."

"Good Jewel because tomorrow is her interview. Let's at least give her a chance."

Jewel leaned towards me with those big eyes of hers and said, "Now JR, what's this about the house on Jensen? How is she going to afford a house like that and she don't even have a job?"

"Well Jewel, we can help her buy the house with the salary she will be making."

Then Jewel stood up and said, "And JR, just what type of salary were you planning on paying her? I think you need to first find out what type of skills she already possesses and I can do the research to find out the best salary offer."

I could very well understand where Jewel was coming from and I realize I sounded really illogical to her. However, I wanted to place Ricky in the right school district so he could play for a good basketball team. I did not care to get into that level of detail with Jewel because I really did not think she would agree nor understand.

If I can get them to stay in the Jensen Subdivision, where there is a boatload of foreclosures, I could possibly get Ricky to attend the top basketball school in the state, two years running. What Jewel did not know and what I had failed to tell her was that I played basketball only because a certain man in my childhood convinced my dad to relocate our family to a certain part of town in Ocala. That move allowed me to play basketball with a good school.

"Jewel," I calmly waved my hands up and down as to signal Jewel to sit down, "let's offer her 60K."

"JR, that is pretty steep for someone you don't even know. Why don't we interview her first and see what type of skills she has and I will derive at the appropriate salary after we get all of her information."

Jewel got the most serious look on her face than I ever seen from her.

"Man, you don't even know this woman. I bet she won't last one week in the office with me. You know I can be a bitch JR. I am not in agreement with paying this no name woman all this money and you have never even seen or met her; don't even know what her work ethic is like."

Jewel was making some very key points and I guess she was right in every respect. Besides, there is a great probability that she may not even work out at the office and especially if she is working for Jewel.

I really don't know why black women have such a rough time working for other black women. That is something I will never understand. Then again, whose to say that Evelyn would even be remotely interested in the job.

"Okay Jewel, we can discuss salary options at a later time okay."

"JR, we can but should I elect to hire Evelyn on tomorrow, I would inform her that salary and benefits would be discussed at a later time," she interjected.

That is what I like about Jewel. I really do like her take-charge attitude and I can trust this woman. She is so honest that if she were ripping me off, she would bring it to my attention. She reminded me so much of the woman who starred in Brewster's Millions; you know the black woman married to the white attorney who was so committed to Mr. Brewster (Richard Pryor).

"By the way Jewel, here is your first check."

I started writing Julie a check from my personal checking account.

"Do you like the 1st and the 15th for paydays? Let me know. By the way, you will be in charge of payroll until you hire someone to manage that department as well."

"Wow JR! I feel so important. I'm like the CEO?"

"Sounds like the title for you. I will get you trained and everything. Welcome aboard partner."

We shook hands and I kissed her on the cheek. Jewel will be a good investment. She tried to talk me out of the weekly Saturday basketball games. She thought it was too risky to have all those hood rats (her words) at the place at one time. I had to let her know that I was a product of the hood and that was a done subject.

CHAPTER 13
The Hook Up

"Hey Coach Bartelone, how are you doing?" I called the basketball coach of the state champion high school in Houston known as the Belmont High School Bearcats.

"What's up JR? How's the realtor extraordinaire doing? I love this house you sold to us. The wife sure won't be leaving me any time soon now."

He started laughing with that comment and I chided him by saying, "Yep, the things a man has got to do. Hey man, that's good to hear. I'm glad I could be of assistance. By the way, have you selected your varsity squad yet?"

"Of course I have JR. You know we are state champions two years running and I don't see any team stopping us this year. I got all my seniors returning and six juniors. Now officially, tryouts are about five weeks from now but I clearly have the best talent in the area and they have played together for about three years. Anyway, why do you ask?"

"Look Coach, I have seen your team and played against all your players but you have got no player who can stand next to this fourteen year old sensation I saw today. He's six feet tall and weighs about 180 and can leap about 38 inches vertically easy and is as quick as a cat. He has an outside and inside game. He can play the one (point guard), two (shooting guard), or three (small forward), or four (power forward) spot. He has the release of a college veteran and the composure and maturity to match. He may need some work with his academics but he also maneuvers right and left evenly dribbling the ball. He is clearly ambidextrous. As a defender, you have no clue what his strong side is. On defense, he is catlike quick and strong as an ox. I'm talking natural talent here coach."

"Wow JR, you sound better at selling this athlete than you do at selling houses. Here's my point! I got a team that isn't broke yet and my philosophy is if it isn't broke, don't fix it. JR, I got five starting seniors who all have scholarships with big NCAA schools and two are McDonald's All Americans. I'm good with my team but once again I do have tryouts in about five weeks. He can come and tryout. However, I am not inclined to play a freshman on my varsity squad. Remember JR, this is the 6A school level and these kids could beat up on any community college with their skills. Perhaps at his age, he can play on our junior varsity or ninth grade squad because fourteen is way too young for a kid to be playing varsity. I mean, come on JR, Jordan was not playing varsity at age fourteen. The kid can only be but so good. Also, I have worked hard to get my boys' grades where they are and I do not welcome any academically challenged kid to the team."

"I hear you Coach but don't mess around and let your archrival pick this kid up and this conversation could come back to haunt you."

He started laughing at my words.

"JR, there is so much talent out there and all I'm saying is I got a team who has attained the highest honors for two years in a row. They are all coming back for a third championship run. Truly, you understand that? Also, pre-season scouting tells me that I got the team to beat. We have destroyed Lake View Academy now for about five consecutive years. We own them more than they own themselves."

Coach Bartelone started laughing after his last comment. I had to accept what Coach Bartelone was saying. He was actually right on point but I was still surprised that he did not at least want to take a peek at this kid.

"You right coach! I understand. Just remember, I gave you the first shot. I'll speak with you at a later time."

"JR, I appreciate that. By the way, we host the region's Christmas tournament on this year and our conference has the toughest teams in the state. Let's see how Lake View does in our tournament. Take care JR."

He did not realize it but he just made one of the biggest mistakes a coach could make, overlooking additional talent. Hell, I played high school and college ball and you never feel like you got it all. Now I have got to find a way to get Ricky to play within another region but I had to definitely have him relocated from where they are currently staying. That could definitely be a problem. If I could sell them one of those foreclosed houses in the Jensen Subdivision, Ricky could easily play for Lake View Academy. Oh well, let me try Coach Charlie Lawson at Lake View Academy and see what he has to say.

"Hello," said Mary, Coach Lawson's wife.

"Hi Mary, this is JR Carter. I was wondering if the Coach was home?"

"Hi JR, where's my house at? I thought you were finding us a house that had our name on it?"

"I did Mary but Coach thought that the price was too high."

"JR, since when did he have you thinking that he made the decisions in this house? That's my call! I am so tired of living in this house. When can you show me the house?"

Coach Lawson picked up another phone. He sounded very apologetic and humble in his tone.

"Mary, please get off the phone. I got it now," said Coach Lawson.

Mrs. Lawson launched out at her husband. "Charlie, JR told me you said that the house was too expensive. I'm looking at the house next week and if that house satisfies my taste, we will be buying that house. You need to stop worrying about being fired by that stupid school and start living."

Coach Lawson seemed very nervous and anxious to get his wife off the phone. He spoke to her in a very low and soft tone.

"Mary, okay baby! We will look at the house next week. Now, can JR and I have some privacy? He isn't trying to get in our business like this."

Mrs. Lawson interjected, "JR, I want to see that house. Don't forget! You promise?"

"Mary, I promise. I will show it to you next week."

"Okay, bye bye!" Mary hung up the phone.

"JR, how are you," said Coach Lawson.

"Coach, let me apologize for I did not mean to get you into any trouble regarding the house. Then again, I should be asking you what's up. Sounds like you should have bought that house!"

I started laughing in a very kind way.

"JR, you know I got three consecutive losing seasons coaching for the most political high school in the city. Dem white folks gonna fire me if I have another losing season. Mary doesn't understand the business. Coaching high school basketball isn't like it used to be when a coach could win or lose forever but only be replaced when he retired. Now, people want you to win or move out the way."

"Charlie, I might have some help for you this season. When are your tryouts?"

"I got tryouts in three weeks. Why? What you got for me?"

"Well, let's just say I have a probable solution for you to build a team around. I tried to hook him up with Coach Bartelone but he got his squad already. Now, I'm giving you a chance."

"Really, well JR nothing like being second choice but I forgive you for that."

"Charlie, the kid was going to be living in Coach Bartelone's school district but now I got to make plans to get him in your school district."

"Well JR, what kind of skills does the kid have?"

"Charlie, can you meet me next Saturday at the Lakes?"

"Sure JR, but if the boy lives out there he must be filthy rich."

"No Charlie, he doesn't live there but I'll meet you there and I'll call you next Friday night to finalize the plan. Matter of fact, why don't we meet and you can check him out and then we can go and pick up Mary and show her the house?"

"JR, I can look at houses until the sky turns red but I am not in the position to purchase some expensive house that I may not be able to afford if I get fired."

"I'm with you Coach and I understand. I don't foresee you getting fired but we can talk more on Friday and meet on Saturday."

"Okay JR, I'll talk back with you then. Thanks for the call too!"

"The pleasure was all mine."

Charlie will be glad to get a player like Ricky on his team. Let's hope all works out to that end.

***

"Loke, what's going on playa?" I finally caught him home at his new residence. I stopped by his crib after calling him and letting him know I was on my way.

"Naw Man! I need to ask you what the hell is going on. Did my purchase of this house pave the way for you to buy the nicest mini mansion in all of Texas?"

"Come on Loke! It's not the nicest mini mansion in all of Texas. I'm the house manager there as I explained to you already. I know some people that know some people that ripped some people off and now they want to make amends."

We both started laughing after saying all that but in those words were the naked truth.

"I'm just joking Loke and no I did not rip you off. As far as business is concerned, I'm just trying to provide a service to the community by selling houses that customers desire to have and can afford."

"I know you didn't rip me off playa." Loke quickly expressed. "I'm just messing with you. Look here, I'm about to plan my pool party to celebrate my birthday. I'm having nothing but honeys up in here in bikini's and I mean thong bikini's at that."

"What day are you having them over? I'd like to chip in if I may."

"Are you going to chip in with more women or what?"

"Actually, I had more like refreshments and food in mind or whatever you need. We can discuss it at length when you are ready."

"Sounds good JR! I'll think about it some and let you know. On a serious note, thanks for hooking me up with this pad in high society."

We were sitting in Loke's den area when this fine honey in a thong bikini walked in and sat in his lap. She looked

Hispanic but she was definitely a hottie. He kissed her in front of me and then she walked out the room.

"JR, guess how I met her?"

I glared at Loke as if I was really trying to read his mind. He quickly interrupted my thoughts. "She was one of the movers that actually moved my property. She's my lady of the quarter."

He started teasing as he was sipping some Gin and Tonic. My displayed look of consternation yielded the following reply: "Lady of the quarter? What's that all about?"

"JR, you need to cycle honeys in and out on a quarterly basis. Just be honest with them and let them know you trying them out for a quarter; that's right, three months."

"Loke, what woman will agree to something that whack? Come on man! You can't treat women like a rental car, use them up and then get rid of them."

I was laughing like I had just heard the funniest joke of my life.

"JR, you can laugh all you like but she just signed up to the program. She gets the right to be my honey for three months and that don't mean I only see her either."

I was laughing like crazy but I must admit I thought Loke had more smarts than that.

"Loke, you should not even lead women on to that degree unless you have sincere interests in them."

"JR, that's what your mom is talking about. I am a divorced man and I am not trying to get serious with no hoe. Think about Debbie and Gina, Sasha and Thomasina. These women all have one thing in common. They love to get laid. You need to treat a hoe like a hoe. Don't get serious and fall in love too soon playa. Make them at least good mileage to tread upon first. You are a young man with much life ahead of you.

Don't fall in love too soon or you will be like me. A young, divorced happy go lucky, horny mutha f.... that views the only good coochie is new coochie. As TUPAC said, f...the world."

I busted out laughing at Loke's crazy perspectives. I knew Loke was mainly joking but there was some truth to his words, not a lot of truth but some.

Debbie, Sasha, Thomasina, and Gina were hoes and Lord knows they all had some good coochie. But then again, there's more to life than just good ass stuff.

"Loke, what happens after a quarter? Do you recycle women around?"

"Oh most certainly in order to get around, you got to recycle. Tai dat ass up for three good months and then bring in the new stuff. Don't hurt nobody's feelings. You must always make it seem like they are kicking you to the curve and you are not kicking them to the curve."

I cracked up listening to Loke because he was so sincere. I must admit that that's the most I've laughed since I been in H-town. He was truly some kind of funny. I also know his bark was much bigger than his bite. We continued to talk noise, both he and I. I got a couple of drinks and joined in his buffoonery. His friend came back in and she had been drinking too. I don't know how Loke does it. A dentist, damn good one at that, but he has such a twisted perspective on the game.

I left Loke when his friend came back into the room with only a towel on. I was still debating with him on my departure as I left to his favorite words: "Don't hate the playa, hate the game." Loke's cell phone was ringing off the hook while I was there and he answered every call. He told those women all that they wanted to hear. Loke was a cool dude who I found much laughter in.

**

"JR," I answered my phone at home.

"JR, do you want me to drive or are you going to drive to pick up Ricky and his mom?"

"I'll drive Jewel. His mom's name is Evelyn."

"Okay, I'm headed to your place and we can go from there."

"Good plan jewel. I'll see you in a few."

I had just returned home from Veronica's house. She wanted me to meet some of her relatives. We had a nice time and they truly enjoyed Veronica's house. As a realtor, some folks really become akin to your ways if you bring happiness in their lives in the form of a brand new house. Veronica was so proud of the house that she wanted to introduce me to her relatives.

Veronica was also someone that I could develop feelings for but I enjoyed our relationship. There was no commitment or nothing like that but we just kind of always hooked up when it was time; time for me to tai dat ass up as she called me most of the time.

CHAPTER 14
Shocked From Head To Toe

I got on the scales today, all to realize I had lost twenty pounds since I had been in H-town. My belly was officially gone and I was determined to keep it off. As a form of celebration, I quietly and privately stopped by the Winn Dixie grocery store and bought me a box of Lorna Doone cookies. I got me some fruit punch and sat in my car eating them cookies as relaxed as someone smoking a cigarette after some darn good lovemaking.

Cookies have always been my weakness but I noticed that I got somewhat full after eating the first row of two rows in the box. I have this love/hate relationship with Lorna Doone cookies. After I have eaten enough to get full, I want to throw away the remaining portion as though I had nothing to do with them at all. It's kind of like that with sex. Once I'm done, its like I want to leave right away as though I did nothing. Perhaps that was the guilt that lied within me from all those years of being preached to not to commit fornication.

Hey, I lost a considerable amount of weight and I deserved a box of cookies though. Anyway, I felt my cookie high coming on and I was full and threw away almost half of the second row. Then, I promised myself that I would never buy those filthy, sugar pills again. It's a conclusion that I derive at every time I frantically eat cookies like that.

Jewel showed up to my place quicker than normal. She

was learning the area real fast. She was excited about the opportunities that were being provided to her. I was glad to be her partner and friend. Just to reflect how close we were, Jewel brought clothes over and said that she had already picked out which guest room she was staying in and that she would be spending the night. I had no problem whatsoever with that and I informed my security staff.

We pulled up to Lennox Projects to pick up Ricky and Evelyn. Wow! Who would have ever thought that Evelyn would have the kind of impact on me that she did. It was truly love at first sight and I really mean it this time. This woman was bad! She was the one. As she was approaching the car, I thought to myself that I had finally found my inamorata. I was so intimidated. I needed Jewel to be there.

She walked out of her complex with a nicely wrapped tweed like dress that had a split in the rear and the front. The color was dark brown with a twirl of subtle, red streaks. Her hair was full and dark as in jet black and it hung all the way down her back. It was real too, not extensions. It had a nice wavy flow where the front had a micro braid and the remainder flowed beautifully off her head.

She had the prettiest face I had ever seen in my life. She had big brown eyes with dark eyebrows, a nice and round nose, thin and narrow, long lips with thick juicy tips and ivory white teeth. Her nails were done and she showed a little cleavage but not too much, and a lot of legs in that dress.

Her butt was one word, perfect with a capital P. She stood about 5'7" but with heels she was easy 5'10". I was going totally against my mother's direction. I was clearly taken out the frame and I was all over the place mentally. Still, nobody knew except me. I had learned how to conceal my feelings but Evelyn was truly my ticket to playa retirement.

Those caramel thighs of hers made me want to say, *Bread of Heaven, Feed Me Till I Want No More.* Man, you know a brother is caving in when he uses a church hymnal to express his feelings about a woman. Within my heart, all of a sudden Evelyn was my Janet Jackson, my Halle Berry, my Beverly Johnson, my Gabrielle Union, my Oprah and my female version of a woman Denzel.

Nevertheless, I played it cool. As I pulled up Evelyn and Ricky approached me and I stood outside the car with the door open.

"Hi Evelyn, I'm JR. It is certainly nice to meet you. Let me introduce you to Jewel."

I kindly shook Evelyn's hands and they were ever so soft.

"Hi JR, it's nice to meet you too," she replied in kind.

As she got in the car, she shook Jewel's hand. "Hi Jewel, nice to meet you home gurl," Evelyn said.

"The pleasure is all mine Evelyn," Jewel responded.

Jewel turned to Ricky and said, "And this must be Ricky! Well, hello there, young man."

Ricky extended his hand and shook Jewel's hand while saying, "Hi Ma'am."

Jewel immediately opened up the conversation.

"I am honored to accompany yawl to dinner," said Jewel.

I looked back at Ricky. "Ricky, what's going on man?"

"Hey JR," Ricky said.

His mother elbowed him in the side. "I'm sorry. I meant to say hey Mr. JR."

I heard Evelyn whisper to Ricky, "Boy, you know I done told you time and time again to respect your elders. Please don't embarrass me on this dinner date."

"Evelyn, Ricky is fine. He doesn't have to call me Mr. JR because all the boys call me JR. So please, allow Ricky to call me JR because any other name would be totally abnormal for me," I quickly uttered.

Evelyn looked at Ricky and said, "Okay Ricky, but I still expect you to say Mr. and Miss to other folks."

Ricky looked at his mom and smiled and said "Yes Ma'am." She lowered her head and looked right into his eyes and said, "You can smile all you like but I'm serious Ricky."

"Yes Ma'am," Ricky responded again. We proceeded to this nice and loquacious restaurant called The Cave on the other side of town and our conversation was flowing like we all knew each other. Evelyn was very inquisitive and I loved her voice and the flow of her thoughts was like beautiful music to my ears. I also adored her natural body communication language. She was somewhat country but very sophisticated. Both she and Ricky were very clean and you could tell they had a tight relationship.

Evelyn seemed as young as I was. I noticed that she had no rings on her fingers and did not wear much jewelry. In addition, Ricky seemed to be a well-mannered kid who was mature beyond his years.

I wanted to marry Evelyn and adopt her son. My overall feeling was clearly, *lights out, game ova for me.* I have finally found the woman God had in store for me. She doesn't know but she will in time.

After we were seated at the restaurant and everyone placed their orders for drinks and food, I proceeded with my proposition.

"Evelyn, I wanted to meet with you and Ricky for a couple of reasons: First, I wanted to help facilitate your transition into the area by perhaps assisting you with employment, as well as linking Ricky up with a real nice school where he can excel academically and play the game his natural talents call for. Jewel is the business manager of my company, On Time Realty and I need an executive administrator and I would like for you to consider my offer. With that comes an opportunity to purchase a nice house within a nice neighborhood that can be automatically deducted from your salary payment. We can discuss the details at a later time. Secondly, I'd like to assist Ricky's transition into the area by helping him get to the right school to augment his educational and basketball skills but I wanted to make certain both you and Ricky were in agreement."

Jewel just kind of stared at me as though she was witnessing a very shocking event. Ricky was smiling with those pretty white teeth of his and Evelyn just stared and listened without emotion.

"Let me make sure I hear what you are saying. You want to give me a job as an executive administrator, help me buy a house outside of the projects, and make certain Ricky is academically smart and able to play basketball? Mind you Ricky has not played ball long and I have no experience as an administrator but I am a paralegal assistant. Now, Ricky is pretty smart in school. He has only gone to private schools but the schools he has attended have not had any sports programs; they were strictly about academics."

I, once again, was not surprised to hear that about Ricky's academics as I was told by Evelyn on yesterday that he was an honor roll student. Also, as I hung around Ricky, he struck me as a very intelligent, young man.

"That is good to know. So what is Ricky an A, B, or C student?" I said to Evelyn.

"My boy better not bring home no C, he knows we don't tolerate that in our household," said Evelyn as she looked at Ricky. Ricky makes As and Bs, mainly As."

Ricky was smiling and Jewel was just staring as though she was still shocked as to what she was hearing.

"Well, that's great! Academics won't be an issue then," I said.

"What's the catch? What do you want from us?" Evelyn impatiently expressed.

"I want you to do a great job as my administrator and I want Ricky to be the best student and ballplayer that he can be," I conveyed without batting an eye.

Ricky interrupted, while staring at his mom, "Mom, I can do that with no problem. I told you I could play basketball."

"Be quiet Ricky while groan folks are talking. Just because you are present at this table and we are discussing you does not give you the right to talk, okay," Evelyn said to Ricky. I must admit that she was very sincere but also somewhat funny.

"Now JR, your offer seems somewhat tempting. To be honest with you I would probably only work for you until I got a paralegal position. Besides, what kind of salary are we talking about that will help me buy a house, and what kind of house are we talking about?"

I looked intensely into Evelyn's eyes. "I can pay you a starting salary of 60K and if you choose to leave for another paralegal job then I will only honor your request."

Evelyn and Jewel both had shocking looks on their faces. Evelyn quickly responded, "What? You will pay me 60K as in $60,000 dollars a year. Jesus! That would take me awhile to make that kind of money in the paralegal field."

"Keep in mind that is just a starting salary. Your pay raises will pay you more than any paralegal job could pay you," I convincingly spoke as though I was justifying my position.

Then Jewel turned to Evelyn and said, "Evelyn, I am an attorney by trade. I understand the paralegal career field and I could use your work ethic as the executive administrator of our company. We need you right away if you are interested."

I was very surprised to hear that from Jewel but she was doing her job, supporting her boss. She was still making faces at me for some reason but only the two of us could tell.

"Now Jewel, you are the business manager," Evelyn exclaimed.

"So would I be working for you or JR?"

I quickly intervened before Jewel had a chance to reply.

"You would technically be working for me but functionally working for Jewel. In essence, you would be working for both of us. Is that okay by you? We can discuss further details at a later time."

"Well, when can I see this house that you have in mind because I hate living in the projects but it's all I can afford right now. Perhaps I need a week to consider the proposition," Evelyn said.

I did not like the way that sounded and I knew this was my wife. Sometimes a man knows when nobody else knows. I had to bum rush her and explain to Jewel on the ride home.

"Evelyn, you can see the house first thing tomorrow as you begin work tomorrow. You can temporarily relocate tomorrow at another house until your house is ready for you to move into. That way, Ricky will be allowed to attend Lake View Academy High School, which is a school known for academics but just added basketball to its sports program about seven years ago."

"Lord Have Mercy! JR, I must admit that I am overwhelmed. The move from the projects is definitely easy because all we have are a few suitcases and that's it. We left Dallas under a surprise sudden notice. We departed right away due to personal reasons."

Jewel once again looked at me as though she was really

going to fix me when we got alone. Then, Jewel said, "JR, we can give her time to think it over for there is no rush. We want Evelyn to take her time and be certain that this is what she wants."

I was not taking no for an answer. I was determined to land this fish.

"Also Evelyn, so goes business capital, so goes your salary. The company has been on an upswing since its very existence."

Evelyn was smiling and she responded, "I can start at $60, 000 dollars. My goodness! That's more money than I would make stripping."

Silence was had with that comment. Evelyn realized the immediate looks and the shocking expressions on both Jewel and my face. She immediately cleaned it up.

"I'm just kidding yawl."

I thought I would follow through with a joke.

"I don't believe you. In fact, I beg to differ with you."

Evelyn looked at me and said, "What?"

I looked her dead straight in her eyes and said, "You would make so much more money stripping."

I laughed but I noticed I was the only one laughing. Jewel gave me that impolite look like I had really said something wrong.

"Look here, if that is what this is really about, you got the wrong woman," she said with a look of anger.

I waved my hands and said, "Evelyn, I'm joking."

"This better not be about anything of the sorts," Evelyn continued.

"I can assure you JR was just kidding," Jewel quickly insisted.

"Evelyn, it is not that kind of party. Trust me," I quickly expressed.

Evelyn looked at me and just smirked and I smiled with my hands up just to indicate I was telling the truth. However, I meant what I said but I imagine the comment was inappropriate. She could make a lot of money stripping.

"Evelyn, the job is yours for the taking and I can go over all the details with you later on in the week," Jewel reiterated.

Mission accomplished. Evelyn seemed positive about the proposal and she should start working sometime this week. Then, I turned to Ricky and said, "Ricky, how would you like to attend Lake View Academy? Its one of the top academic high schools in the nation and they offer a lot in terms of college preparatory courses."

Ricky stared at his mom and then looked at me and said, "JR, I was already sold when you said they have a basketball team."

"The basketball team has been struggling over the past four years. I don't think they have had a winning season for sometime now. However, their high school to college percentage for students is clearly the highest in the state. The school is more known for its college preparatory curriculum than it is for sports. However, the community became more interested in a competitive sports program, namely the basketball program."

Ricky had a smile like that of Gomer Pyle.

"It will be so good to be able to go to a school that has a basketball team. I can't wait," replied Ricky.

"Ricky," Evelyn interrupted, "I don't care how many basketball teams they got at this school, you had better not allow your grades to drop beneath a B or you won't be seeing no basketball. Do you hear me?"

Ricky quickly answered back with a smile, while saying, "Yes Ma'am. I hear you loud and clear."

Ricky and Evelyn truly impressed me. All he wanted to

do was play basketball and from what his mom interjected, his academics were very much stronger than I was informed. Thus, the stage was set and I was more anxious about meeting Evelyn than I was about making sure Ricky went to school where he could play basketball. I've got to be careful with my feelings because Evelyn has truly taken me to love at first sight. I never really believed in that concept but I honestly think I am experiencing it as I speak.

CHAPTER 15
At War With Jewel

We dropped both Evelyn and Ricky off after dinner. Ricky and I were wrestling for a moment as I was telling him how I used to take young boys like him to the hoop before I suffered my major injury. He jokingly called me an old man. I enjoyed hanging out with the kid and his mom. Now, the following weeks would be the toughest period of my time in Texas as far as feelings were concerned.

Evelyn truly captured my interest and I had to find a way to make my interest known without running her off. I had to find a way to lure her and perhaps help her see what was so obvious to me, which was, that she was mine!

As soon as we dropped Evelyn and Ricky off, Jewel laid into me like an ax chopping down a tree. In essence, we had our first major argument. I knew it was coming and I really was not mad at Jewel. She did not like how I had moved so far ahead. She was upset for several reasons: she felt that I did not include her in on all the plans, she felt that I changed the salary for Evelyn by too significant an amount without consulting her, and she felt that I should have consulted her on the moving and relocation of Evelyn and Ricky.

I was very quiet and I accepted my scolding like a guilty kid with his hands in the cookie jar. I just showed no facial expression but I really did admire Jewel for beating me up like this. To some degree, she was like my mom away from home.

I really appreciated her and I knew I would have no concrete answers to most of her questions regarding Evelyn and Ricky. I did not think 60K was too much to offer and all the other company perks should be automatic anyway for such a position. Then again, could it be that these perks that I mentioned just honestly came out of nowhere as I was not about to accept a negative answer from Evelyn. I will probably live to regret it but I felt like I did what I had to do for the moment.

Thus, I continued to listen to Jewel as she was literally cursing me out. Let me tune back in to her words.

"JR, we definitely need to talk. How can you afford to pay her 60K and where is this so-called house that you plan to help her buy. Where in the hell are you planning on boarding them while this house is ready? Please enlighten me! You are going to pay a woman 60K and you don't even know her skills nor do you know how good she is. You could have gotten her for 45K and without all the perks!"

I had to respond to Jewel because I definitely did not want to lose her.

"Jewel, let me first apologize. I will never do that again. I do however feel good about her."

"In what way JR, about her working skills or her stripping skills?"

That comment triggered my anger to some degree.

"Okay Jewel! I deserved that." She quickly interrupted, "Why JR? Why? I'm starting to feel like JADAKISS! Why?"

I looked over at her as I was driving back to my house and she was sternly serious and really upset.

"Jewel, trust me on this. She is a winner. I will make good by this move, trust me okay. There are times when a businessman feels he must take a chance and this is that time for me. Trust me now! Please show her the three bedroom houses in the Fuquay Varina development."

Jewel looked down and away from me and then she looked back up and said, "Okay boss, whatever you say."

"Come on Jewel! Don't be that way about this. Please! Trust a brother okay," I implored.

"Okay JR, but where are you boarding her on tomorrow?"

Oh Boy! This is really going to get heated now as I was beginning to feel like I was talking to my mom. I could sense that Jewel would have a cow over this. I tried to break it to her as gently as I could without showing my full deck of cards.

"Jewel, Evelyn and Ricky can stay at my place. I got plenty of space and her house will be ready within a month's time."

She quickly turned her head and shouted at me, "JR, stop the damn car right now! You are out of your country ass mind. You don't even know this hood rat from any other hood rat. What in the hell is wrong with you? You got too many women as it is. Why are you treating this bitch so special? I mean, you date elegant, well to do women and now you do all of this for a project hoe whose son can shoot a basketball. What in God's name are you trying to prove? That woman doesn't want you. She doesn't even want your money so what is your point? Don't be stupid man! She damn show ain't worth all that."

I pulled over on the side as Jewel requested and I said to Jewel, "Look partner, I know what I am doing. I'm just lending a hand. I really do have a good feeling about this."

Jewel stared me in my eyes and then without hesitation hit me with these words, "JR, how many times have you had a good feel about something and you were wrong? I tell you what. Just take me to my car so I can go home. I refuse to say another word."

Jewel may not have realized it but she sounded more and more like my mom, especially with that last comment of how many times I been wrong. She did hurt my feelings and I guess this is what my mom was always talking about when it came to women and I. I mean, what if Evelyn tries to use me. It's not like it hasn't ever happened before. Besides, she clearly does not display any interest in me whatsoever. What is it within me that makes me feel I can actually pull this woman? She might be too street smart for me anyway. *Damn! Is this God giving me such a strong attraction for her or is it I? I have been wrong before. Wow! Is it love at first sight or stupidity at first right? Is it cupid or stupid? Jewel really set me back. I felt a little stupid right now.*

"JR, you told me about how women have hurt you in the past. Why are you putting yourself out like this? You told me your mom warns you all the time about falling in love too fast and putting all your marbles on the line. Is this business with Evelyn and this kid about real business JR or are you personally attracted to her?" Jewel continued.

Jewel looked at me real hard and then quickly said, "I know the answer to that. It's strictly business because I see the caliber of women you attract and they are very much on a greater economic scale than Evelyn. For crying out loud, you would have been trying to get up my skirt before you would show interests in her. Besides, I know you got better business sense than to mix business and pleasure, and to my knowledge you already supposedly have a significant other somewhere. I just have yet to meet her."

Wow! Jewel really knocked me up side my head. I had to respond appropriately and refrain from embarrassing myself.

"Jewel, I had and have interests in developing Ricky's basketball talents. Anything else is gravy. Remember, I played basketball when I was his age and I really think this kid has talent."

I did not want to show my hand yet because I did feel

somewhat dumbfounded talking to Jewel about Evelyn. Therefore, I felt a need to share only the basketball line and force my own self to do some serious thinking as to how foolish I may really be regarding Evelyn. Who knows? I could be wrong about Ricky as well. *Wow! Listen to me. I went from definitely knowing to definitely doubting just that fast.*

I told Jewel to get herself a company car. She turned to me while sitting in the car as though she was disgusted.

"Do you really think I give a damn about a company car JR? Is this all that you have deduced your foolishness to? Please answer my questions JR because I am trying at this very moment to decide whether or not I need to renege on working with you at all. I am clearly at a crossroads right at this moment so you had better come with a logical explanation before I just vault."

I really felt the pressure of not knowing exactly what to say but I knew I had to say something or the second most important person in Houston, Texas was about to kick a brother to the curve. I turned and twisted in the car and then I looked over to Jewel and into her fiery but gorgeous eyes.

"Jewel, I realize that I may be coming across as an absolute fool and I perhaps am an absolute fool. However, I value your support and your business savvy ways that I cannot afford to lose you as my business partner. You mean more to me than this job by the way. You are like family to me, like a sister that I never had. I need you in my life and that's real. Forgive me for my errors and please understand my heart. I plan to go to the top Jewel and I vouch to take you with me. There will be times when I will make risky calls but I need your support. Aside from you, Julie, and Loke that's all I really have here in Houston."

I begin to wipe my eyes as though a teardrop was about

to drop. There was total silence as Jewel stared into my eyes. I had no idea what she was thinking but I did not get the feeling that it would be anything that I wanted to hear. I wanted to say more words to Jewel but my mind was so devastated by the anticipation of what she would say next.

This quiet period had to be one of the most torturing periods of my life. Then Jewel looked forward as to face the front windshield of the car, took a deep breath and said, "Tomorrow I will show Evelyn the Fuquay Varina Subdivision as you so desire and I will also make certain they are moved into the house that you are managing. "

Wow, the greatest sigh of relief passed right over me as I grabbed Jewel's hand and kissed it. She quickly snatched her hand away and said, "JR, get your mouth off my hand because I don't know where your mouth has been."

We both just started laughing.

"Jewel, thanks for hanging on and I really do apologize. Now, on a different note, why do you think I have so many women when you never seen me with one."

She laughed again.

"JR, are you denying the fact that you see a variety of women."

"Jewel, I don't see no way near as many women as you imply. What have you seen out of me?"

"JR, I have not seen anything but I just noticed that you have never even as much as winked at me, which has been a shocker for me. I always figured it was because you had too many women and not enough time to see them all." I looked at Jewel and she stared back at me.

"Jewel, I have not hit on you because I respect your engagement and I highly respect our friendship way too much to risk destroying our relations. In addition, you have not thrown yourself at me like some women in Texas have done."

She snapped her head up and declared: "Oh that will never happen at all. I would never try and hit on you, as I have always been faithful to my fiancé. You can try all the sweet-talking efforts you like and flash all the money you have but you will not be getting up this skirt. I am committed to my man."

I laughed with Jewel and said, "I can tell you are truly committed and that is very admirable of you. Are we okay now? You still my boo?"

She smiled and said, "Hell To The Naw! I am not yo boo because I'm more important than that. I'm your business manager and co-conspirator of your newly owned real estate company."

Jewel, stroked the sides of her hair and she always did that just before she was about to say something very thought provoking.

"Well JR, I don't mean no harm but before that hood rat gets to have all the bennies, I should at least experience them before her since I am the one supposedly hiring her. Besides, I do not feel like driving all the way cross town to my condo." She said that with a smile.

"Jewel, take my nicest guest bedroom and bunk here for the night if you so choose. You can feel free to stay here anytime my sista."

"Look my brotha, I have already picked my room out and my belongings are already in the room. Do you see how I am always a step or two ahead of you JR?"

I responded to myself, *whatever?* I was truly tired. I got back on the road and drove to my place. My house was so big that Jewel could be staying in one of the guest rooms and I wouldn't even know it.

"Jewel, let's press with the decisions made and perhaps we may have more insight on tomorrow."

We both opened the car doors and got out and Jewel looked at me with one of those smart looks, "next time, let me do my job," she said.

I came around the car and hugged her and kissed her on the cheek and I asked her, "You still love me baby? We down for whatever?" I laughed as I held her tight and would not let her go.

She pushed me away and said, "get off me JR, you are a trip if ever I seen one," and she started walking away. I spanked her on that big ass of hers and she turned around and chased me with her purse and I ran like I used to run when my friends and I would steal apples from white folks' backyards. Sometimes we would hop over a fence all to be met by a huge German shepherd and we would hustle back over the fence and run like crazy.

Anyway, by time I stopped running I was out of gas and in front of my swimming pool on the deep end, which was 12 foot high. I did not realize Jewel was so close on my tracks until all of a sudden I was pushed into the swimming pool, Hugo Boss suit and all.

"HAHAHA! I bet you won't ever grab my ass again." Jewel just laughed like crazy.

"Bet you didn't know I ran track in high school," she said. Ahahahahah!"

The security staff came over my global intercom speaker system and said, "Mr. Carter, is everything okay?"

Jewel, who was laughing so feverishly at me, heard the sound and it literally horrified her and she gradually tipped over into the pool as well. As she came up above the water, she cried, "Oh hell naw! I just got my hair done.... UUGHHH!"

I laughed so hard that my stomach muscles started hurting, as I told Johnson, one of the security guys, that everything was "A" okay over here. I helped Jewel out the pool and she punched on me the whole while we walked back to the house, until we parted for the night.

CHAPTER 16
One House, One Family

I just finished attending five closings, two for my company and three for Julie. I gave a lot of thought to what Jewel said on last night. However, I have at least returned to the first motive of mine, which was to lend a hand to a kid that may lack a father figure and may need some push and academic support.

Now, Jewel was very busy as well this morning. She left my house very early and I had not gotten a chance to speak with her. She did call me later in the day to give me an update. She leased three company vehicles on today, all Infinity. Why Infinity? Well, I did not get a chance to ask her but I'm sure it was due to some economy package, knowing Jewel. After all, the vehicles were leased through one of Julie's car dealerships where I get a very nice discount, unbeknown to Jewel.

Julie owned some of everything in Houston from oil companies to land development firms and the list goes on and on. The beauty of her ownership is how all these companies do not bear her name, nor does she flaunt the fact that she owns them.

Jewel also informed me that Evelyn decided to start work on tomorrow, loved all the houses in Fuquay, and they got Ricky into Lake View Academy High School, the same school that Charlie Lawson coaches basketball.

Jewel also got Evelyn and Ricky moved into my house.

Evelyn thinks that I am merely keeping the house for someone, like most people already believe. Ricky reassured her of that fact. I intentionally did not see Evelyn today but I was meeting with Ricky tonight in my gym. Jewel called me later in the evening as I was at Star Top Realty, with much excitement in her voice.

"Evelyn could not believe the house when she saw it. She told me she felt like she had died and gone to heaven. JR, why don't you make Evelyn your house manager and you can definitely justify her reason for staying with you. Also, I told the house attendant that nobody stays in my room without my approval. In addition to that, I made a corporate decision to stay at your place for now so Evelyn would not get the wrong idea and feel uncomfortable."

I was quickly concerned about Evelyn's impression.

"Jewel, did Evelyn express that she felt uncomfortable or something? I think that was an excellent decision for you to stay at my place to at least preclude Evelyn from becoming uncomfortable. That way, she will understand that you live there as well and that's no big deal for her and Ricky to be there."

"JR, once again, I am already steps ahead of you as far as that is concerned. I have explained everything to your house attendant and the security staff as well."

Actually, I had already considered making Evelyn the manager of my house but I did not want Jewel to take it the wrong way. I could not afford another beat down from my partner. Now that she has officially produced the idea, I've got to pounce on her recommendation.

"JR, Evelyn did seem uncomfortable at first until we drove out to the house and for some reason all her discomfort disappeared. Also, Evelyn can take her time about selecting a house of her choosing. That way she does not have to rush and buy a house but she can wait until more money has been saved."

"Jewel, since you have spent some time with Evelyn, do tell me what you think about her so far. Just give me your honest opinion."

"JR, you know I'm going to tell you exactly how I feel. Honestly, I like her alot. She is really a nice and kind woman, once you get beyond the country flare that she showcases. I also find her to be very intelligent which really did not come as a surprise to me but I think she's going to be okay for business."

"Jewel, I really do appreciate your support."

She interrupted me.

"By the way JR, am I reading the wrong figures? Our company has an account of well over two million dollars in it. JR, are you not telling me something again? Where in the world did all that money come from?"

Jewel has yet to be told about how the company was totally generating funds and how I had turned some investments over to expand our business. I will sit down with her in the next few days.

***

Two weeks had gone by and I have not heard a peep out of Evelyn. It's funny to live in a house and not see everyone that lives there. That really speaks to the massive size of this house.

"Jewel, how has Evelyn been doing at work?"

I called Jewel from Star Top after I had gotten out of meetings all day.

"JR, she is a natural. She has made my job so much easy

for me. She organized everything and even arranged the office in a much better fashion. She is a take-charge kind of leader and I like that. Overall, I think she is going to be fine. That's why I recommend her for the job at your house as well. Her paralegal experience does make her more than qualified. She took my computerized calendar and practically made it a breathing document. I knew everything I had to do for the next week and she planned out my tomorrow for me."

"Jewel, that sounds like a good report. Evelyn is making us money and so I was not wrong after all," I said.

"JR, you are fortunate. You happened to be right on target regarding Evelyn but that was a very risky move. By the way, Evelyn and I shopped for her some business outfits and her business cell phone. She is already too critical for me not to have around the clock access to her."

I was not surprised at all. Evelyn will make us money and now I got to get Ricky off and headed straight.

"Jewel, once again, you are doing a great job."

"JR, will you talk to me soon about the company's account? Do you know how I discovered it? Evelyn showed me on the computer how we can access the account."

"Right Jewel, I laid those instructions out for you under that password you must have given Evelyn."

"Okay, yeah she had to have the password and she did inform me that the law firm she worked for never eclipsed half that amount in their funds and they been around for nearly seven years. She was impressed by that and she is very proud to be a part of building a company."

"Jewel, I'm glad she's happy and I trust you will manage the account appropriately. We will discuss further in a few days. We need to have a business meeting soon to firm up further plans. Jewel, you are certain that Evelyn would be good for managing the house?"

"JR, she would be fine managing the house. Be careful though. You don't want to make her want to stay at the house forever. She could get used to that arrangement. Well, I know I am. I have not even thought about stopping by my condo because I have been so comfortable staying at your place. I brought all my clothes over because the guest room in your house is bigger than that entire condo."

I started laughing at Jewel and knew exactly what she was talking about, having owned the condo prior to her. My guest rooms are like apartments or suites in a hotel. To me, Jewel was just too funny. I have no idea how she is doing this in light of her engagement to her beau.

"JR, I got to run. I'll see you later."

Wow, I can foresee Evelyn becoming very pleased with the office manager job. Next up, I've got to sell her into the house manager position and perhaps get her to see how reasonable it is for her and Ricky to stay at the house permanently. *Come on JR, what are you doing? Kill those thoughts!*

***

"Get up Rickey! Push it!"

I was working out with Ricky in the gym. We played a game of basketball where he destroyed me like 15-3. He shot outside jumpers and when I went to guard him outside, he drove right past me and even dunked on me four times. I went over some drills with him and now I was having him run sprints with the ball up and down the court. I was literally wearing him out but he was responding real well to my drills.

This kid was rugged, tough, and had the confidence of a much older player. He outran me in sprints and wore me out as well, which is why I was just blowing the whistle and telling him what to do. My body was so sore and tired but I know I had to push him.

This routine had become a daily routine at least until he started playing school ball and participated in their practices. I would also have him take about 200 to 250 shots per evening, depending on how late it got at night. On tonight, Evelyn whom I had not seen in about three days came into the gym. I can't lie one second but as soon as I saw her I had to fight being totally mesmerized by her and I could tell that she had no clue.

Ricky had just finished sprinting and he was telling me how much he really liked the high school. Evelyn walked over and had on exercise attire like she had been working out in my mini fitness center in another part of the house.

"Are you trying to kill my boy? He seems to be so tired."

I turned around and got those same feelings about her once again. The immediate attraction and feelings that she was meant to be mine had not evaporated. She had on tight white shorts and a nice body top. I got to admit that she was the finest woman I had ever laid eyes on.

"Ricky, let's pick it up tomorrow after the tutorial session. Nice workout kid. Don't forget to do those post workout stretches that I showed you earlier, so you won't get any senseless injuries and you won't be too sore for tomorrow."

I lightly hit him in the chest and he said, "JR, I really do love my room. This house is the bomb."

As soon as he said that Evelyn was quick to say, "Ricky, this is just for a short period until our house is ready dear. Don't get too latched on this place. For this is not our home. Now, you go and take a good shower and I'll check on you later."

Evelyn just killed my spirit with those words but I had to take the high road. I looked towards Evelyn and said, "Can we talk? I got another proposition for you."

She looked with curiosity and said, "Okay but I need to shower up first so why don't you meet me in the media room."

I quickly said, "Okay, I guess I need to shower as well. Say we meet in the media room about thirty minutes from now?"

She nodded her head and started walking away and said, "About forty-five minutes, give or take five or ten, just before Soul Food comes on."

I agreed and I departed the gym from a different direction as my room was on the East Wing of the house and they were on the West Wing.

I took a nice shower and threw on some casual shorts and a tee shirt. It actually took Evelyn about 60 minutes but once again her presence just captivated my heart. She wore a big jersey over some tights but still looked as sexy as ever. By no means was she dressed in any way provocative at all.

"I hope I didn't keep you waiting too long," she said as she walked in the media room.

"No problem Evelyn! How was work today and just tell me how you feel about everything?"

"JR, I owe you for looking out for a sista. I love the job, the challenge and everything. I also love the school Ricky is going to and of course I love this house."

"I'm glad you do because I want you to consider being the house manager. The job entails an additional salary and of course you have free room and board and food and shelter."

"JR, what about the owners? How do they feel about that? Aren't you the house manager?"

"I am but I don't have time and the owners have already agreed to the idea. You and Ricky can stay here and save more money to buy a house of your choosing, aside from settling in Fuquay."

"JR, the houses in Fuquay are nice. I would love to move in either one of those as soon as they are ready."

"I know you would Evelyn but all I'm saying is that those will always be a possibility but right now you can save money and move out when you have to."

"JR, how long are we talking about? When do the owners return?"

"Evelyn, the owners live in Germany primarily and they rarely come to Houston when they come back to the United States. They also have a house in New York and they normally travel there and not here. My father is a close friend of the owner and he decided to hit two birds with one stone by having me keep his friend's place while also providing me a place to stay."

"But JR, don't you want your own place one day?"

I looked at her and my eyes melted.

"I do Evelyn, just like I want my own wife and family one day but now is not the time."

Damn, why did I say that? I was sounding good with that lie about the owners living in Germany and knowing my dad and all that and then I stumble with some stupid words like I finished with.

"Evelyn, you can stay here as long as you like and when you are ready to resign from the job, all the owner would like is a two month advance notice. His attorney will get everything for you in writing. This would be great for Ricky. He could work on his game every day if he so desired with the indoor basketball court."

"What? Ricky? Please JR, I would be so spoiled living here," she said.

"If you feel you need to do the job full time Evelyn, then the salary you make with me will be transferred to this position. It's really that simple. It's your call but Jewel tells me you have been a God sent at the office so I definitely don't want to lose you there either."

"JR, are you going to continue to remain here too?"

"Well, I do travel a lot and I stay here most of the time but not all the time. Lately, I been staying here to rest and manage the house with much effort the best I can. You will see me most days but most days I won't be here but I will always be a phone call away. Consult me on the house issues as I deal direct with the owner."

"JR. My son is so happy and I know I have to be careful not to allow him to get too attached to you. He's not used to having a father figure in his life and I can tell he is enjoying this. I promise I won't let you down though. I feel like I owe you for life."

"You won't let me down Evelyn. I feel certain of that. I'll get you a list of rules for managing the house and let me know if you have any questions. By the way, your son wore me out on the basketball court and I got these closings first off in the morning."

While I was talking, Jewel walked into the media room. She shouted out, "Soul Food, anybody?"

Evelyn turned around and said, "I'm with you gurl. It should be on in five minutes."

"Well ladies, I'm going to let yawl enjoy your show, as I need to call it a night. I got some business meetings first off in the morning and I don't want to be in there dozing off, u feel me?"

They both were listening until Soul Food started coming on and their eyes were glued to my theatre screen and I trickled out without them seeming to notice. It seemed to me that Jewel and Evelyn were becoming very close with that sista gurl talk and all. As I got half way down the hall I decided to return to tell the ladies about Lydia serving breakfast every morning around 6:30 am. I walked back into the media room and they were glaring at the screen and talking to each other like women watching a soap opera.

"Also ladies, Lydia serves breakfast every morning around 6:30 am if you let her know the night prior what you would like to eat."

Jewel turned around and said, "JR, you are late with that information. We have been eating breakfast every morning at the table. Myself, Ricky and Evelyn love Lydia's breakfast layout. Lydia has been taking real good care of us. We got this, okay. Now stop interrupting us from watching our favorite show. Get lost and let us ladies bond. Everything is taken care of. You go to bed and get some sleep so you can make breakfast in the morning and we can talk then."

I just started laughing but I loved it. I left out after that revelation and Evelyn didn't even turn around to look at me. She definitely seemed to have no interest in me, then again, who can compete with Soul Food? However, before I decided to depart to bed, I thought I would check on Ricky and see if he was asleep already. I knocked on the door and true to form the boy was in there playing Madden 2005, Play station football. I thought I would go ahead and give the boy a beating real quick but we played for quite awhile.

Matter of fact, I probably got the boy in trouble as we were playing and Evelyn walked in on us.

"JR, you cheated," Ricky said like he was shocked.

"You got in my way on that play! I could have scored a three pointer if you had not gotten in my way."

I acted like I was so surprised although I intentionally got in Ricky's way.

"I did? I'm sorry Ricky but the game is over champ and its bedtime."

Evelyn intervened as though she was surprised.

"JR, I thought you were dead set for sleep over two hours ago and Ricky you know it is well past your bedtime."

I got up and headed towards the door and said, "That's right Ricky, you need to get some sleep and I'll beat up on you later on in the week."

I was laughing so hard and Evelyn quickly said, "You should be ashamed of yourself, cheating on a kid."

I could not stop laughing fast enough to even respond. Ricky's room was designed with virtual reality sound systems. Whenever you played play station 2, it would seem as though the crowd was in the room watching you play. It had the true reality effects. I kind of had that installed while he was in school and Evelyn was at work. The boy loves the whole setup. It really made you feel as though you were really present in the real atmosphere of the games you played whether you were in a football stadium or basketball coliseum.

I beat Ricky in NBA Live after he practically killed me in Madden football. The game was a close one and I won 109—107 and we were in the Staple Center in Los Angeles, California where the Lakers play. Of course I had the Lakers team and he had the Detroit Pistons.

I did kind of cheat on the boy but it was so funny how I won. I was beginning to leave as Evelyn was talking to Ricky.

"JR, I will pay you back tomorrow and you won't have a chance to cheat," Ricky said.

"Yeah right, whatever dude...get some sleep so you can get over your beating...nahnahnahnahna...Be a man and accept your beating from the mighty J to the R."

I was laughing so hard.

"Okay boys, it is bedtime for both of yawl."

"Good night Evelyn," I said.

"Mom, JR cheated in play station 2. He intentionally

blocked my view so I could not execute the final play just before time ran out."

"JR should be ashamed of himself but that's okay honey you can beat him back on tomorrow. Besides, he told me that you slaughtered him on the basketball court in the gym," Evelyn said.

I jumped in from behind the door entry area and said, "Evelyn, how was I supposed to know that I had obstructed Ricky's view. It was a mistake because I just got so excited."

My laughter gave it away and Ricky was repeating, "That's not true mom. JR knew what he was doing."

I was laughing so hard and I told both of them good night. However, I slowly walked down the hallway, hoping to see another shot of Evelyn before I went to my side of the house.

Evelyn walked out and shut his door and loudly whispered, "JR, I have never seen him so happy. You have a very strong influence on him, so you better stop teaching my boy how to cheat."

She was smiling. She also told me thanks again and this time she planted a wet kiss on my cheeks. Now, my mom always told me that there was a difference from a wet kiss compared to a dry kiss. A wet kiss meant that a woman was interested whereas a dry kiss was more of a display or formality.

Anyway, I said good night and I went to bed and I swore to myself that I would not wash my face for months, at least the spot where Evelyn kissed me. It's amazing how you can become so attracted to someone that they bring out the kid in you all over again as though you have been reborn. I went to my room and shouted out a New Day, which is Pattie Labelle's song and it immediately played as I laid down to sleep after saying my prayers.

CHAPTER 17
Ricky Blows Up

My company was blowing up! God was blessing me on all fronts. Whoever would have thought that this Ocala reject would shoot up amongst the stars? I went from feeling like there was no hope to where I am now. I think it all started with God placing Julie in my life. She has been able to help me and I have been able to help others.

***

"JR, I don't know where you got this kid from but he has saved my job and the wife loves the new house." Coach Charlie Lawson ran over to me after his high school basketball team won the Invitational Christmas Tournament Championship at Belmont High School. They did it by beating their archrival, the very team that won the state championship two years in a row, the very team that said they had no room for Ricky.

Well, I'm sure Coach Bartelone feels like he made a critical mistake as Ricky got off. They had just finished presenting the championship trophy to Coach Lawson and the team. However, prior to that they presented Ricky the MVP trophy for the tournament. Directly after Coach Lawson came over, Coach Bartelone came over and congratulated Ricky. He also pulled me off to the side and said, "I was wrong and you were right. That kid is awesome."

Check this out! Ricky scored 31 points, pulled down 11

rebounds, 10 assists and 4 steals, all against the two starting McDonald's All Americans on one team. Whoever thought that a ninth grader would be so much of a threat to opposing varsity players. Much less, how does a ninth grader do this against the #1 ranked team in the state?

They had no defense that could stop Ricky as his team soared to an 87-66 victory, pushing their record to a perfect 5-0.

"Good game kid. I'm very proud of you. Remember these moments because they don't always last long. You literally had a Jordanesque like game," I said to Ricky as I patted him on the head.

"Thanks JR, can I ride home with you?" He said.

Evelyn had walked up and I said, "Ricky, I'd love to take you home but your mom probably wants that honor."

Evelyn spoke and hugged Ricky and said, "good game son! Ricky, you were awesome."

He gave the trophy to his mom as he talked to different people. Ricky was smiling from cheek to cheek as several people from coaches to fans and players wanted to congratulate him.

"Mom, can I ride home with JR?"

I had rushed to the game straight from work but Evelyn had driven to the game and Ricky traveled with his team but his team was cleared to return home with their parents if they so chose.

Anyway, Evelyn replied to Ricky's request, "I can't believe you gonna let your mom ride home by herself."

I intervened and said, "Actually, we can all ride home together! I'll have someone pick up your car Evelyn, if that's okay by you."

She replied with an excited but cautious smile, "JR, you are too sweet but who do you have in mind?"

She made me laugh with uncontrollable joy. She was looking some kind of good to me. I hung around Ricky along with Evelyn and I contacted one of my security staff members to pick up Evelyn's car and take it to the house.

"JR, what about my stuff," Evelyn asked. I got all kinds of personal stuff in the car?"

"Evelyn, trust me! Walker will pick up your car and he won't even touch your stuff. It would appear as though you drove it yourself."

"Oh, Walker! Okay, he's cool."

Actually, my entire security staff was trained like Walker, the Chief of Security. No one would touch Evelyn's stuff nor would they even act as though they noticed it. Evelyn and I stood near Ricky as everybody approached him to congratulate him on his game. I was floored to notice one exchange that got my attention.

"Great game freshman, but you played every bit like a senior. My name is Dante Vickson and this is Robert Matron. We just wanted to congratulate you on the game. We have only one other way for our team to play against your team again and that's in the state championship as we compete in different districts on the playoff tree. Now, Belmont High will be there, having taken the state two years running. If Lake View Academy can make it there, which I doubt, revenge will be ours freshman."

They were the two McDonald's All Americans and they were laughing and joking with Ricky. I was madly impressed by the way Ricky responded back to these superstars.

"Wow! Thanks guys! I guess we will play against yawl again in the state championship game and guess what, yawl will lose again because your time is up!"

He started laughing as he said that but for some reason,

he even convinced me that he was giving some early prophecy. They all shook hands and hugged as they walked away from each other.

Ricky had his share of groupie high school girls that came by to speak as well. Ricky was now six feet two and weighed about 185 pounds and had the natural wavy hair, was a pecan tan with a Rick Fox, Shemar Moore like appeal. Even women gawk at him when he and I travel around town, all to realize he's a young kid.

"Hey Ricky, that was a good game," said another man that Ricky did not know. This message was repeated several times by some high school girls who were obviously checking Ricky out.

"He is so fine gurl," said one young high school girl to another after they greeted Ricky.

I also noticed that as Ricky was leaving towards his locker room to hear his coach give a departing speech, this Caucasian gentleman in a nice suit approached Evelyn and I. "Hi Mr. and Mrs. Lyles I presume, I'm John Newman with NIKE! I was wondering if I could get a minute of your time."

I turned and corrected the gentleman by saying, "I'm sorry but I am JR and this is Miss Lyles, Ricky's mom as I am an acquaintance of the family."

"Perhaps I misunderstood Ricky for he said you were his father and Miss Lyles was his mom. I guess I just assumed you two were married."

"Well, like many, you too have assumed wrong! How may I help you Mr. Newman?" Evelyn said.

I know Evelyn was merely correcting him but I sure took that as a slam. She was too quick to make sure this guy knew I was not her husband. Oh well, that was once again taken as a big hint.

I was so embarrassed that I created a reason to leave the two alone.

"Excuse me; I have to find the rest room."

I walked off like I was going to the bathroom with a great need to relieve myself. Actually, I did not need to use the bathroom but I went anyway just to hide my facial expression, that of rejection. When I returned the NIKE guy was still there so I diverted away from them. I knew what he wanted, to see if Ricky would be interested in wearing their tennis shoes, which is a big deal as it eventually allows that kid who they predict to be a superstar to be an ambassador for their shoes. Ricky and I already talked about the perks and offers that will emerge from being a recognized superstar. I also know that he has referred to me as his father on numerous occasions and I have never corrected him nor told Evelyn. I realize I am like a father to him.

"JR, we are waiting on you."

Evelyn waved me over as she and the NIKE agent were still standing there. To my surprise, Evelyn did not want to hear his pitch until I had returned. That was a nice gesture, I think. We listened to his pitch and he left a card for us to contact him when our schedule was available. He gave both of us cards. As soon as he walked off, Evelyn gave me the card and just looked at me at a glance. I took the card and put it in my suit coat pocket.

No words were exchanged. I guess I was still thinking about that comment. Ricky came walking out about fifteen minutes later but prior to that Evelyn was on the phone.

After she got off the phone, she said, "I met Loke today. He stopped by the office looking for you and I told him you were not there and he said he would call you on your cell phone."

Oh my goodness! Loke saw Evelyn in my swimming pool

one day and I told him the deal but I did not let him know how I felt about her. He only knows that she works for me and that was it. I told him how he could meet her and he followed suit. Loke, however sees her as a piece of meat but I see her as my wife.

"Loke's a good man. He's been a good friend of mine. He also takes care of my teeth. I recommend him for you and Ricky, as far as being your dentist that is."

"Is he really that good JR?"

"Evelyn, you will learn that whenever I recommend you to someone they are the best in the business. He takes care of my teeth and Jewel's as well. Get her cut on Loke if you don't trust mine."

"Actually, I already have. That was Loke who just called me. He wants to take me to dinner tomorrow night. Jewel told me that you guys were pretty close."

I was thinking to myself that, *Loke didn't waste any time whatsoever.*

"Yeah, we are very close but different in a lot of ways. I guess you gave him your cell phone number?"

She looked at me and put her hands on her hips.

"Don't play JR. Loke said that you gave him my cell phone number?"

I was surprised at that piece of information. Not the fact that she was telling me that but the contents were not true.

"Evelyn, if I did, I sure don't remember doing that. I apologize. I mean, I don't even have your cell phone number come to think of it."

"Come on JR! You should have my cell phone number in case you need to contact me when I'm not around. That's okay! I was going to talk with you about giving my number to Loke but now I don't have to."

"Please don't hesitate to talk to me about anything," I quickly responded. "By no means would I remotely think of offering you up to anybody. Evelyn, I sure do like you."

Man! Where did that come from? Am I reaching a point of desperate measures or what? I know I don't want her to even associate me with Loke because if she gets to know him, she would realize that he is a dog and assume that I am the same.

"JR, you don't even know me," Evelyn said as she smiled. "Besides, what man will toss you up to his best friend if he liked you? You don't even act like I exist, especially in the same house that we live in. Also, what's this one week trip that you and Jewel are about to take, calling it business?"

I had to respond, although I knew there would not be much time for discussion.

"I'm sorry but I did not offer you up to Loke. Once again, I would not do that. Jewel and I are going out on business alone. Our relationship is strictly business and plutonic. If you think there is something more to it, you can come along yourself. So, I guess you and Loke are going out to dinner?"

"JR, what is this you have with Loke? I asked him not to call me again on this cell phone, for it is strictly for business and I declined dinner. I also told him that if I wanted him to call me I would give him a number to reach me at the house and he said that he had your number. I told him that if I did not give him the number, I ain't taking no calls from him.

I looked at her and smiled. Then I said to her "Good reply."

She also said, "he also invited me to his swimsuit party but I declined. I guess yawl got some real hoochie momma action going on there?"

I backed off like I was totally innocent.

"No yawl at all. I was just going to support my boy's

birthday party but since I will be away on business I have to miss it."

Ricky came running over and we all headed outside to the car.

"Hey JR, we got a game on Thursday night against the New Ridge High School Titans. Are you gonna make it?"

I was already in the car driving and I leaned back and said, "You know what son, I will miss the game on Thursday because I won't be back until late Friday evening next week but I will have it recorded."

Ricky leaned forward from the back seat and said, "Back from where JR?"

Evelyn stared at me real hard when I said son to Ricky. She was still looking at me real hard.

"I got to make a business trip from here to Georgia and Virginia but I'm sure you guys will play real well. The Titans should be no match for you guys," I said.

"JR, can I go with you on a business trip one day?"

Evelyn interrupted him, "Ricky, you know the answer to that already. You got school and a game to play."

I hashed in right after Evelyn. "Ricky, you can't make this one but I promise to take you on one at another time. There will be plenty of business trips and perhaps the summertime may be the best time for you since you will be out of school."

"You promise JR," he said. I affirmed my promise. "Cool, I can't wait. Are you gonna call back everyday about two or three times like I call you?" He said.

I leaned back again and said, "You can call me with your cell phone at anytime like normal."

"JR, I took that phone away from Ricky," Evelyn interrupted. "He is too young to have a phone and you are too busy to talk to him two to three times during the day like that. I told him to come through me and then I would call you."

"That's cool! As long as both of you know that I am only one phone call away."

The drive home seemed fairly quiet after that because Ricky fell asleep as though he was an infant in a moving car. We pulled up to the house and Ricky was still sleep in the back seat. Evelyn wanted me to lift the other garage door to make sure her car was back, like for some reason it would not be returned. I hit the remote button and lifted the other garage door and there it was. She woke Ricky up, told him to shower and go to bed.

"Mom, I already took a shower at the gym after the game," Ricky replied.

"Good, then you can go straight to bed," Evelyn said with a stern look on her face.

He got out the car and I signaled to him thumbs up. That was my way of saying I would be by to play some PS2 before he went to bed.

Evelyn and I went and sat in the sitting room.

"JR, what time are you leaving Wednesday?" Evelyn asked.

"I'm not for sure but I will check with Jewel or you can check when you see her in the morning. I'm sure she is asleep by now."

"That's okay! I think I scheduled yawl for a 10am ride to the airport. I'll pack your clothes on tomorrow night if you don't mind?"

"Okay," I said in utter but joyful surprise.

"You are so beautiful to me."

She looked at me and took off her shoes and said, "Beauty can be only temporary. What's behind the looks are so much more important."

I walked over to her and got on my knees and I said,

"That's exactly what I mean. Your beauty shines through from your soul."

I got real bold and leaned unto her lap and I rubbed her face. Then, I kissed her on her lips. Its like I was so drawn to her that I overcame my shyness and became prone to romance with her. She kissed me back and rubbed my head and then asked me, "What took you so long?"

I grabbed her and we passionately kissed for at least three minutes. Then, we stopped and she just got up and grabbed her shoes and walked out. I also left afterwards but her leaving confused me. I went and took a shower, grabbed a bite to eat from the kitchen and then I went to Ricky's room and he was out cold. He had the remote in his hand and the other one setup for me. I turned the game off and made sure he was in the bed comfortably and little did I know Evelyn was watching me and when I turned to leave the room she walked away.

However, she seemed to have dropped her house robe near the door and I picked it up. Then, I saw her slip and then her bra and then her panties were right at her door. I opened the door and she was in bed underneath the sheets with one leg showing. I walked in and closed the door and turned the lights out. She said, "What took you so long?"

I licked every inch of her body and made the best love I ever made in my life. We made love twice throughout the night. I woke up with her looking in my eyes.

"Hey gorgeous," I said to her and then I kissed her on her lips. She kissed me back and rolled over into my arms.

"Evelyn, be my lady."

"What about that professional being mixed up with personal speech you gave me?"

"I said that?"

"Yes JR, you sure did."

"Evelyn, bump all that. I want you to be my girl, my woman, my boo."

"JR, are you sure about all that? I'm no hoochie for hire now."

"I know that Evelyn. You are all I want. I just got to close some business with some other folks."

"Other folks? How many other folks JR? Never mind, you handle your business! I guess we can date for a minute. I am not going anywhere unless you give me reason to. JR, we won't rush anything though. Make sure this is what you want."

I left her room about 6am before Ricky woke up. I felt so complete and I was ready to call some other women and let them know that JR was done, turning in my playa card, calling it a day. I'm done! *Lights Out, Game Ova!*

When I went to my room early in the morning I yelled out, "Sports center" and my plasma television came out from the wall and I literally could not believe what I saw on ESPN television. Check this out.

"Good morning ladies and gentleman, I'm Stuart Scott and this is Stephen A. Smith for a very special coverage of Sports center. Not many times do we track the progress of pre-college athletes on sports center. Matter of fact the last pre-college phenom that we covered was a kid by the name of Danny Armano, the Bronx, New York pitcher who attracted our scope with incredible pitching ability. Nevertheless, after further review it was revealed that he was not in fact the age at which we were all led to believe, that of 12. Danny is still throwing that ball and it is highly likely that we will see him emerge back on the scene as his arm is still very deadly for would be sluggers, even at the age of 14 years old.

Speaking of 14 year olds, our coverage shifts to Houston, Texas at the Belmont High School Christmas Invitational

Tournament. Now, what's significant about this tournament is that the host, Belmont High, is the Texas state champion two years running with a starting lineup of two reigning McDonald's All American All-stars. Get a load of this! Six of the 18 teams participating in this tournament are currently ranked within the top ten in the state of Texas with the host team ranked number one. Having said that, who would have imagined who would reign as the champion of this tournament?"

"Let's go straight to the game and take a good look at some of these highlights. First off, the very reason why we are covering this game is for this reason. Let us introduce to you the man-child whom many have dubbed as the second coming of Jordan. This freshman phenomenon has shocked the world of high school basketball with stellar steals and incredible dunks like this one. (They show a highlight reel of Ricky stealing the ball, going coast to coast and then doing a 360-degree dunk.) Can he dunk in traffic? Well, how about this, shorty dribbles left and does a crossover to his right and then quickly accelerates towards the hoop and then makes a complete poster child out of Dante Vickson, one of the reigning McDonald's All Americans. Let's watch this again in slow motion. (They play the highlight reel again in slow motion.) Then we move to the 4th quarter, can the kid shoot it from outside? Are you kidding me? Shorty is shooting the 3 ball from the NBA range not the high school range. Take a good look here. (They show Ricky shooting a 3 pointer.) Take another look at another three pointer and another one and another one...Guess what...this kid sank six 3 pointers in the game and his shots hit nothing but net! (They show all of Ricky's six 3 pointers that he made.) Oh by the way, can the kid play defense? Let's look here as he comes out of nowhere and slaps shots all over the court. Somebody say it isn't so! Shorty breaking off something proper!

(They show all the shots Ricky blocked.) Yo, this kid's defense was pure BUTTA as he was all over the court. The current top ranked school in the state had no answers for this previously unknown but now nationally renown freshman superstar who erupted out of nowhere unto the national scope. Ricky finished with 31 points, 11 boards, 10 dimes (assists) and six blocked shots, literally taking the tournament MVP honors by storm as Lake View Academy went on to bury Belmont High by a score of 87-66; pushing their record to a perfect 5-0.

"Stephen A, what do you think? Is this kid the second coming of Jordan or what?"

Stephen A. begins to share his opinion.

"The next Jordan? Let me break this down for you. This kid is 14 years old at 6 feet 2 and weighing 185 pounds with a smooth jump shot that is as nice as any current NBA ballplayer. Oh by the way, the kid is believed to have a 37 inch vertical jump which will get higher as he is still growing; all these superior talents at the mere age of 14. Stuart, Jordan was not putting out these kind of numbers at 14. I would vouch to say that this kid could write his own destiny. To me, he could clearly be a superstar right now today but I cannot fathom him surpassing his airness (Jordan) as an individual performer and I'm not for sure if he will be able to bring home the number of championship rings that Jordan brought home. But the mere fact that we are discussing this kid's future while he is only 14 years old clearly defines him as destined with the potential to become one of the greatest ballplayers of all time. Now, having said that I don't want to ruin what this kid is doing right now and I think we should acknowledge the fact that if he continues to put up numbers like this, he will definitely be one of the best pre-college ballplayers to play the game. All I got to say is that this boy is bad! This boy will rewrite the history books if he continues to perform as he has in his first 5 games. I mean, come on Stuart, the boy is averaging 37 points and 18 boards a game. Hey, we need to get tickets to this kid's game so we can witness on the scene this historical shifting of the guard."

I was in such a stare struck mode. Ricky is on ESPN already at the age of 14. That coverage alone will attract many more scouts on all circuits. I was proud of Ricky and very uncertain as to how this will all play out. This success is happening all for a kid who in his own words is just glad to be able to play basketball. I am so happy as well for his coach as Lake View Academy, traditionally known for pre-college academics, is about to rise on the competitive basketball level platform. I can't predict the future but this is sure getting dicey at best.

After the coverage of Ricky, they showed an interview of Coach Charlie Lawson where he was addressing the fact that ticket sales have skyrocketed and there were reports that all games away and home for the rest of the season were sold out. Ricky was clearly filling up the stands as everybody was coming out to see this kid play. I was both happy and confused. I was hoping to myself that all this attention Ricky was getting would not have a detrimental impact on my relationship with his mom. I guess I was being selfish in my own way but for some reason I had a fear within that I clearly could not explain at this juncture.

CHAPTER 18
Am I Being Played?

I got home early on Wednesday. Loke called on my cell.

"What's up playa?" he said.

"You da man Doc. What's going on?"

"Hey man, I just wanted you to know that I'm moving my pool party to next weekend and that way you will be able to attend."

I was quite surprised to say the least.

"Loke, are you sure? I was going to stop by and chat with you before I left."

"Not tonight dude, I got some hot company coming over. By the way, won't you invite that fine ass woman working for you? She is a supermodel if ever I seen one. Hey man, you should hook me up with her, that's retirement material."

"Well Loke, I'm already seeing her."

"Really? Since when JR?"

"Since this morning."

"Okay, then that explains why she does not want me calling her and why she turned me down for dinner. I got to admit JR, she would be good for you if you could land that one. Shoot, I'd retire my playa card for her. But JR, don't turn that playa card in so fast now, we got a lot more coochie to hit before you retire."

"Loke, it might be too late. I could be done already. I enjoy being with her and her son."

"Son? Son? What? She got a son? Oh hell naw! Her stock value just dropped significantly. You aren't about to be involved with somebody else's baby daddy are you? JR, don't go there man! Trust me that is nothing but a full time headache. Man, kick that hoe out yo house and run like hell. I did not realize she had a son. Man, that's baggage and we got too much going for us than to tote around a lot of baggage. Shoooooot! No wonder that hoe done moved in with you."

I was quiet for a moment and I felt very dejected to say the least.

"Loke, she ain't a hoe okay. Please don't refer to her that way. Let me let you go and I'll talk with you later."

"Dang, you already sound like you been brainwashed. JR, don't take it personal now. You know you my boy and all. I'm speaking for your interests only. Keep in mind, you are talking to a father who is divorced and I don't let any niggas get involved with my kids. They do whatever with my ex-wife but those kids are my bloods and ain't no stranger going to move in and replace me as dad. Her son has a dad somewhere out there. Be careful man!"

I was quiet and I knew where Loke was coming from. He was just looking out for my interest. However, I did not want to further discuss what I strongly felt deep within; that Evelyn and I were meant to be.

"Loke, I'll call you later okay. It's all good."

"JR, come on man. Don't turn on me dude over some hoe out the projects that already has a kid. Come on JR! See the light on this simple issue man. Her coochie isn't that good bruh! Matter of fact, ain't no coochie that good." Loke said.

"By the way, aren't you leaving tomorrow? So when are you going to call me back. All I'm saying JR is that how you know she ain't just after your money and hooked into what you can do for her. Be smart playa. You know we normally hang out with women that have more money anyway. Hey, I'll let you go right now but don't forget, hollaatyaboy!"

I hung up the phone without saying goodbye to Loke. I knew that at least some of the words he spoke made a lot of sense. I went straight to my Jacuzzi bathtub. I had my sound system play Usher's song entitled "Burn." I was deep in thought and looking straight ahead at the wall just replaying Loke's words in my head, while also anticipating what my mom, Jewel, Veronica and Julie would all say. I really wanted to talk to someone but whom could I talk to? Besides, if I tell anyone that I am involved with a woman who already has a kid and really describe their background, they will all come to the same conclusion: that this woman was using me. My mom would really have a fit.

Deep down inside, I could really care less about the thoughts of everyone else. This is what I want and the hell with everybody and their thoughts of what should be and what should not be. *Lord, if I am wrong this time, at least I am wrong for going with what I feel is in my heart and your desire for me. Therefore, I can't be that screwed up.* This is where I really miss my father. I need a man to look me in my eyes and tell me to go for what I know and let whatever fall, fall.

"Any regrets?"

I looked up and Evelyn was in my bathroom doorway just staring at me.

"You seem to be in deep thought," she said.

I looked up and I was more confirmed than ever by her presence.

"No baby. I got no regrets at all. For I got what you need and I need what you got. Take them clothes off and join me."

She laughed and said, "JR, its still broad daylight outside."

"So, take them clothes off and join me. I don't care who knows about us. I'm not going to hide my feelings any longer. I told Loke today."

She started taking off her clothes and joined me in the Jacuzzi. I made love to her in the Jacuzzi and she just made me feel so justified beyond description. I held her in my arms and we were relaxed in the tub together. She told me about her day and I told her about mine, with exception of the hard feelings I had after talking to Loke. While we were talking, the phone rang and it was Veronica.

"JR," I bellowed into the air.

"What's up JR?" Veronica said on the other line.

Evelyn was so amazed about my phone system in my room. I never told her about it.

"Hi Veronica! I am busy right now but I can call you back later."

"JR, what you doing? Are you busy with your not so serious friend?"

Veronica started laughing as though it was a joke but she noticed that I was not laughing as I would normally in the past. There was silence and Evelyn still laid in my arms.

"Actually Veronica, I know we have not talked in awhile but I can meet with you later on perhaps next weekend because my not so serious friend is about to become, my so serious friend."

Evelyn just turned and looked at me. Veronica paused and responded, "JR, are you serious?"

She paused with the longest silence ever, it seemed and then replied, "Yeah, we need to talk face to face. I hope you are happy. I'll see you on next weekend if I got to wait that long."

"Well, I leave out of town on a business trip on tomorrow and I will be gone for a week. I'll call you next week."

Veronica hung up the phone and Evelyn said, "JR, are

you serious? You have described me as a not so serious friend. I should have known you were about games."

She started to get out of the Jacuzzi and I held her.

"Evelyn, I have been in love with you from the moment you walked out that house back in the projects. I have always told Veronica I had such a friend but that was before your time. I always told women I had a not so serious friend just to keep them in check. I have not had the chance to readdress with anyone since you have come into my life. My life has been all about work and you, and that's real baby."

Much to my surprise, Evelyn was not upset nor did she act as though she did not believe me.

"Well JR, perhaps we need to slow down anyway. You seem to have business that you need to resolve internally and externally with all your friends. I also have concerns as to how folks may be looking at the way I am affecting you. I mean, JR you got to admit that this is happening kind of fast; perhaps a little too fast."

I could feel the discomfort in Evelyn's voice but I was not done yet.

"Evelyn, its fast for people that don't know our chemistry. It's fast for outsiders who may envy what we have. It's fast for people who don't want to believe what we have. Only you and I can determine the velocity of our love and the hell with anybody else as long as our love for one another is real. I don't consider God's timing fast but I consider it on time. Not that I am so intunned with God as I should be but just by being able to be with you, God's got to be nearby because baby you are definitely a slice of heaven for me."

She kissed me and we made love again and fell asleep on my bed.

***

I woke up to Lydia ringing for dinner. I quickly hurried and got dressed and went to eat dinner with everyone. Evelyn had cooked and while Ricky and I were eating, he told me about his day and what kind of defense they were going to play against the Titans. He said he loved playing full court press because he gets to make a lot of steals, assists, and dunks. After dinner, we went to play PS2 sports while Evelyn went and started packing for my trip. Afterwards, I left Ricky because he had some homework but he beat me in a PS2 game first.

I went to my bedroom and Evelyn was packing and looking at television. I walked in from behind and grabbed her and wrestled her to the bed.

"JR, we need to talk about the house."

"You don't like the house?" I said.

"I love the house but it ain't ours. We need to get our own house baby."

"Okay, we got plenty of time to work that out," I said.

I started kissing her but I noticed she did not respond. Then came the bomb.

"JR, I mean Ricky and I need to get our own house. I do not want people to think that I am seeing you so I can stay in this house with you. I do not want to be viewed at as a gold digger."

I was somewhat surprised to hear that but I could understand where Evelyn was coming from. I continued to caress her and she replied, "stop JR, you know Ricky is home."

"I know but we got a sound proof room and we can just lock the door."

"No, not now! I'll be in here all night after he goes to bed."

"You promise?" She kissed me and said, "Yes, my dear."

Afterwards, I called Julie and let her know I was leaving out of town and I told her I needed to see her sometime when I returned and she of course consented.

I went back to check Ricky's homework and Evelyn was already going over his homework. Evelyn told me Ricky was making A's and B's, with exception of a C in Biology. She was talking to him about raising that grade. I went back to look over some paperwork and I fell asleep. Ricky woke me up and wanted to say he would see me in the morning. After he went to bed, Evelyn confirmed he was asleep by checking his room. She came to my room and woke me up by easing her nice, naked, warm body in bed with me. God! I love this woman.

CHAPTER 19
Jewel Or Diamond In The Ruff

J ewel and I caught our flight as planned. She was looking good as usual.

"Jewel, we need to find another executive administrator."

She looked at me and said, "JR, why is that? Evelyn is doing a great job. She has made the company a lot of money and I can definitely trust her."

"I agree Jewel." She looked, yawned, and then said, "Why are you talking about replacing her then? This doesn't have anything to do with your friend Loke, does it?"

I laughed and quickly lifted my head up at her as to show my surprising look.

"First of all, I'm not trying to replace her; at least not in the negative sense of the word. I'm actually promoting her."

Jewel looked at me real hard.

"The next move up is assistant business manager or my job. JR, are you trying to tell me something?"

"Yeah, I just want to make her the house manager full time. I'm promoting Evelyn to the position of wife, my wife."

She looked at me with her mouth wide open.

"JR, are you serious? What about all your other lady friends? You know you got a lot of them. I don't know about that. JR, you really need to think about that. I don't know that time has proven her worthy to be your wife?"

I looked at Jewel and said, "what in the world are you talking about?"

"JR, it really does not even matter with me talking to you because you are going to do what's already in your head anyway. There is no need for me to try and talk you out of it."

"Come on now Jewel! Why has it got to be like that?"

"JR, don't even play because you know I'm right. I will admit, however, from the weeks I've noticed Evelyn she does turn down a lot of men. You would be surprised as to how much traffic comes her way. I have been very impressed with how she handles men; practically taught me a thang or two. She even turned down your handsome friend Loke. She cracked me up when she said she don't date no man that looks as good as she does. She had me laughing for dayz. All your male employees act like they would drink Evelyn's bath water."

Jewel and I sat beside each other in the First Class section on our Delta Airlines Flight. She leaned over to me while yawning and continued talking.

"I just want my friend, you, to be happy. Now JR, she has never talked about you to me other than professionally. She has not given me any indication that she likes you but she is devoted to you professionally."

I just listened to Jewel and then I told her, "Evelyn probably wanted to see what you would say and try and tell whether or not we had something going on."

"I kind of doubt that JR because we have discussed your many women together and she knew that I would not go there on that realization alone."

These words did startle me and I had to get to the bottom line as Jewel continued to tell me I have a lot of women.

"Jewel, why do you insist that I have a lot of women? Where are you getting this from?"

She immediately laughed and leaned over to cough from the sudden laughter.

"JR, anyone that is a close partner of Loke has to be in the same ballpark as he's in. My fiancé had a friend like Loke and when he met me he told me how he pulled away from his friend because he attracted too many women for him to stay focused. I assumed the same with you and Loke."

I leaned over to Jewel and sincerely responded to her words.

"Jewel, that is not at all the case. I'm not saying I'm a virgin but it is possible for two oranges to hang on the same tree and have different tastes. We have an orange tree in my yard back home and I know what I am talking about."

She looked at me with a smirk on her face.

"JR, you don't have to lie to me. You are a single man and what you do behind the door is your business."

I casually stated, "well Jewel, if that's the case then why are you always picking at me by saying I have so many women?"

"Honestly JR, I just be joking with you. However, I have been led to believe that you have many women which is probably why you never tried to hit on me."

I stared at Jewel as she stared at me. I really did not know what thoughts were in her head but I had to find out because it could really be messy from here if I am in a total naive state as to what is really going on. Nevertheless, I elected to be very indirect in my approach to get to her inner feelings.

"Jewel, I refuse to put Loke's business out on the street because you could be wrong about him as well. We both have similar interests for the most part but look at our backgrounds. I am single and Loke is divorced. In essence, we both view women from a totally different perspective. I appreciate his perspective and I'm certain he can understand mine."

Jewel sipped on her cup of coffee and then she continued to stare at me with those mysterious eyes of hers that had no hint as to where her mind was. I call them alligator eyes.

"JR, why have you never made a move on me?"

Okay, I got to admit that I did not expect to hear that. I looked down and away from Jewel and this was when playa tactics came into play. Jewel reminded me of Alicia Keys. She was so beautiful that you just did not want to touch her. All of us watched the 2005 Grammy Awards at the house together and I told them that I fell in love with Alicia Keys when she sang that song, "If I Ain't Got You." They all laughed at me. Anyway, Jewel's hair was just as full with body as Alicia Keys' hair looked during the night of the Grammy Awards.

Now, back to the task at hand, how do I answer Jewel's question? I had to give it an attempt. Here is what I said, "Jewel, when I saw you, you reminded me of how I was when I arrived here in Houston. You were so professional and so sincere with business. Although I am very much attracted to you, I really valued your friendship because I was already involved with a few women and I refused to involve you in that manner. Also, I respected your engagement ring and I was also intimidated by your beauty."

"Hush JR! That is about the biggest bunch of bull crap I have heard in awhile. I was just curious because you have always acted like a big brother to me and I wondered how you refrained from trying to hit on me. I mean, most men that I have this type of proximity with still attempt to get up my skirt and I'm trying to figure out what made you so different. I was just curious."

I smiled at Jewel and said, "so I did not disappoint you, did I?"

She quickly turned her head and gave me that elevator look and said, "JR, I hope you don't think I'm interested in you. You are not even my type. Don't for one-minute think you have it like that with me because we are like brother and sister and that's it? To have anything beyond that with you would be taboo."

Although I was surprised to hear that from Jewel, I found myself inclined to believe her. Jewel is a very honest and straightforward woman and she has no reason to lie. I played off her comments with a small laugh and then I told her, "look here little sister, we are going to become very close over the years and I'm glad to know that we have a mutual understanding of our relationship."

"Whatever JR," she smiled and leaned her head on the corner of my shoulder and fell asleep. I stared at her and I just thought about how I love this woman in such a sisterly type fashion. It's like I want to be with her for the rest of my life. The feeling was that soothing. I leaned my head back and fell asleep as well.

***

My phone rang as Jewel and I were returning to the hotel from one of the land development sites and I answered, "JR."

"JR, we won again."

Ricky called me directly after the game as I could hear the surrounding noise.

"Hey boy, congrats to you! How close was the game?"

"Well, the score was 94–52. I didn't play the last quarter. Coach said my job was done at the end of the third quarter. He seemed to think I might get hurt."

"That's good Ricky! Keep working hard and listening to your coach."

"Okay JR, I got to go. I'll call you later. Here is mom."

"Hello," Evelyn said.

"Hey gorgeous! How was the game baby?"

"It was good. They really did not have much competition.

Ricky made this real pretty play where he went up in the air and pinned the ball to the backboard and brought the ball back down and made a real pretty pass. The crowd went crazy. He jumped real high. I told him he would be under punishment if he did that again. I ain't trying to see my baby get hurt. Hold on JR."

She turned away from the phone and yelled at someone in the background.

"Look here boy! If you ever grab my butt again I will beat you up in here, do you hear me?"

I heard some mumbling in the background of Evelyn's conversation.

"Are you there JR?"

"Yeah baby, I'm here. What was that all about?"

"Just some stupid, young kid feeling my butt like he crazy. JR let me get out this crowd. I'll call you when we get home."

"Okay baby, bye bye."

Wow! It sounded like Ricky did a high pin block on the backboard. I'll call Coach Lawson later on and get the details. Jewel and I had been interviewing all day for a local business manager to lead the subdivision project in Georgia.

We also discussed a possible replacement for Evelyn in the office. Jewel was an outstanding partner for me. We got along so well. I asked her to help me find an engagement ring for Evelyn and she said we would do that in Virginia. At first she said that she would have no parts of trying to help me marry someone that I have known for such a short period of time. Then, not long afterwards, she started telling me how she wish her fiancé' would get a grip and realize that they need to be married or perhaps maybe not, since she was still having her doubts. Jewel just really did not seem to be as head over heals with Sidney as it appeared. I even noticed that she stopped wearing her engagement ring. I was going to inquire about that but I thought maybe I would wait and allow her to initiate that conversation. All I know is that if he hurts her in anyway, he would definitely get a very unpleasant visit from me. That's just how close I came to be with Jewel.

**

"Hey Coach, how's it going?"

Coach Lawson answered the phone as I was calling to get his assessment on the game. He sounded a little grumpy however.

"JR, I am glad to get a call from someone I know. My phone has been ringing off the hook. Everybody is asking about this 14 year old, eighth wonder of the world. Are we at eight or nine so-called wonders now, I forget? Anyway, JR, that boy could be the next LEBRON, but going straight to pro before graduating from high school. He did a 360-degree, jacknife dunk tonight after catching the ball off an alley OOP that brought the whole gymnasium down. It's just amazing how he stayed in the air so high for so long. I have not seen those types of moves since Jordan."

"Are you serious?" I said.

"Look JR, I got pro, college, and other high school scouts calling me and asking about Ricky. I took him out the game in the third quarter and mind you, he did not play any at all in the fourth quarter and still scored 29 points, 11 rebounds, 5 assists and get a load of this: he broke the high school record for steals. That boy stole the ball 13 times. JR, we got something special in him. I am still excited from the game."

"Wow, sounds like he will have no problem getting scholarship money."

"What? Scholarship money? JR, that boy ain't going to no

college. He is going straight to the NBA. Unfortunately, I'm worried that he may not even finish out his high school years, much less this school year. I got pro scouts saying they could use him right now."

I was so excited to hear the news.

"Coach, I hear you but Ricky ain't going nowhere. He will finish high school if I got anything to do with it. Please don't inform him of all this attention. I don't want him distracted with all this post game talk."

"JR, I hear you but I must say this boy's game is more complete than college seniors. I have to carry his birth certificate with me because other coaches don't believe me when I tell them this child-man is only 14 years old."

"Well, he has a birthday in a couple of months. I'm glad he is a good fit for your team."

"Good fit? Ricky Lyles is the team! Trust me JR, he will go far as long as he stays healthy. I do disagree with you on this one thing; that boy will be the first to leave high school and go to the NBA. His talents are that great. I mean he could start on an NBA team, I'm not talking about just barely making it."

"I hear you Coach. Well, I'm out of town but I'll be in touch. I just wanted to hear from the coach how Ricky did. I'll be in touch later on."

Coach Lawson seemed really happy! I am so glad for him! I am truly happy for Ricky too.

***

"JR, that is a real nice engagement set, trust me."

Jewel and I were shopping for an engagement ring for Evelyn.

"I don't know Jewel; I like that one there better."

She looked and stared at me real hard and said, "JR, that's about $6,800."

I looked and said I know but that's what I want my wife to be, to have."

She took a hard stare at me as though she was saying, "DYAMMN, why can't that nigga be mine, paying that much for an engagement set?"

We got the ring set I liked.

Jewel gave me a speech about walking around with so much cash on me. As we were departing the store, my cell phone rang and when I recognized it was from my house, I answered. Oh yeah, Jewel strongly nagged me about always using the calling ID feature on my phone more frequently rather than just answering the phone cold turkey.

"JR," I said.

"Hey baby! I miss you! Whatchu doing?"

It was Evelyn and she sounded so sexy.

"Jewel and I just finished doing some shopping."

"That's all yawl better be doing together."

There was a quick pause and then Evelyn uttered, "I'm just kidding JR, but my message is serious."

In the background I heard Ricky asking for the phone.

"Ricky, you have to wait. Look, let me let you talk to your biggest fan. I'll call you later after I send him to bed."

I was so glad to hear those words.

"Okay Evelyn, I'll talk with you later."

Ricky got on the phone.

"JR how's the business trip?"

"It's going well Ricky. I sure do miss you boy!"

"I miss you too JR. By the way, I raised my Biology grade up to an A minus and did mom tell you about all the gifts people are trying to give me?"

"Ricky, I'm glad to hear that on the grades. Push that A minus into an A and we might be talking about driving lessons real soon after you turn 15 that is."

I heard him screaming, "oh yes" as to show his excitement at possibly being able to drive.

"Also Ricky, please do not take any gifts from anyone, particularly strangers and companies. A lot of kids get into trouble like that. I'll explain it to you more when I return. What have you been doing aside from school and basketball?"

"Mom and I went to dinner and I beat her in tennis. She kept hitting the ball like a baseball. She was real funny. JR, can we get a dog? I saw this pretty one today."

"What did your mom say?"

"She says wait until we get our own house."

"Okay, that's good advice but how bout we start looking when I get home okay. Now, you do realize a dog is a major responsibility and you will be held liable for maintaining the dog, okay?"

He got excited real fast.

"Alright JR, that's what I'm talking about."

"Ricky, can you keep a secret?"

"Sure JR, what's the secret?"

"SH-SH! Don't say that word too loud. I got your mom an engagement ring."

He shouted out "What? I mean, really....YES!...YES!"

Then, he started to whisper.

"I won't say a word JR. I am so happy to hear that. So, that means we get to be together forever, right?"

"That's right son! We will be together forever."

"JR, I am so glad because I like you as though you were my dad and now you can actually act like him."

I started laughing but I knew what Ricky was trying to say.

"That's right son, I will continue to be like a father and I'm proud to have you as my son. Okay, keep that engagement stuff quiet for now and I'll talk with you later. You need to get some sleep. You got a game tomorrow right?"

"Yes Sir! I am too happy to go to bed."

"Well, sneak and practice on your PS2 games until you fall asleep. That will also be our secret, okay?"

"Okay dad, oops...I said that too loud...I mean JR."

"Good night son."

Wow that sounded nice hearing that word: dad. I greeted the two of them goodbye and Jewel and I pressed on with business. Jewel shared a lot with me about her problems with her fiancé and why they were not married yet. I thought Jewel would be a good wedding coordinator but I'd leave that to Evelyn to decide.

***

The following evening after working our business endeavors, Jewel nagged me about taking her to the movies to see Ice Cube's new movie "Are We There Yet?" We had dinner and then went to the Potomac Mills Mall and watched the movie. I really enjoyed it in every respect and laughed my butt off. Jewel stared at me with a smile on her face. I pretended not to notice but I did.

Towards the end of the movie I was very mushy. I had nothing but tears flooding my eyes as I realized how thankful, happy, and ready I was to have my own family. To me, this is where Loke does not get it. This is where my mom does not get it. I realize I am young but I am ready to have my own family. I want kids to play with and one woman to come home to everyday. In this day and generation, why should a man be treated as though he's losing his mind to desire those things?

Loke should understand because he has kids and he is divorced. Hell, it's my turn. Let me live my life.

"JR, are you okay?"

I was sitting there in a daze with my lachrymose expression as the movie credits were being shown and Jewel had already stood up as though she was ready to leave. I got up and gathered my thoughts and we returned to the hotel.

***

I called Julie and told her about my latest developments, particularly that I was engaged and about to be married. She was very surprised but said she was happy for me, although she really did not sound happy. She told me that we could resume as business partners and just friends and that she would honor that as she stated early in our relationship. I did not think it would be this easy but it somehow seemed to be. I felt relieved but I was also fearful; fearful of the fact that I could never turn Julie down. I thought she would renege on everything once I told her but she was totally supportive. She still said we could meet face to face and go over everything after I returned.

Later on in the evening I got a call from Ricky and he was still at the gym where they played and you could tell that the game was just over because I could hear people trying to talk to him.

"JR, we won another one but this game was really tough. Corrolton High had a very tall team and they played a tough zone defense. The game went down to the wire. JR, I got to go, my coach is signaling me over. Here is mom."

"JR, this game was a thriller. They barely won by three points," said Evelyn as she spoke on the phone.

"Was Corrolton that good?" I asked.

"Yeah! They got like three seven footers that are triplets

but you would have been proud of Ricky again. He showed out tonight."

"Really, what did he do?"

"You know, everything. He played a great game. Matter of fact, they are interviewing him right now with his coach and television cameras around and everything. Let me call you later okay."

"Okay baby, I'll talk with you later."

My phone was ringing off the hook for some reason. I had already spoken with Penelope, Juanita, and Debbie and pretty much told them I was engaged. The only problem with these women is that they thought I was really committed all along so they did not see a problem still but I had to let them know that we could remain friends but I would only sleep with one woman.

They were not happy campers but I was not worried about them. Well, actually, I really felt bad because as Loke would always say I did not want to break up with anyone on bad terms where they could come back and haunt me. Thus, I did feel the slightest bit insecure. Loke said you should always place yourself in a position for them to kick you to the curve and that way you are not the bad guy.

Afterwards, Jewel and I had dinner and we were returning to the hotel and I did not realize it but I had my cell phone turned off. When I turned it back on, everybody had called. I called in time to talk with Evelyn but Ricky had already fallen asleep. She emphasized that he really wanted to talk to me. After I got off the phone with Evelyn, I returned Coach Lawson's phone call.

"Hey Coach, this is JR! I'm sorry to call so late but I just got your message."

I could tell the coach was sleep as his voice sounded so lethargic.

"JR, no problem man. Did you hear about the game?"

"Not the details, I just heard it was close. Since when did Corrolton High become so tough?"

"JR, they got the strongest frontcourt in the state. I'm surprised you have not heard about the Russell triplets. They are all seniors and stand about seven foot and they got skills. Not to worry though because we had Ricky Lyles. JR, that boy is bad! He put on one of the best high school performances I have ever seen. Ricky was like an untamed tiger on the court tonight. He broke three records tonight."

"What?"

"That's right! He had 11 blocked shots, scored...you might want to sit down on this if you are not sitting already...the boy scored 67 points, hit 15 three pointers, grabbed 13 boards and still had 9 assists and 7 steals.... he broke the record for most points scored in a game, most blocked shots and most three pointers...JR, this boy is something special...do you know how we won the game? Ricky hit a three pointer at the buzzer...nothing but net!"

I was so astonished and totally devoid of words.

"Coach, the boy did all that? You have got to be kidding me!"

"JR, he slammed on one of the Russell triplets where I swear he took off from the top of the key...oh I'm sorry.... Ricky broke 4 school records...He also hit 13 consecutive free throws...the boy did not miss one, do you hear me? The stands were full of scouts from everywhere. I think there were more NBA scouts than college scouts. I have been asked nearly a thousand times, where did I get this boy? All I say is that he relocated here from Dallas. They wanna know what school did he play with in Dallas and I have to tell them, he played nowhere for the boy is only 14 years old."

"Wow Coach! So Ricky Lyles ain't no joke?"

"JR, Ricky Lyles is the second coming of Jordan.... no, I am not so certain that he won't be better! I assure you! Check out the news! The boy had his first interview on television tonight. This boy is a man on the court JR. He will be playing in the NBA next year...the boy is just too good for this level as well as college level. I been coaching basketball for over 25 years, I know what I'm talking about. For our high school, Ricky is like the second coming of Christ and Lord please don't strike me down for saying this. I'm just painting a picture JR because you don't seem to get it."

"Coach, I did not know Ricky was such an outside threat to where he was raining three pointers like that. I always thought he was great for mid range shooting."

"JR, I am learning more and more about this kid every game. When the Triplets seem to bother his inside game, the boy took his game outside and literally dared them to follow. On a couple of plays, Ricky faked a three to get one of them to leave their feet and then he went inside and posterized at least one of the other two with a ferocious dunk. He did just what he needed to get the results leading to a win. In practice, he does the basic fundamental stuff and works hard but come game night, all that adrenaline produces another animal. He was a beast on the boards."

Coach Lawson sounded really compelling. I guess time will definitely tell. I got off the phone with the coach, as I knew he was already asleep before I called. Jewel and I were preparing to return back to Houston. Our trip was very successful.

Jewel and I bonded real well on the trip. She became more of a sister to me. I like to think I became more of a brother to her. She told me how she had wanted to do a lot of things in New York but her fiancé was very much a controller and he kept her isolated from society in some respects to such a degree that she had to get away. I definitely was glad to have her.

CHAPTER 20
Surprises Galore!

After we landed back in Houston, Evelyn and Ricky greeted us at the airport. Ricky just seemed so happy and he just kept punching me on my shoulders, a gesture he got from me. When we got in the car, I played my CD that I had in my bag. I played "A New Day" by Patti Labelle. We listened to that song all the way home. I felt just like it was a new day. After we arrived home, I went through the newspaper articles that they had on Ricky. Wow! He was all over the place. The media was clearly dubbing him as the second coming of Jordan.

Next up, I had to go meet with the boss. It was important for me to get Julie's cut on everything. She was like a mentor to me and I really valued her opinion. I called her and she wanted to meet me at a coffee shop adjacent to Star Top Realty.

We met there and I told her all about my trip. Julie was looking good as usual. I told her all about my personal life.

"JR, are you happy?"

"Yes Julie!"

"Well, that's all that matters. This woman loves you very much huh?"

"She does as well as her son. He is a superstar basketball player."

"Oh really!" Julie replied as she lifted up her eyeglasses.

"He sure is Julie. Matter of fact, he has been all over the news here lately."

"Wait a minute. How old is he JR?"

"Ricky is 14 years old," I quickly replied.

"JR, is he the kid the whole town has been ranting and raving about? I saw him on television a couple of nights ago and they said he broke like four major high school records. Are we talking about Ricky Lyles?"

"Yes Julie! We as a family are nearly a perfect fit. Matter of fact, I want you to meet us for dinner one evening next week if you can slow down from your busy schedule?"

"Sure JR, I would love to do that. Does Ricky have an agent yet?"

"No Julie, he's only 14 years old and way too early for that kind of stuff."

"Actually JR, he's really not. If all is true that I hear about this kid, he may be the first to leave high school for the NBA?"

I started modestly laughing, like I had something to do with his skills.

"Julie, that's media hype. I don't foresee Ricky leaving high school for the NBA."

"JR, have you considered being his agent, or perhaps Jewel if you are too swamped which I imagine you are. I can hook you up with the right folks to get the training. Besides, who will care more for his interests than you?"

Julie may have guided me onto something big. I never thought about any of these possible realities. Ricky will need an agent and she's right, who better to serve his interests than I, unless I could get Jewel to do it.

"Julie, Jewel is an attorney, perhaps she could represent Ricky as his agent. She knows all the legal circles and avenues to derive at reasonable business goals."

"You are right JR, Jewel could do it but would she be

willing? Anyway, it's something for you all to discuss. Besides, it sounds like Jewel's hands are quite full right now," Julie said.

Julie had such an incredible business mind.

"I will definitely study that thought Julie. Once again, I owe you."

"JR, stop saying you owe me. I'm sure I will miss us, but we won't dwell on that. I feel committed to treat you as though you were like my father when he was your age."

"Julie, I'm sure I will miss us too."

We departed from the coffee shop and I told her I would get back with her on the dinner timeframe. I must admit I could still feel the strong attraction coming from both of us. I was starting to feel somewhat guilty but should I just expect to go cold turkey like this or should it take some time. The only person I felt comfortable talking to about that was Julie, but I elected not to at this time. I did not want to let her know how I really felt deep down within.

***

"JR, I love this suit! I really like these shoes too." Ricky was excited. I brought him back a couple of Hugo Boss suits from Atlanta when Jewel and I went shopping on my trip. We were at Boston's Restaurant and it was a very special occasion. Ricky had just led his team to a come from behind victory over another high school arch rival basketball team. They were behind by 16 points going into the 4th quarter and then Ricky just got stupid on the court. He had early foul trouble in which he had to sit out the early portion of the game, but still led his team to a 78-73 victory as he poured in 31 points (17 in the 4th quarter), grabbed 15 rebounds, six steals, 9 assists, 8 blocked shots (5 in the 4th quarter). He literally put the team on his shoulder and took them to their perfect 10-0 undefeated record.

I was nicely dressed with my black Hugo Boss suite on and so was Evelyn as I bought her about four sexy dresses from Atlanta. The three of us were at dinner and we had just finished eating. I told them I had a surprise and what I did was have Jewel show up after I made a phone call. Evelyn was way too anxious.

"Okay everybody! I called this dinner for one reason alone," I said with excitement. I stood at the table and Jewel showed up to everybody's surprise but mine. I went around to Evelyn and kneeled before her.

"Evelyn, will you marry me?" She started crying and was nodding her head.

"Yes, Yes JR! Of course I will marry you. Damn, what took you so long?"

She was wiping tears from her eyes as I slipped that nice rock on her finger, after Jewel handed it to me. Ricky was just smiling like he was the happiest kid alive.

"JR told me he bought you an engagement ring and it was our secret until now, right JR?"

"That's right playa and you kept my secret too."

The whole restaurant stood still and witnessed my proposal. They applauded with a standing ovation as she said yes. I stood up and jumped in the air like I had just won the lottery and then we hugged each other. I waved Ricky over and we hugged in a circle and I said, "I know it will be tough and Ricky I regret that we arrived in each other's lives so late. I wish I could have been there when you were a little boy but I promise to be a father to you for the rest of my life. Evelyn, I know it will be tough but our love will overcome any challenge whatsoever. May God richly bless our newfound family and let this be the beginning of many joys for us. With God at the front and center of our lives, we have no need to fear or worry."

Evelyn was just crying tears of joy. Even Jewel started crying. It was more than just a Kodak moment. Thus, it was official. Evelyn and I were engaged.

Jewel said as she joined our circle, "Okay now, have yawl set a wedding date?" I responded, "Nope, but I'm thinking within the next month or so."

Evelyn was still just crying tears of joy.

"Then again, you need to come up with the perfect date Miss Wedding Coordinator," I said to Jewel in a very conservative way. Jewel looked, as her eyes and mouth were wide open with excitement.

"What? You mean? Okay folks, no problem, I just need to get busy. Evelyn and I will come up with the best date. We need time to get invitations out. I will direct this wedding and put my best effort in it as though it's my own. I would love to be the director of your wedding."

"JR, do you think the owner of the house would mind if we had the wedding at the house?"

Jewel stared at me and then she stared back at Evelyn and said, "The owner? JR, you still have not told Evelyn who the owner of the house really is?"

I looked at Jewel and said, "Not yet!" Jewel looked at Evelyn and said, "Girl, if you don't realize it, let me be the first to tell you that you are marrying a very wealthy man. JR owns the house and is about to own another 25 more, not to include a portion of the properties we just visited on that business trip. Evelyn, I know it may not concern you, but you have landed someone bigger than a lottery ticket. Can you say Cha-Ching?"

Evelyn and Ricky both looked very shocked.

Ricky said, "Wait a minute! JR, you really own the house? No wonder you did not want me to accept any gifts," he said with that marquee grin of his.

He had the look of amazement on his face. Evelyn also interrupted, "Ricky, please keep that information quiet. Don't repeat this to anyone and I'm sure JR can tell you why later. Besides, you bring way too much attention to this family already."

I was glad to hear my baby share her wisdom considering these matters. I was clearly at peace. I still sense that Evelyn thought that people would call her a gold digger. I guess I should perhaps have the same concern: about to marry the mother of the next Jordan to be basketball player.

Then, out of nowhere, this old white couple came over to the table and I thought they were gonna congratulate us for our engagement but I was certainly surprised as the elder man spoke to us.

"Excuse me but I really do not mean to disturb your celebration over here. I was wondering if this young man was Ricky Lyles?"

I responded, "Yes Sir, he sure is."

Then the old man and woman who were holding hands together started smiling and the man said, "Could we get your autograph? We saw you on television the other night and in the newspapers and we know you will be one of the greatest ballplayers to ever play the game."

Ricky was literally floored. He looked at me as to gain approval and I said, "Go ahead boy and sign your first autograph."

Ricky did it without hesitation. I looked at his signature and said, "Boy, we need to work on that autograph. Perhaps your agent sitting beside you can work with you on that."

Jewel's face lit up again as the couple said thanks and walked away. Evelyn was smiling as though she was in heaven.

"JR, are you serious?" Jewel asked.

"Well Jewel, Evelyn, Ricky and I talked about it and if you got the time the job is yours. You won't be too busy until probably another year or so from now."

"JR, I am so ecstatic. I don't even watch basketball but I have seen nothing but his handsome face all over the media. You are wrong about one thing. He does have activity now and I will be busy with him right away. Ricky, is that what you want?"

"Yes Ma'am! JR and mom say you will serve our best interests as my attorney and agent."

"Attorney too! Oh my goodness. Yawl are so much full of surprises. This is the best news I've had since I was engaged. Lord have mercy!"

She got up and kissed Ricky, Evelyn and myself on the cheeks. This was a celebration of all sorts. Evelyn came over to me with blood shot eyes as she was still recovering from the ring on her finger.

"JR, I had no idea who the owner was. I don't care if you didn't even have a house or job; I was in love with you the moment I laid eyes on you. I don't know why but somehow I felt in my soul that you were mine."

She kissed me on my lips and I held her with the most complete feeling I ever had in my life.

"Jewel, please plan the wedding for next month because this family is overdue."

"JR, I'll get on that tonight," she said.

Ricky intervened, "JR, since you own the house, we can get that dog can't we?"

I looked at Evelyn and I said, "Ricky that is strictly your mom's call because she runs the house." I held my face where Evelyn could not see me and I winked at Ricky as to say, "Yeah Right!"

Then, I continued with, "matter of fact, effective tomorrow, that is Evelyn's full time job as she is being promoted from the executive administrator position to my wife to be."

Evelyn looked with her mouth wide open again.

"What JR? Am I being fired?"

"No way baby! You are being promoted. Ain't no wife of mine working that hard no more."

Jewel raised her hand and said, "Let me clarify what JR is saying. Evelyn, you need to be free to plan your wedding and after that you help make the calls on the business as co-owner. Girl, you will prefer that position much more anyway."

The dinner was now complete and I was the happiest guy alive, knowing that I was finally about to be united with my mate. All I need to do now is talk with my mentor again and meet with Veronica. But first and foremost, I must get some serious dialogue with my momma.

CHAPTER 21
Momma Drama

When I got back to the house, I went and took a quick shower as I was supposed to join Evelyn and Jewel in the media room to watch some movie that they had been ranting and raving about. I don't even know what the movie was all about but all I know was it had something to do with a true story and Oprah was involved with the production.

As I got out of the shower, for some reason, I felt an urging to call my mom. The very thought of having this conversation about marriage with my mom created a serious turn in my stomach as I knew I was about to get into a very stressful conversation just from the call alone. Nevertheless, the call had to be made.

I sounded out in my room, "call momma." My computerized telephone system immediately dialed the numbers.

"Hello," sounded the voice on the other line.

"Cousin Mike, what's going on man?"

"Hey JR, its all good in da hood. How you doing man?"

"I'm doing good man! I'm just working hard and trying to keep the bills low. You know how that is."

"I feel ya man! Every time I look, it seems like I got a bill collector knocking on my door."

Mike needs to quit. Who in the world does he think he talking to? He is a leech in every respect of the word. Every since I bought my momma a new house, he has practically moved in and my mom says bill collectors be calling him all the time. I remember when he would charge up his credit cards and then would call the bank and lie by saying somebody stole his card. The boy would max the card out and then call the company after the collections department got involved, as if that was not a dead giveaway.

Mike was lazy and was known for always coming up with a reason to stay out of work. He would always talk about "white folks this and white folks that" as he carried his "Thunderbird" alcohol brand practically everywhere he went.

Anyway, I really was not feeling Mike, as I was getting more and more nervous by the moment, anticipating my talk with mom.

"Mike, I love to talk with you at a later time but is momma there?"

He quickly replied, "hold on JR, I got somebody on the other line."

Now, why am I not surprised? That's typical Mike for you. Next, he's going to come on the line and tell me momma is asleep, watch!

Five minutes passed by and I was getting furious. He finally came back to the phone.

"I'm sorry JR but Auntie Em is already asleep."

I angrily replied, "Mike, if you don't get off that phone and get momma on the phone I will catch a flight back right now just to kick yo butt! Stop playing man! This is serious."

He actually tried to argue with me.

"JR, I ain't playing man. I'm serious, your mom is asleep. She went to bed early ton..." I interrupted and said, "boy, get off the phone now Mike and put my mom on the phone, you hear me!"

All of a sudden I hear momma's voice.

"Hey son, I want to tell you that I am loving this house. You really took care of mom this time."

I was glad to hear that momma enjoyed the house. It was a foreclosed house that I got as a steal.

"Mom, I'm glad you like the house and you should enjoy it as much as you can. Momma, I thought you were gonna run Mike home to his house."

My mom started clearing her throat.

"Look son, since I got plenty of room here, I figure he's okay."

"Momma, please don't tell me you still selling that bootleg, moonshine whiskey? Mike will be selling them quarter shots for dayz if you are."

My mom seemed aggravated and she said without shame, "Jamie Randell Carter, you better stay out groan folks business. You forget that I had you and you did not have me, okay.... okay. Now, what did you call for anyway? Did you get a speeding ticket or something because it takes damn near a miracle for you to call home? What's the problem?"

I slowly denied that there was any problem and I tried to figure out what would be the best transition to lead off the conversation. Then I said to myself, *what the heck, here it goes.*

"Momma, I have finally found the woman of my dreams."

There was silence and she replied, "okay?" I was afraid to say anything else but I had to.

"Well momma, we are going to get married later on in the year."

She loudly cleared her throat and lashed out at me with, "JR, you got jokes. I ain't got no time for no jokes tonight because I'm tired; do you hear me?"

I quickly expressed, "momma this is not about no joke. I'm serious."

She raised her voice and said, "now son who in the world are you talking about marrying? I know you ain't talking about that ghetto hood rat who you brought home a couple of weeks ago with her illegitimate son?"

I got a little pissed by the comment but I was cool.

"Momma, please don't refer to Evelyn as a hood rat and please don't call Ricky illegitimate. For this will be my family real soon momma."

"Jamie Randell Carter, I sure hope you ain't made no plans for marriage because you are not about to marry nobody like that. That boy of hers is a grown man and she ain't after nothing but yo money and I'm frankly disappointed that you can't see through her pretentious ways."

I vehemently disagreed with momma.

"Momma, you don't know her nor do you know Ricky."

"And JR how long have you known her and how long have you known Ricky and where the hell is his father? You best tell that hood rat to keep on sniffing because she ain't getting no cheese from this family, a trifling ass hoe."

"Momma, I can't believe you cursing like this and talking about the woman of my dreams."

"Look here boy! You don't even know how to choose a woman. Now, Ima Jean has returned back to Ocala with her credentials and she is opening up her own physician's practice right here in town. That woman has been crazy about you all her life JR. That's the kind of woman you need to marry."

There goes my mom again trying to tell me who I need to marry.

"Momma, I do not like Ima Jean like that. I'm glad she finished med school and is a big time physician but we did not have chemistry."

"Yeah right JR! Only reason why you did not was because of you. Look here boy, you need to realize that you ain't all that and a good woman is hard to find. Now that woman has been asking about you since she arrived back in town. I feel bad that you won't even allow me to give her your phone number. You should at least hear what she gots to say."

Momma just don't understand. Ima Jean was truly fine in every respect and as smart as any intelligent woman. I was crazy in love with her. In high school, we were the couple most likely to get married. Well, at least until I found out that she had practically slept with my whole basketball team. That's the information that momma does not know. I was not one to continue to ruin one's reputation. As if that was not enough, when Ima Jean and I went to college, I caught her sleeping with my roommate. To this day, I have not said anything to her nor Larry Smith about how I would get out of night class early and here them moaning and groaning in my room. They carried on not once, not twice, but at least over five times.

Bottom line, Ima Jean was weak at the knees when it came to attention. She would give up her coochie to anybody, it would seem, if they said the right words. Thus, Ima Jean clearly was not the one for me. Oh well, back to the standoff with mom as she was talking up a storm…"and another thang JR, you need to stop acting like you done left yo country roots and went to the big city and wiped that ole Ocala dirt off yo shoes. Son, you ain't nothing but a country boy gone to the city, so you need to stop acting like you all that and a phat box of chips. You still the former snotty nosed, knotty head boy that I raised. Do you hear me, and don't you forget that?"

"Momma, I did not want to get into a long argument with you."

"What?" She interrupted me. "You watch your tone young

man. I am still yo momma and I will drive my car up to Texas in a heartbeat and beat you just like you still a kid. Do you hear me? I don't wanna hear no more talk about you getting married anytime soon boy! I can't wait to tell yo dad. You know you should be ashamed of yourself."

I could see that I was at a perfect stalemate with mom. My recourse was to diplomatically get off the phone and press on.

"Okay Momma, well I'm gonna let you go and I did not mean to upset you by any means. I will be sending you an invitation concerning the wedding date. I hope you and most my relatives will be here for my wedding. I realize you don't think I'm making the right move momma but I have chosen to follow my heart and my heart is with Evelyn and Ricky."

There was total silence on the phone and momma came back with a very straight and direct tone in her voice.

"JR, if you marry that hood rat, you can consider yourself no son of mine. I refuse to allow my son to be manipulated by some fly by night hoe. You done got my blood pressure rising and my heart pounding and I don't care to talk with you about this anymore son. Make the right decision."

Click! What? My momma hung up on me. Can you believe that? I was in a complete state of shock. What makes my mom feel like she can dictate who I marry? I'm a twenty six year old man and I should be able to marry who I choose, not who she thinks I should marry. Damn, I am so confused now. I mean, next to Julie, the biggest voice and influence on me was my mom. I'm not trying to be disowned. Wow! What's a man to do in my shoes? I guess I need to reevaluate all over again. That conversation clearly set me back.

I got on my knees to pray. "God, I am at a major crossroads in my life. Please help me to make the right decision. I know I have not been good by bible standards but I really do mean well. Let me know which way to go Lord." Phew! I got off my knees and did what I always do when I got depressed: laid down and went to sleep.

CHAPTER 22
Cutting My Losses

Jewel hired the next administrator! That is after I consulted Julie for support as I told her about the change going on in my life. Julie's endorsement was all I needed. I was leaving the office and I also informed Julie about Ricky's upcoming game because she wanted to attend the next home game.

Veronica asked me to stop by as I was leaving the office. I stopped by and she wanted to have sex. I told her I was getting married within a month and she responded like it was no big deal. I told her that we could not have sex any more and she was not having it. I told her I was madly in love now and life had changed.

"So you mean to tell me you don't care for me. JR, I thought you and I were going to become a serious couple. I know you and that lady you let move in would be an item but I never thought you would marry her."

"Can we be friends? I will always care for you and I really thought you and I were gonna be a couple but Veronica I'm ready for marriage and you were just coming out of one."

"JR, that's ridiculous and you know it. It sure did not keep you from making love to me. Don't throw anything at me and expect me to believe it."

I felt real bad.

I hugged her and she hugged me back.

"Veronica, I'm sorry."

"JR, make love to me one last time, please!"

I said no to Veronica. She put both my hands on that backyard of hers and it was almost lights out, game ova.

"Veronica, I'm sorry but I can't."

"JR, just one last time!" I removed my arms from around her but she would not let me go.

"JR, you will at least see me off the right way."

"Veronica, I only have desires for one woman in that way and I'm sorry but I really cannot help that."

She pushed me away.

"Get out my house! You good for nothing son of a b...." I met her lips with mine before she could complete her sentence.

I rotated them tires and screwed her like she was a hoe. Some of it was inside anger on my part and guilt for cheating. Nevertheless, I got to admit, that coochie was good. I left right away and Veronica said as I was leaving, "JR, I don't want to mess up what you have but you can come by to see me whenever you so desire. You can get this whenever you want it or at least until I get in a serious relationship. My feelings are still hurt but I still care for you."

I told her to feel free to call me if she needed anything and then I left. As I was traveling home I took a call from Debbie. "JR, I miss you."

"Debbie, I'm about to get married in a month."

She got quiet. "JR, I was hoping you would dump that woman and have me."

"Debbie, I'm sorry but that won't happen."

She went on to say, "You can still come and see me sometimes like you been doing. My legs are always wide open for you."

"You will be okay Debbie. You won't miss me that much. Besides, I know that Loke has been tearing dat ass up. You won't miss me that much."

She got quiet for a moment and then she finally replied, "JR, that was just that one time and I was half way drunk."

I quickly replied, "Debbie don't lie. It's no need to. I know Loke has been wearing dat ass out okay. Remember now, that's my boy."

She quickly countered with, "JR, I was screwing him only because I was missing you. He can't handle this coochie like you can baby."

She was talking all sexy. I told her I was done but we could be friends.

"You don't understand! I wanted Loke to tell you about he and I so I could make you jealous, as you would always run off to your so-called woman. Look JR, she can't keep yo little soldier happy like I can. That's why you been creeping to me anyway."

Debbie, like Veronica, both think I have been seeing Evelyn all the while I was seeing them. This is where my lie may have created more of a problem for me rather than bailing me out of a problem.

"Debbie, we will be friends. I got to go now."

"JR, if she don't treat you right, remember this pure butta is right here for you baby."

I got a few more ladies out the way as far as letting them know I won't be seeing them again. I still need to call Juanita one day. Then again, I don't even need to call anyone else. The phone rang again!

"JR."

"JR, when will you be home," Evelyn said with a sweetly pleasant voice.

"I'm about 15 minutes out sweetheart."

"Okay! I'll see you then."

I pulled up to my first garage shortly there afterwards and Evelyn walked out to meet me. As soon as I opened and closed the car door she jumped all over me.

"How was your first day home honey?"

She just started kissing me and I returned her kisses.

"JR, our wedding date is gonna be the 15th of March, about six weeks away."

I tried to be funny. "Man, why so far away? I got to wait that long?"

"Stop it JR! You know JR, since we have a wedding date nearby, we will not be making love anymore until our honeymoon. Then again, I should say until our wedding day because we really can't take a honeymoon until after school is out, in the summertime. Don't you agree?"

"Well, can we just keep making love up until we are married? I do agree on the honeymoon being taken during the summer."

Evelyn put her hands on her hips and said, "JR, we can go a few weeks until we're married. Trust me, all the love we made last night should keep us for a while. I could barely walk this morning."

"Good, that means I'm doing my job."

I started laughing and then she said, "I saw a dog today that would be perfect for the house, after he is trained. He's a pretty black Golden Retriever. Those dogs are known for being very smart."

"Okay baby, that sounds good. We can have the dog trained and then purchase or whatever you want to do."

"Well JR, I was talking with one of the security guards and they said that they have dog training experience and they would like to do the honors. We could get the dog and they could work on training the dog."

"Okay Evelyn, whatever works. That's cool by me. You think Ricky will like the dog?"

"Are you kidding JR, of course he will."

We walked into the house together and she told me about the wedding plans. I was truly loving life.

"By the way sweetheart, are we set for dinner on tomorrow night?" She got excited.

"Oh yeah, Jewel and I want to try out this brand new restaurant that's been open for only two weeks. The name of the restaurant is called Houston's. Now JR, who's all supposed to be going to this dinner?"

"Its just a nice birthday dinner for Loke. I had in mind, my boss, Julie, Jewel, you, Ricky and Loke."

"Should Ricky be there since its all adults?"

We walked into the conference room together and I said, "I wanted Julie to meet Ricky and I think that's a perfect time."

She grabbed my hand and said, "Oh by the way, do you have a problem with the fact that we are getting married on Ricky's birthday?"

I replied nonchalantly, "I don't mind if yawl don't mind?"

"Okay! I was just checking because we don't mind, meaning Ricky and I. I told him we would celebrate his birthday the whole weekend. Then again, we will work it in because I have a bridal shower on Friday night and you have a Bachelor's Party at Loke's place.

I looked stunned. "I don't know anything about a Bachelor's Party?"

"Loke scheduled it through Jewel. That's all I know. You can discuss that with him. I understand his swimsuit party is this Saturday?"

"Yep! I wasn't gonna go but since he rescheduled it for me to attend, I figure I would go."

She nudged me as I walked into the bedroom and said, "Yeah right JR! You know you won't miss that party. Its not like he's got a gun to your head making you go. JR, you didn't even notice the bedroom."

I looked around and she had moved her things into the bedroom, which was fine with me. My bedroom was huge anyway. The size of a penthouse suite. We had closet space the size of another master bedroom altogether.

"Great honey! Now if you think we are going to be sleeping in the same bed and not making love, you got another thang coming."

She wrestled me to the bed and said, "We will see." We started kissing again and Ricky walked in. I alerted Evelyn by speaking to Ricky as her back was towards the door. "Hey Ricky, what's going on son?"

He held a suit up while smiling and said, "mom, I'm gonna wear this after the game Thursday night."

Evelyn quickly said, "Ricky, I wanted you to wear that tomorrow night at Loke's birthday dinner."

He stepped back as though he was surprised.

"I got to go to that after practice?"

"That's right big guy! You need to get used to practicing and then getting pretty for social engagements. I predict you will be doing that for quite sometime. Hey! Don't I owe you some revenge?" I said.

"Not until Ricky finishes his homework," Evelyn quickly stated. Ricky lowered the suit and said, "didn't I kick your butt enough the last time. Just stop by in about two hours."

"I don't think so young man, another two hours is

bedtime." Evelyn said as she playfully hit Ricky in his broad chest.

"Don't worry Ricky! We got plenty of time for me to spank that butt of yours. By the way, we meet with the NIKE agent sometime next week. We will keep you posted because Addidas, Jordan, and Reebok also have agents that would like to meet with us." I was delighted to pass on that information to Ricky.

CHAPTER 23
The Family Reunion

J ulie, it was so very nice meeting you! By the way, do you have a card? Here is my information. We should get together sometime."

Loke was definitely making a move on Julie. The night was truly fantastic and we sang happy birthday to Loke, and Julie met Evelyn and Ricky as well. She vowed to attend his basketball game on tomorrow night. As Loke was talking to Julie, this older but nicely dressed man at the restaurant came over and introduced himself as the owner. He also thanked us for coming and he gave us all a card.

As Julie was getting ready to leave, Loke offered to walk her to her car. However, this older gentleman came over to Julie again.

"I really hope you enjoyed the restaurant," said the older gentleman as he stared into Julie's eyes. Julie stared back with a great level of intensity. She noticed his height, his eyes, and his overall features.

"Sir, I really enjoyed your restaurant. The food was outstanding and I definitely will recommend it," Julie said. Then, she looked again in his eyes and said, "I know you from somewhere."

"You are more beautiful than I ever imagined you to be. I see your mom all over you," he said.

"Excuse me Sir but this is an A and B conversation and..."

said Loke but he was quickly interrupted by Julie. "Dad! Oh my God! Is that you? Oh my God! That is you! I thought I would never ever see you again in my life."

She became so jubilant, as her eyes were flooded with tears. She reached out her arms to hug him.

"Julie, I returned here hoping to find you. I have missed you all my life. You are every bit of what your mom described!" He hugged her for a long time.

Loke gently eased away and stared at me and I stared at them. Julie held her father's hand as tears were now rushing from her eyes.

"JR, this is my father that I told you about."

We both greeted one another with a conservative handshake and I introduced him to everybody else. Julie turned to her father again and said, "Where is Corey?"

"Corey is in New York, managing my hotel chain. He would be so glad to finally meet his older sister."

Julie cried even harder and her father hugged her again. Loke stood by helplessly as I explained their story to everyone else. They must have talked for a good fifteen minutes. Afterwards, Julie came over.

"JR, Jewel, I'm gonna catch a ride home with my father. Loke, I will call you on tomorrow. Evelyn, you have a fine young man in JR and JR you have a very beautiful woman in Evelyn and a fine son to boot. You both did well. I envy you. Ricky, I will be at your game on tomorrow night and I'm gonna try and get my father to come."

She looked at her father again and they just hugged each other again.

"This is truly a happy day for me." Julie and her father walked off.

Loke came over and asked me why he seemed like he had

not been around Julie for sometime. He also said that Julie was special and I added that she was more special than he would know. He also commented on the fact that Julie had a father of African American descent, which in his mind explained her body features.

We left the restaurant and Loke wanted to make sure I had a kitchen pass for the party on Saturday. Jewel and I were walking back to our cars as Loke, Evelyn and Ricky were talking. Jewel was talking business and I noticed her engagement ring was not on her hand again. I noticed it for a couple of days now but I never said anything.

"JR, I broke up with Sidney. It's a long story but there will be no wedding for me. I imagined Evelyn told you by now."

"No Jewel, she did not but I am so sorry to hear that. You are staying at the house tonight, aren't you? I don't want you being alone. I'm serious Jewel. That's a directive not an invite."

"JR, I been staying at your house since the first time I moved in. You haven't even noticed that I have practically brought all my things there. I mean I have my clothes and stuff like that there. I would be crazy to try and do all that I am doing and to stay thirty minutes out. Matter of fact, Evelyn has been trying to get me to move in the house permanently and that way Ricky's agent can live in the same house with him."

I hugged Jewel and said, "Jewel, that's an excellent idea. Of course you won't have to pay a penny either." We hugged each other as to have our own little celebration.

"Jewel, I also think you should take some time off work to free your mind and properly move on from this pain."

"JR, are you out of your mind? The best therapy that I have right now is being so busy with work and, of course being around yawl. I feel like I'm apart of this family too."

I grabbed her hand and said, "look here Jewel, you are apart of this family. I want to adopt you as my sister right away."

Jewel started laughing and pushed me off jokingly.

"On a serious note JR, I would go crazy if I stopped working now. No Sir my friend, work is all good."

Jewel rode back in the mini limousine that Julie, Evelyn and Ricky and I rode in. My security guard came to pick up her vehicle. Loke had driven off and he called me on his cell phone.

"Why didn't you tell me how fine Julie was? I think I'm in love JR."

I listened to Loke but I knew I would not talk too expressively with everyone in the limousine with me.

"Loke, you are too funny."

"I'm serious JR! By the way, what's the status on Jewel? She is also fine as a mutha! I noticed I did not see her engagement ring on tonight?"

"Well Loke, I will fill you in a little later but I need to go right now, okay. We definitely will hook up at your party this weekend."

"Oh yeah JR, before I forget, I been reading the newspapers and seeing the news on this boy wonder Ricky Lyles. I plan to come to the game on tomorrow night. Also, tell me about Julie some more. Is that your limousine or hers?"

"Okay Loke, we will talk at length this weekend if not tomorrow."

I knew loke would ask about the limousine. I actually had that purchased and had one of my security guards drive it and they also picked up Julie.

Actually, I have been trying to convince Julie that she needs to travel in a mini limousine as well and that the driver should be trained as a security guard. I told her that even though most do not know her status, if some knucklehead managed to act up she would be at his mercy. She did not agree with me, and thought that would advertise too much of her fame. I pleaded with her and from our conversation I went out and purchased me a mini limousine and I will use Walker as my driver whenever Evelyn, Ricky, and I need to go on dinners and events where we all travel together, like tonight. I also purchased a Hummer because it's more room for all of us, including Jewel to travel in. Julie complimented the limo when Walker picked her up. I ordered one more just like it but instead of black, its white. I also ordered Evelyn a cherry wood top Bentley that she will get on our wedding day, so of course she knows nothing about it now.

Jewel snapped me out of daydreaming.

"JR, what's Loke talking about?"

"He was talking about you and yo fine self."

"PUHLEASE! As I have told a few of my friends, Loke is as fine as they come but I lost a little love for him when he asked me to come to his swimsuit party and told me I had to wear a thong bikini. I told him I could not believe he was gonna throw me in the pot with his hoochie mommas."

"I know exactly what you mean! I gave him the same reply when he invited me to come," said Evelyn.

Ricky looked at me and posed a question that resulted in an immediate response. "JR, am I going to the party with you on Saturday?"

Before I even had a chance to respond, both Evelyn and Jewel said emphatically, "no" at the same time. Then, they looked at each other and just busted out laughing.

"Ricky knows better than to even ask a question like that," Evelyn said.

I just looked over as I stroked Evelyn's hair and said, "Trust me Ricky! You will have plenty of time in your life for that."

"JR, don't you introduce that innocent kid to the wolves so fast," Jewel said.

I laughed as I replied, "Why yawl staring at me as though I could contaminate Ricky?"

We all started laughing.

CHAPTER 24
Julie's Acknowledgment

When we got to the house, Jewel and I started talking about how business was going. She had recently completed the Broker Certification course and had already left Star Top Realty. I thought this was a good time to tell her that our overall business, On Time Realty, had processed enough business for her to earn an increase in her annual salary by $15K.

"JR, are you sure? I know business is going great but I also know that we have spent lots of money."

"That's true but we have earned a pretty penny under your leadership. I appreciate your support Jewel!"

"JR, I appreciate your unwavering confidence in my abilities," she said as she looked at me.

The three of us all talked about the business in general and actually had much unexpected laughter.

**

"Ricky, take the shot!"

Somebody yelled at him from the stands. Instead, he faked a three point shot and put his defender in the air and then he drove around him for one of the most ferocious slamdunks in the game, leaving the crowd speechless at the manchild sensation. On the very next play, Ricky stole the ball from his opponent's end of the court near the three-second line and he busted off into a breakaway move where he passed the ball to his teammate. Ricky accelerated like he had jets in his legs, outrunning everybody on the floor. His teammate threw the ball up near the hoop at the other end and Ricky came out of nowhere and caught the ball in mid air and did a perfect Tommy Hawk slam-dunk. Loke stood up and stared at me as the crowd erupted with a roar of celebration. This game had quickly become the Ricky Lyles' show. When the buzzer sounded, Lake View Academy had demolished another historical giant in the league with a score of 84–63.

They literally had no answer for Ricky as he hit 5 of 7 three pointers and finished with 36 points, 11 rebounds, 9 steals, 6 assists, while taking his team to a perfect 21-0. Evelyn and I were so proud of Ricky. Julie and her father attended the game as well. I went over to greet them after I grabbed Ricky by the head and congratulated him in our personal way.

"Hi Mr. Coles (Julie's dad), I'm glad to see you again." He returned the greeting with a handshake and a smile, then said, "JR, it is nice seeing you again as well. Ricky is truly a phenomenal ball player."

I agreed with him and said to Julie, "Hi boss, you're looking finer than ever." I kissed Julie on her cheeks and hugged her as well.

"JR, can we talk sometime soon?" Julie asked.

"Yes Ma'am! I sure can talk anytime."

"I will call you and we can go from there."

I had no idea what Julie wanted. She also spoke with Evelyn and gave Ricky a hug and said, "You are special. Your talent is so natural and pure."

"Thanks Ma'am! I appreciate the compliment," Ricky said in response.

"JR, that boy is clearly the next Jordan. I was in total awe

of every move he made. Are you sure he is only 14 years old?"
Loke inquired as he came over to join us.

"Loke, he will be 15 soon but there are no mistakes about
his age. I am so intrigued with Ricky's basketball talent. I
recognized his skills the first time I played with him."

Loke was talking as though he was truly surprised about
Ricky's game.

"JR, he seems so much more mature for his age. I really
cannot believe that move that I saw tonight. Also, the boy is
clearly shooting NBA 3 pointers. All I got to say is this boy is
headed for the top."

"Let's hope so because he truly has the whole package: the
looks, the smarts, and the skills," I replied

Loke put his hand on my shoulder and looked down as
though he was ashamed and said, "JR, I apologize for what I
said about Evelyn and Ricky. You guys make such a beautiful
family."

I interrupted and said, "hey Loke, don't even worry about
that man. You were just looking out for my well being and I
truly appreciate that."

Then he took me by total surprise and made a comment
that took me back. "Besides JR, you bouts to get paid yo?
Hell, if I had known Ricky was the next Jordan I would be
trying to marry Evelyn too."

I was really thrown by that comment and I looked Loke
square in the eyes and said, "Latrell Oliver King, I don't
appreciate that comment. Heaven knows I would marry Evelyn
if Ricky was handicapped and could not walk. You had your
chance at love Loke which is why you are divorced, now let me
have my chance okay."

He grabbed me and said, "JR, come on man, you know I
was just kidding. I know that you are not the predatory type.

I was just joking man, lighten up on a brotha. Evelyn is the finest in Houston and Ricky just happened to have skills. You are the luckiest man alive and I envy you to some degree."

I looked at Loke and we hugged each other in a very manly sort of fashion.

"Are you going to be my best man or what?"

He looked at me with the dear in the headlights look.

"Are you asking me to be your best man? Oh Hell Yeah! Hell yeah! You damn straight! I'm your best man, who else could it be?"

We both laughed and hugged each other again like real brothers.

Loke grabbed Ricky by the shoulders and hugged him. They started talking. Numerous scouts and coaches came over to Evelyn and I, sharing their interests in Ricky basically. I pulled Evelyn off and we waited near the departing bleachers. Loke was talking with Julie. I could imagine what he was saying. He was definitely trying to get with her. Her father was just smiling as though he understood where Loke was coming from.

I went over to Coach Lawson as soon as he had a brief moment alone.

"Did I lie to you about Ricky?" I asked.

"You most certainly did. You did not tell me this boy was this good. JR, I'm going to tell you the bottom line truth. Ricky has injected new life into my coaching career. You would be surprised at how many job offers I've been getting and how many ballplayers want to come and play with Ricky. Some will be seniors next year. Scouts are calling me around the clock about Ricky. The college scouts say he is ready now and some pro scouts also contend that he is ready now."

"Ricky isn't going anywhere Charlie. The boy is learning and growing up. We won't rush him to that."

"JR, I agree with you but you have got to realize that Ricky will go far and he has pretty much mastered high school level basketball."

Coach and I greeted one another as he was being swamped with reporters. Now, as I saw it, my job was to keep as much pressure as possible off that kid. I am certain that Charlie agreed in principal.

Evelyn and I waited for Ricky and then we all left like one big happy family. Walker came over and said, "JR, that boy is special. He owns his own destiny. I have seen a lot come and go and that boy is as good as they come." I carried on small talk with Walker and then Jewel caught up with us.

"JR, you know Ricky's going to get a lot of offers before long. I was just listening to some of the conversations as I was waiting for you guys. He seems to be viewed as a God sent in this area.

***

The following day, on Friday morning, as I was leaving the house I got a call from Julie. She wanted me to meet her on Quarters Way, one of her subdivisions about fifteen minutes out from downtown. I must admit, the call did concern me as the last time we met at a residence, well, I was not engaged nor was I committed to Evelyn and all sexual sparks went off.

Julie was fully dressed and looked good as usual. I was actually glad to see that because that clearly conveyed how we had grown as friends. I had a lot of questions for her on the business side. Initially, she told me how she was glad to see her father and told me her brother would be in town the weekend of my wedding and she had been talking to him on the phone.

She was very impressed with Evelyn and expressed that she thought I got a wife for a lifetime.

"JR, don't you ever leave her because I firmly believe she will never leave you."

She told me how she shared her business plans with her father and how he gave her more ideas as to how she could really retire and let the businesses run themselves. I consulted her on my business plans and as usual she gave me some very valuable inputs. In addition, I collaborated with her on the land under development and shared with her my strategic approach as to how I could oversee local management in sales, expansion and overall community development efforts.

Out of much surprise, Julie told me about a CEO position that was about to become vacant and she wanted to know if I was interested. She told me that the job required a lot of hiring and firing and it would only augment the business I already had. She asked me to think about it for a while, as the job is not available for about six months. She did inform me that the job required a lot of traveling and that she understood if I declined due to present business ventures. She firmly expressed that she wanted to give me first choice at the position. Last but not least, she said to me what literally floored me in every way.

"JR, I want you to just listen to me for a few minutes. Of all the people I have ever worked with, I consider you one of my most trusted agents and thus you are the type of person I would like to surrender my businesses over to as I give serious consideration to retirement. I promise I won't overload you however but let's just hold off on anything for now as you work those new real estate gold mines that I assigned to you."

I listened very intently as Julie spoke and I did not utter a word but merely nodded my head in approval and acceptance as to what she was saying.

"JR, do you remember I told you I was the owner of a sports team?"

I looked up from thinking about the CEO position with her manufacturing firm and brought my mind back into the room.

"Yes Julie, you just never told me what team you owned."

JR, I am majority owner of the Houston Rockets. As with everything else, please keep that with us."

I looked with total shock, as my mouth was wide open.

"You got to be kidding," I said.

She nodded her head and smiled.

"I just traded for Tracy McGrady earlier in the season and I want to put something mind boggling before you. Ricky will never finish high school like a traditional kid would finish high school; his skills are too good. Hear me out on this JR. He will get a diploma but I want you to consider allowing him to be a future first round draft pick of the Houston Rockets in possibly next year's draft and if not then, the year after."

I was totally flabbergasted in every respect. I had no words to say for the moment.

"JR, just think about it. He will be the first 15 or 16 year old drafted by the NBA and he will already be grounded due to the fact his parents will be in the home with him. My coaching and managing staff has placed him as the number one long-term acquisition on our desire list. He's only going to grow taller, get faster, shoot better, and be that much more of a dominant player. Did you hear what Michael Jordan said the other night on ESPN?"

She quickly answered the question herself without waiting on my reply. "He said and I quote: I would rather have Ricky Lyles' future than my past."

"JR, just think about it and let's just keep that between us. Who knows? Anything can happen."

I listened and in all sincerity I never thought about Ricky

leaving early to play pro. Hell, I didn't even imagine him leaving college early to play pro. Instead, I wanted him to do the things a normal kid did. Besides, there is no hurry for him. Its not like he is coming from a poor family now. I really had to mull over this and even get Evelyn and Ricky's inputs. To me, if money or survival were not the key motive, what would be? He's an overall A minus, B plus student in one of the toughest academic institutions for high school kids, and he's got the world ahead of him. He's 6'2" now and he hadn't even entered a growth spurt yet which could result in another 4 to 6 inches of growth or he could be done growing, which is very unlikely.

"Julie, you have really surprised me with the NBA perspective. I honestly had not looked that far down the road but perhaps I should."

"JR, a blind man could not miss this! You got more owners and coaches talking about Ricky more than you realize. I can possibly foresee him playing another high school year but after that, his skills would be so far ahead of his competitors, assuming that he will only get better. This year alone he will be a McDonald's All American MVP, a state champion, a first team all star, and his team will probably be ranked as the top team in the nation."

Wow, and to think that I did not think that Julie followed the game.

"Julie, you are very confident. I don't know if Ricky will be all that this year."

"JR, you are about the only one that feels that way. You need to wake up and smell the coffee. Ricky Lyles is already commanding national fame and attention."

Julie was very convincing and I must admit I had not been staying abreast of all the chatter about Ricky because I have been too busy with work.

"Julie, I'm with you. I just need to study it some more."

She stood from the sofa and told me that the decision was ultimately Ricky's but Evelyn and I should have the greatest influence on that decision.

Then Julie walked away from the sofa and said, "Now, what's the deal with your dentist friend?" I laughed uncontrollably with the thought of her even mentioning Loke.

"Julie, what on earth do you mean?"

She put her hands on her hips.

"JR, you know darn well what I'm talking about. He has been calling me like I owe him some money. He claims he is in love with me. What's his story? I sense that he is a player, am I correct?"

I threw my hands up in the air as to seem unsure and said, "He told me the same thing that he was in love with you but Loke has been divorced and I'm not sure he's over his wife. He's not seeking any early commitment from what I would guess, unless you have inspired him otherwise. Also, he does not know how powerfully rich you are. He has no clue. Is he currently a playa? I really don't know how to answer that without misrepresenting Loke. Has he been approached by a lot of women? Yes." She sat down and had that pensive look on her face.

"Well, he is extremely attractive and has the smarts of a genius, has the gift of gab and all that but I just want to make certain he knows that I'm not impressed and his money and occupation does not wet my panties."

I started laughing and I told Julie not to feel obligated to respond to Loke but I did tell her he was an outstanding dentist and did have a real good heart.

"Julie, all I can do is recommend that you at least be open minded and perhaps see if he could be worth your time. Then again, I am a big supporter and friend of his but of course I am a bigger supporter and friend of yours."

Her cell phone rang and it was her father. She was running late with meeting him for breakfast. We hugged each other and kissed each other on the cheeks.

"JR, we will talk again sometime. I appreciate you making yourself available, knowing that you probably have a busy day ahead of you."

"Julie, you are my top priority boss. I am always available for you. That's the way it is and that's the way it will always be."

CHAPTER 25
Close Call

J R, I need to get your recommendation real fast," Jewel called me as I was headed home after a busy day with Star Top and my business.

"What seems to be the issue Jewel?" I spoke to her on my speakerphone in my car.

"Well JR, we are scheduled to return to Atlanta two days from now to interview ten candidates for regional manager; remember, our short list? However, I just got a call from the Jordan Camp and they would like to meet with us on Thursday as well. I wanted to turn it down but they informed me that Michael's schedule is so busy that he would not be available again for another month or so."

I almost ran into the car ahead of me as I lost focus on my driving while focusing in on Jewel's words.

"Jewel, I don't understand. Are you telling me that Michael Jordan wants to meet with us to discuss his sneaker shoe options for Ricky?"

I could hear the excitement in Jewel's voice.

"JR, that's exactly what I am saying. His camp emphasized that Michael himself would be the one meeting with us to discuss this business venture."

To say I was lost for words was truly an understatement.

"Jewel, you mean I got a chance to meet Michael Jordan under business alternatives?"

"Well JR, actually I am the one meeting with Michael and of course he wanted to meet Ricky as well. I mean, you can be in attendance but it's not mandatory for you to be. Besides, we are behind schedule with hiring a regional manager for the Stockbridge area property."

I chuckled and said, "I get your point Jewel. It sounds like you don't want me present for the Jordan meeting."

"JR, that is not true at all. It really does not matter to me. I did not want to cancel out however, realizing that this opportunity may not come around again. I view it as a big opportunity for Ricky," Jewel quickly replied.

Jewel actually was declaring an understatement, as this would be a grand opportunity for Ricky, one that we should not miss out on.

"Wow, it would have been nice to meet his airness but I can only hope to have that opportunity later at another time."

"JR, if you are that anxious to meet Michael, why don't you and Ricky meet with him and I will take the trip to Georgia to interview potential managers."

"Jewel, don't you want to meet Michael Jordan?"

"JR, of course I would but business dictates that it would not be feasible for both of us to be present."

That is why I need Jewel in my business life. She keeps me on track in so many ways. However, she is Ricky's agent and not I, and therefore she should be the one meeting with Michael.

"Jewel, you press on and meet with Michael. I will press on with the Georgia trip. You are Ricky's agent and that's your job."

She coughed and quickly replied with the most concerned voice, "JR, are you for sure? I really mean what I said. I do not have to meet Michael Jordan."

"No Jewel, once again, it's your job and I know you will handle business. Now, I would imagine you could cancel our meetings with those other companies. I mean, whose gonna turn down Michael Jordan?"

"JR, I totally disagree with you on that. We need to be fair and listen to all offers as well as Jordan's. I figure there are so many kids out there that would desire to be a part of the Jordan camp that they may not offer the better option of all the other companies. I mean, think about it. If everybody wants to work with or for Michael, can you foresee how his company could possibly use that to their advantage and offer only a portion of what the other companies may offer."

Once again, Jewel was conveying nothing but absolute business sense. Wow, I was starting to feel like a door knob in this process.

"Jewel, you are right on point. Press ahead with your plan and don't listen to me. Your decisions will give Ricky the better option throughout this whole process."

"MMMMM HUMMMMM! I'm glad you can see my logic. I will press with the plans and you need to get ready for that Georgia trip. I will cancel my portion of the trip. By the way, the trip was for three days. That way you can take your time comparing the applicants and seeing who really stacks up. We can talk via telephone as well."

I did not like the idea of being gone three days, although it made a lot of sense.

"Jewel, I probably won't be there for no more than two days max. It won't take me that long. I will be interviewing about ten candidates and I can do that within a two day period, trust me."

"Alright JR, I hear what you are saying and I will contact the applicants and have them set up to meet you within the two day period. That would mean that you interview five the first day and five the second day and we will get you back here on the red eye."

"That's fine Jewel."

"JR, are you sure you're gonna be okay going without me?"

I started laughing and said, "yeah, I will have to do my own driving now; Ahahahahah!"

"Okay JR, I see you got jokes but that's okay. One day you will learn how to appreciate a sister," Jewel jokingly replied.

I was laughing but then I stopped and said, "Jewel, I tell you I appreciate you all the time. You know I was just kidding. I will miss you on this trip."

"Yeah, whatever JR! You go ahead and try and fix it now but the words have already been stated. Look, I got to go! I just wanted to let you know about Jordan."

"Okay Jewel, I'll see you at home tonight, bye bye."

We had to get a special telephone line for Ricky and all his infrastructure support. He starting getting all types of invites from Hollywood to local grocery stores, asking him to appear for special groups, charities, and the whole nine. This kid was definitely attracting fame and fortune at such an early age. I mean, people referred to me as Ricky's dad. It did not bother me but I thought it was extremely humorous, although I was very happy for Ricky.

***

"Come on Evelyn baby. You mean I can't get any before I go on my trip. That is not fair."

Evelyn rolled over in bed and looked me in my face and said, "JR, we have been doing real well baby and we are so close to our wedding day. We can still hold out until then."

I acted like I was mad but really I was not. I was just trying to get me some good loving from the woman of my life before I went on this two-day trip to Atlanta. I really did not want to go but business had to be taken care of.

"Evelyn, you sure you don't want to go with me to Atlanta?"

She rose up in the bed on that question.

"And miss out on meeting Michael Jordan? Are you out yo mind JR? Do you realize what you just asked me to do?"

I chuckled at her words.

"Oh so, Michael is more important than I am, huh?"

She laid back down and kissed me on my cheek and said, "of course not boo. He just got more money than you do."

"Oh, its like that huh?"

She kissed me again and said, "Yeah, basically it really is."

I playfully pushed her away and then she playfully responded, "JR, how you just gonna push me away like that?"

Then she kissed me again on my forehead and said, "baby, you know I need to be here for Ricky. He's got the playoffs and then the next day he's got that meeting with Michael Jordan. By the way, did you know that Michael Jordan was flying in early to attend Ricky's game?"

I almost fell out the bed. I quickly responded like I had been hit up side the head with a bunch of rocks.

"Are you serious honey? Jewel did not tell me that."

"JR, in Jewel's defense, she probably did not get a chance to tell you. I think his camp wanted to keep it very private as in secret."

I got up out the bed and I told Evelyn I had to go talk to Jewel.

"JR, don't go waking Jewel up. You know she is extremely busy. Besides, she told me not to tell anyone."

I turned and looked at Evelyn and said, "I'm not just anyone. I should have been informed. How many dads find out by mistake that Michael Jordan is coming to town to see their son play basketball?"

Evelyn grabbed me and said, "am I gonna have to give you some to shut you down for the night?"

I looked and said, "baby you know I would love to have some but I must talk to Jewel."

She grabbed me and said, "okay but you will do it on the phone and not forcing her to have to get up out her bed."

I consented without any problem. Jewel also had the voice communication system in her room and it answered only to her voice.

"Okay honey, I will call her on the phone."

I shouted out, "Jewel's room" and her phone in her private penthouse rang.

"Hello," she answered.

"Jewel, wake up little gurl. How in the world are you gonna coordinate the trip of the greatest player to play the game coming to see Ricky play and not tell me?"

She replied with a very slow and mumbling like voice.

"JR, check your cell phone. I left a message because you came home so late and I called you earlier and all I got was your voice mail. It's all on your cell phone, okay. I'm going back to bed. I will see you in the morning before you leave the house to catch your plane. Good night."

Click went the phone. I turned and looked at Evelyn and said, "She hung up too early. I was not finished with her."

"JR, Jewel was not totally awake, now don't call her and wake her again. Check your cell phone baby."

I went and got my cell phone, which was lodged, deep into my coat suit pocket. I played back all my messages, which three were from Jewel.

The most urgent one from her expressed, "JR, where are you when I need you most? I told you about turning your cell phone off. Look, Michael Jordan is coming into town early to discretely attend Ricky's playoff game and then we meet with him after Ricky gets out of school, the following day, which will also be after Michael's charity golf tournament. I have left you two other messages. Oh well, I'll see you in the morning for breakfast. Now, please keep it quiet. Ricky knows nothing about Jordan attending his game and I don't intend to tell him because I don't want him distracted."

I looked at Evelyn and she said, "See, she did try to tell you what was going on."

I could not imagine this happening. I turned to Evelyn and said, "Michael Jordan has always been my hero and I hate that I will miss all of this fun."

I got back in bed and started rubbing Evelyn's juicy butt and she grabbed my hand.

"But Evelyn, you said I could," she interrupted me right away, "I said you could if you did not call and wake up Jewel but you did and so now you ain't getting none until our wedding day."

I pouted like a kid and just held her in my arms and rolled over and eventually fell asleep.

CHAPTER 26
ATL

The following morning I had breakfast with everyone. Ricky was filling me in on the defensive strategy their high school was intending to play against Kingwood High School. Kingwood was another school in northern Houston that had a proud tradition of basketball excellence. They also finished third place in the Christmas tournament but they had not played Lake View Academy this year. They had only lost one game all season to Belmont High and they had a very talented team.

Matter of fact, superstar Belonte Coley was the talk of the town until Ricky broke out of nowhere. Belonte was destined for the pro ranks and he had accepted a basketball scholarship from Duke University. Kingwood was ranked second in the state while Lake View was ranked seventh, although they were yet undefeated. The stage was set for a very good game and I had to miss it, not to mention missing Jordan.

Jewel and I talked on the fly as she and Evelyn took me to the airport after Ricky left for school. Jewel was so excited about her visit with Jordan. She was going to be one of the select few to meet him at the airport. Of course, she had Evelyn tagging along with her as well.

"JR, enjoy your flight and remember you don't have to make any decisions until we sit down together and decide who's the best candidate," said Jewel as she gave me a hug.

Evelyn followed with, "be safe honey and call us when you get there. I'll let you know how the game went. I love you."

"I love you too honey. Wow, I am not feeling this trip but oh well."

Jewel interjected, "JR, you should no longer be thinking about that. You go ahead and handle business and get back here safe and sound. I'll let you know how the Jordan trip goes."

I greeted both of them before proceeding through to the security line. After processing through security, I stopped and purchased some chewing gum and I was looking at the list of candidates and the schedule that Jewel had prepared for me. I had an interview scheduled about two hours after my scheduled time of arrival and then it was at one hour intervals from there.

After I was seated in the first class section of my Delta Airlines flight, I was just reflecting back on how life had gone for me over the past year. I did some serious thinking as to how I came to be where I am now. I was in such deep thought that I didn't even read the newspaper, which was totally unlike me.

The flight to ATL was nice and peaceful. I did not pig out on the Delta peanuts like I normally would. I just drank my water and that was pretty much it. I landed, picked up my rental car, and drove on out to Stockbridge, Georgia which was only about a twenty minute drive from Hartsfield International Airport.

I arrived at my Stockbridge office without fail. The administrator, whom Jewel and I hired after our first trip was there to greet me and she provided the same itinerary that Jewel had given me. I spoke with Leslie about thirty minutes, as she was updating me on anything she thought was important. Afterwards, she left me alone and I just went over the resumes of the applicants again as I was gathering my thoughts and questions to ask.

Roughly thirty minutes after Leslie left my office, she rang the intercom.

"Yes, Leslie," I replied.

"Mr. Carter, your first candidate has arrived. I was wondering if you wanted to see her ahead of time as she was forty-five minutes early."

I cleared my throat and told Leslie to give me ten more minutes and I would come out to introduce myself. I quickly organized my desk and put away all the resumes and went over the questions in my mind that I would ask. My plan was to ask each and every candidate the same question. After I felt comfortable with my office setting, I went out to meet my first candidate.

I opened the door to my office and there sat the second most beautiful woman I had ever seen in my life. She was sitting in a comfortable waiting chair with her legs crossed while looking into an office magazine. She had on a burgundy skirt suit that had subtle, thin and lightly toned stripes that matched the red high heel shoes she wore. She was showcasing a cleavage that was out of this world. Her hair was thick and nicely laid with curls in the front banks and looped curls at the ends. She was racking, stacking and packing. I mean this woman was electrifying, mesmerizing, and magnetizing all in one. She was of Italian descent but she was dark in complexion like a fully tanned Caucasian. I went over to meet her and I extended my hand.

"Hi Mrs. Mayberry, I'm Jamie Carter but please call me JR."

She stood up, as she did not see me coming at first and extended her hand.

"Hi JR, I'm very pleased to meet you."

"Why don't we assemble in my office and we will press forward with the interview."

"Okay, sounds good to me," she said.

We both went into my office and of course I let her walk ahead of me. I can't lie. Baby gurl was banging all upside a nigga's head. This may seem like some sort of lust or fantasy but this felt differently than something so simple.

We sat down in an enclosed area of my office where there were nice chairs and a coffee table that served as the centerpiece.

"So Mrs. Mayberry," she interrupted me and said, "please call me Doralee for I am no longer married but I am divorced."

I apologetically replied, "I'm sorry, for I did not know."

"Oh that's okay JR! It has not been that long since it was official so don't even bother to apologize."

She sat right in front of me but for some reason I felt very intimidated although I was the one conducting the interview. I probably should have just sat behind my big desk like I had planned, but I didn't. I imagined that Doralee was about 30 years old, which was kind of young for what I had in mind as far as a regional manager was concerned.

"Okay Doralee, can you tell me about yourself."

The first thing she did when I said that was cross her legs. She had the nicest, phatest, juiciest legs that I have seen in awhile. I mean, since seeing Evelyn's legs. Her legs just looked like they had vanilla ice cream all over them and I loved the taste of vanilla ice cream. The sad part is that when she started talking I did not really pay attention to a word she said. Instead, I found myself trying to hide my focus on her deep, inner thigh which she covertly flashed a couple of times.

When I was not looking at her thighs, I was glancing at her crease, her lips, her eyes, her hair, and I was not hearing a word she said. Her lips were moving but I just could not hear her, although I pretended as though I did. She broke up my daydreaming with the following question.

"JR, I take it that you are single as well. I notice you don't have a ring on your finger and you seem so young?"

I snapped out of it in the subtlest way and I replied, "So Doralee, can you share with me what you envision this job to be all about."

She replied in a very slow but creative way.

"I think this job is about property management to the fullest: developing and modernizing the land into a nice subdivision like community and doing so in the most efficient way. I foresee this job as being a job where you manage different stages toward a final goal."

I noticed that as Doralee was talking her body was slowly but continuously moving. For instance, she kept rubbing her legs up and down up towards her thigh. I saw it initially as a nervous reaction to just being in an interview. I also noticed that she kept leaning forward and every time she did, her humvees (boobs) were standing out in the utmost way. Anyway, she kept on talking as to answering the question I had asked her. She really answered all the questions I had with deep substance and on target replies. I was very impressed with Doralee. I was so impressed that I knew the job was hers. Her youth was my only concern but then again, I'm young too. Jewel is young and Evelyn is young. In other words, I should not hold that against her.

"Doralee, how would you go about hiring your own staff here?"

She bit on every question and really gave some good replies.

While she was talking, I found my eyes gravitating back to her thighs and I noticed that she had moved so inconspicuously that she had actually created some gap between her thighs. *Hold up! Wait a minute. Doralee was not wearing any panties. Lights Out, Game Ova, she's got the job!*

I still did not think she realized what she was doing because she was moving so slowly and I just think she was so nervous. I was content as to what I saw and she gave me all her information again.

I concluded the interview and before she walked out she turned to me and said, "So JR, how long will it be before you hire and how many more candidates do you have to interview?"

"I will let you know within a week's time Doralee. You were the first of ten candidates."

She turned around and said, "I was. Well, I feel at such a disadvantage because how will you remember me if I'm the first of ten candidates?"

"Doralee, not to worry for I have my ways of remembering you. All candidates, whether first or last will be given the same opportunity."

"JR, is there anything else I can do to get this job. I really would love it and I would do a superior job. Just please give me a chance and I will not prove you wrong."

"Thanks for the words Doralee and I will keep that in consideration."

"Can I call to check on the job if I don't hear anything after a period of time?"

"Sure Doralee, matter of fact take my card and feel free to call to check on our decision."

She took the card and then said, "I don't see a cell phone number up here. I would like to call direct to you to get the news."

Without hesitation, I wrote my cell phone number on the back of the card. She received it and I escorted her out the office. Just before I could reach the door, Doralee turned around and dropped a pen and quickly picked it up. She bent down right in front of me and boy did I accidentally get an eye full of her humvees.

Damn, I thought to myself but I think she noticed my expression. This Italian woman was bad in a lot of ways. I had to snap out of it though but I sure did not seem to want to.

She finally left and I was really done for the day. In other words I was mentally tired after that one interview, but I went ahead and interviewed two more and asked Leslie to contact the others for an early morning interview as opposed to a late evening interview.

The other two applicants were really what I had in mine in terms of a regional manager for this subdivision project. Both men were currently managers with major real estate companies and they were mutually equivalent in terms of project development experience. Those two were clearly far ahead of Doralee. Tomorrow will be a very busy day in that I have to interview the remaining seven candidates.

As I was getting drained, I begin to gather my personal belongings to leave the office. I finally did depart around 5:30 pm. My plan was to go to my hotel room and crash, as I was too tired. Once again, that was my plan.

As I was just about to leave the office, my cell phone rang.

"Hello," I said.

"Hi JR, this is Doralee. You do remember me from the interview earlier today?"

"Of course I remember you Doralee. How could I forget you?"

She chuckled a bit.

"I was wondering if we could just take off our roles as we were earlier today and be friends. I know you are visiting the area and I was wondering if you had dinner plans."

MMMM! I really did not even think about dinner plans. I had in mind driving through a fast food establishment prior to going to my hotel room and calling it a day. Then again, I had to be careful. This could be a ploy for her to try and influence my decision on the management position. As I thought about the job however, it was kind of funny how she went from having the job to not even being a contender as I talked with seemingly more qualified applicants.

"Well actually Doralee, I was going to just hit like a McDonald's enroute to my hotel room and then rest for the evening."

"JR, don't you dare yield to the fast food temptation when I have a better offer for you right here at my place."

I must admit I was curious as to what she had in mind although I knew I was not about to take her up on her offer. I guess I wanted to do a little flirting just to see where she was coming from and what she had in mind.

"Well Doralee, what exactly did you have in mind although I can't really make any promises."

"I am in the process of cooking my family's heirloom recipe of Neapolitan Pastiera and Lamb Roast with Pecorino, a dinner that will clearly be one of the best ever, topped off with a vintage bottle of Castello-Brolio wine. You probably have never heard of the dish but trust me you will love the taste of it."

Now, I must admit I had a clear weakness for Italian food along with the wine. However, I really had to take the high road and not even go there. The thought of going there and something happening really placed a lot of fear in my heart.

"JR, are you there?"

"Yes Doralee, I am here. I think I'm going to pass on dinner. Besides, I am so tired from the flight plus the interviewing that I would desire to be knocked out sleep by 8 pm tonight."

"JR, I understand. By the way how far is your drive from the office to the hotel? You do realize the traffic on I-85 is terribly stacked up by now. I would hate for you to be on the highway for hours. Just keep in mind its peak hours traveling south to North on that highway."

I must admit Doralee did remind me of the hectic traffic Jewel and I experienced the last time we were here. We were totally clueless and spent more time on the highway than necessary all because we did not travel via I-85 during the best traveling hours. Fortunately, that experience was why Jewel had me booked in a Hampton Inn just a few more miles south of here.

"Doralee, you are right on point about the traffic but I'm traveling just a few miles further South to my room in the Hampton Inn Hotel so thus I will be fine. I don't even plan to go anywhere but straight to my room after hitting up a fast food restaurant."

"Are you sure JR? I mean I live just five minutes from your office, which is another reason why that job would be so convenient for me. Oopps, I forgot. We are not talking about the job. Anyway, I tell you what. I will check on you later to make certain you got in okay, fair enough?"

Well, I really did not need Doralee checking in on me but at this stage I just wanted to get off the phone with her and I saw this as a quick exit.

"Fair enough Doralee! I need to run now and get situated. It was nice talking with you."

She finally hung up the phone and boy was I relieved.

Honestly, I did not trust myself around Doralee. She has what I call flaming beauty, which could only burn someone like fire. I did not want to jeopardize anything at this juncture of my status quo. Thus, I finally got out the office and went out to my rental car.

When I got to the rental car I noticed an envelope underneath my windshield wiper. I quickly opened the envelope and it was from Doralee. It was a thank you card for the interview but what really captured my attention was the words at the bottom of the inside layer of the card. It read, "Please forgive me but did anyone tell you that you are so powerfully attractive. I hope your significant other, if you have one, is taking real good care of you because I know I would."

That was nice of Doralee. Wow, powerfully attractive? Now I got to admit that was a first that anyone had ever coined to describe me. I read the card and studied it as I noticed it also had some nice perfume fragrance attached that clearly outdid the new car fragrance that existed in my rental. By my honest estimation I presumed the card to be totally inappropriate for business matters but it did make a stab as far as her making her interests known. Then again, what do I care? I am a happily spoken for man.

***

I arrived at the Hampton Inn Hotel after driving through McDonald's. I got my suitcase and went to my room and took a nice bath, just soaking in the efforts of the day. I practically almost fell asleep in the tub. Directly following my bath, I found ESPN on the television and I crashed in the bed.

***

My phone rang and it woke me up around 8:50pm. At

first, I just let the phone ring, as I did not expect anyone to be calling me on the hotel line. I expected Evelyn, Ricky, or Jewel to call my cell after the game so I did not answer the hotel phone. Then, I noticed the phone just kept ringing and I was somewhat startled and I eventually answered it.

"Hello."

"Sir, this is Carlos from downstairs. I have been ringing your phone for awhile but I have a guest here who would like to speak with you."

MMMM! A guest downstairs for me? I begin to wonder who in the world could that be. I had no idea whatsoever but I did not want to confuse the desk clerk.

"Okay Carlos, put them on."

"Hi JR, how are you doing?"

To my surprise, it was Doralee. She was sounding all bubbly and everything.

"Hi Doralee, I was knocked out cold and sleeping hard and good."

"I figured you were and I just brought a plate by for you because I knew that fast food would not last long."

"Doralee, that is quite alright. I am still full from McDonald's. Let me pass on the offer and continue my sleep?"

"JR, truly you are not going to let me come all the way over here with a plate all to be turned away by you. Come on now. I can bring the plate up in just a few minutes, drop it off and then I'm done bothering you for the night."

Jesus! This woman must be in the dictionary for persistence. I did not even want to get out of bed for nothing, not even to open the door. I was really that tired. Next thing I know the phone on her end was hung up. I thought to myself that she must have gotten the point, got upset and just hung up. I was not mad at her but instead I just rolled over and proceeded to go back to sleep. It seemed about twenty minutes later there was a knock on my room door. I was not a happy camper. I got up and opened the door and it was, *guess who*, Doralee.

"JR, I just came on up with your plate. Can you smell this?"

She lifted the plate to my nose and of course it smelled good. She also had a bottle of wine. The fact that she had on a beige trench coat did not mean fifty cent to me, at least not at this time.

"Doralee, I am sorry but I am so tired and I really need some sleep."

"No problem JR! Here is the food and wine and if I could make a quick phone call I will be out of your hair."

I took the food and wine and let Doralee into the room. I placed the food on the desk counter and while she was using the phone, I quickly used the bathroom. When I returned from the bathroom, I was still somewhat lethargic but I thought I had walked into a dream.

Doralee had taken off her trench coat and she had her back towards me while holding the phone to her ear. She had on a red thong and her butt cheeks were hanging out as though they had escaped from Rikers Island. She had on no top and when she turned around, those bazookas had a J on one side and R on the twin side. I stood there watching like I was in a Trans. Talk about lights out, game ova.

Doralee approached me with a wine glass and she served the drink to my mouth. I drank and drank and drank. Next thing I know, she was downstairs bobbing for apples. She even dipped junior in a glass of wine and she licked every crevice that existed on my lower half from my navel on down.

"See JR, I know what you need," were the words she said as she licked, sucked, and gently bit all boundaries of junior. I was a vegetable. Its as if my mind was saying, "no, hell no" but my body was saying, "yes, oh hell yeah." My body clearly won that battle. I was powerless with Doralee. She guided me to every stage of sex. She sat on my face and I ate her coochie like a starving man. I licked her clit it seemed a thousand times as her juices were flowing all over my face.

She then positioned herself in a position she called the power driver position where her legs went up near her head as she laid on her back and I just pounced down on that coochie, going deep between her folds. Her bazookas were bouncing all over the bed and as I was driving into her like a hammer driving a nail into wood. I laid my junior across her with her legs angled back towards her head and I thrusted with all my energy as though I was freeing myself from demonic spirits.

"Give it to me baby, get all up in dere! Bounce it baby, bounce it hard," she was thwarting those words out without any pattern.

Then, she got on top of me and I rolled her forward so at least one of those bazookas was in my mouth. I lifted her body up in the air with my muscular thrusts that quickly went into hyperspeed, which is when she just went crazy with all types of noises.

"Oh, Oh, Oh, F…me baby, oh…oh..oh.. oh."

Then she got a little base in her voice and started scratching my skin while boldly saying, "F…me nigga! Oh..oh, u bettta f…me! You mutha f…in nigga. U betta f…me harder you slave ass mutha fuka…gimme all dat cock. Gimme all dat cock…u trifling ass nigga…f…me hard!..hard!…hard!…suit wearing bastard..f…me harddd!…. AHAHHHHHHHHHH!"

Her coming was making me come hard and strong as I released the hounds all up inside of her. She screamed as though she was being attacked. Wow, she seemed to have released a lot of tension as she called me all kinds of names while slapping my butt and scratching my chest.

She was so loud that I'm surprised the hotel management did not come and warn us to be quiet. We must have screwed like that about four times all through the night. It was so darn good that I clearly lost all sight of who I was and where I was and what was going on in my life.

***

I woke up the next morning to the phone ringing. I unconsciously answered the phone like it was a natural reaction to stop the noise.

"Hello," I said.

"JR, where have you been? We left all sorts of messages on your cell phone. It's a good thing Jewel had the information to the hotel or we would have been sending out an APB out on you," Evelyn said over the phone.

"Hey honey, I have just been busy interviewing and I did not realize how draining this was," I said. Then, out of the blue I heard a yawning sound and I looked over my shoulder and there was Doralee rolling over like a little baby in a comatose state of sleep.

I quickly covered the speaker to the phone, as I was surprised to see her there. I almost urinated in my drawers, all to realize I didn't have any on. I panicked like a pimp being caught by the cops and knew the first thing I had to do was get Evelyn off the phone.

"JR, are you there?" she said.

"Yeah baby, ahhhm, let me call you back honey okay. I got to find my cell phone. I think I left it in the car."

"Okay JR, I can't wait to tell you about the game and Jordan."

"What? Oh yeah, do give me the skinny on the game. I will call you right back. Love you!"

I hung up the phone and just stared at Doralee. She was sleeping like an angel in heaven, so peacefully. I asked myself what in the world am I doing here as though I had literally woke up from a dream.

I battled my mind into thinking that nothing at all happened on last night but all evidence indicated that something did happen. Doralee's perfume, her juices, and any other kind of evidence were all over my junior and me.

I thought to myself, *God, I am so screwed.*

Doralee rolled over and put her hand between my legs and I grabbed her hand.

"Hey baby, did you sleep good last night?

"Doralee, you have to leave right now. No, I have to leave right now."

I got up from the bed very abruptly and she replied, "but JR, its 6:30am in the morning. Where are you going so early? Your first interview is not until 9am and your drive is only ten minutes up the road."

Okay, I'm wondering to myself how did she know what time my first interview was. I was so upset with myself moreso than her. I felt like I had been had!

"Doralee, this is wrong! This is so very wrong. Please leave so I can collect my faculties."

She got up out of the bed all butt naked and everything. She approached me as to try and hug me and said, "but sugar daddy there is nothing wrong with us. We made love because we both felt it for one another and we both needed it."

I pushed her away as she tried to hug me. I was not feeling it.

"Doralee, I am going to take a shower and I'm going to

ask you one more time to leave and if you are still here when I return from my shower I will call security."

"JR, why are you stressing baby? Okay, I will leave but let me remind you that you did what you wanted to do. It was all over your face the first time you introduced yourself to me. That's when the screwing really started. We just went through the motions on last night from what we really felt together in your office. You wanted me which is why you kept staring between my thighs."

I threw my hand as to push her off and I went to take a shower. I had to take a shower and try and clean the very filth of infidelity off my body. I never scrubbed my body so hard before in my life, trying to cleanse myself of what seemed to be the dirtiest smut I have ever been apart of.

I stayed in that shower for at least a half hour. Afterwards I got out the shower and checked to see if Doralee had left and I was relieved that she had. I quickly got dressed and went downstairs to my rental car to get my cell phone. There were numerous messages left on my cell phone from Jewel to Evelyn to Ricky to Coach Lawson. I listened to all there messages and then I returned to my hotel room and called Evelyn.

"Hey Evelyn, how are you?" I said.

"No JR, the question is how are you? Did you just call me Evelyn? That's different. You normally just say baby. Hold on for a minute. Here is Ricky."

Damn! I messed up already by calling her name in a formal way. Shoot! I am so paranoid right now that it's clearly unhealthy for me.

"Hey JR, did you know that Michael Jordan attended the game on last night? I got to shake his hand and he gave me a real nice compliment."

"Wow Ricky, that is good! Not many kids your age get to meet his airness," I said. "What was the compliment Ricky?"

"Oh! He said that I would break all his records if I keep playing the way I'm playing. We meet with him later on this evening to talk about the shoe deal."

"Ricky, how was the game on last night? Did you guys win?"

"Yes Sir! It was real close but we pulled it out. Hey JR, Jewel is signaling for me to give her the phone. I got to leave for school anyway because I'm running late. I'll talk with you later today. Are you gonna have your phone on this time?"

God, I was holding steady until he asked me that one question. Tears just rushed down my face and I had to keep it tight because I did not want to convey to anyone my current state.

"Son, I will for certain have my phone on this evening. I made a mistake and left it in the car, my bad," I said.

"Okay JR, I got to go. Here is Jewel." Ricky gave the phone to Jewel.

"Hello there Mr. MIA (missing in action). I realize you done talked to your family and all but how in the hell do you justify not returning your business partner's phone calls. I'm not going to be as easy on you as Evelyn was. I want to know where the hell have you been?"

"Evelyn, it's been real busy here. My mind is so stressed and tired," I said.

Jewel interrupted me and said, "I can tell you are tired JR, calling me Evelyn." *Ouch! I am really screwing up, calling Jewel by Evelyn's name.* "You need to get some rest before you finish interviewing. I just wanted to tell you that our first public relations effort with Jordan went very well and we meet later today to talk the specifics of the shoe deal," Jewel echoed.

"Sounds good Jewel. I also understand the game went real well on last night?"

"Ricky had a monsta game! That's what I heard one of the news reporters say. They almost lost but he stole the ball and went coast to coast for a slam-dunk with nine seconds left in the game. He was absolutely phenomenal."

I was glad to hear that about Ricky and I was still slightly nervous about my situation.

"JR, let me give you back to Evelyn as I have to leave right away."

"Hey baby, you sound like you need to get some rest and get on back home. Will you be finished today?" Evelyn inquired.

"I am definitely trying to get back tonight. I don't care how late it is. I got seven to interview today and I'm beating feet to the airport directly afterwards. Look baby, I need to run now as I am running late but I will call back later on after I'm done, okay."

"Okay baby! Take it easy honey and don't stress too hard over this. Take care of yourself. I miss you," Evelyn said.

"I miss you too baby. Bye, bye!"

I got off the phone with Evelyn and got myself together for the rest of the day. I checked out of the hotel and rushed to my office in Stockbridge.

***

I finished up at the office after interviewing seven other candidates. These men were very competitive and I got a chance to feel them all out. Honestly, I'm at a stalemate as far as selecting the manager. The only certainty that I knew was that it would not be that trifling hoe. I would show Jewel my notes on each candidate with exception of the one on her and then I will let Jewel choose from those candidates.

They all pretty much had the same credentials and

similar experience. I may lean on one vice another based on their interview performance. Jewel called as I was headed to return my rental car just prior to catching my evening flight back to Texas.

"JR, the meeting with Jordan was such a success. I was totally wrong about what they had to offer as he literally brought out all the goods in his effort to land Ricky. I was very pleased. We can discuss the details when you get back but I just wanted you to know the deal."

"Cool Jewel! I'm sure Ricky was ecstatic to be their talking with Jordan."

"Oh JR, Ricky was in heaven, just smiling all over the place. You could have threatened to take away his PS2 games and he still would have been smiling. JR, what's wrong? You seem somewhat different. You know I know you now."

Dang, Jewel was right. I feared being around her because she really did know me well. Its almost like she had radar locked on to my emotions and could tell where I was mentally at all times. Nevertheless, I had to keep this secret with me. I had to take this one straight to my grave.

"Jewel, I'm just tired. Interviewing ten people within two days was a lot of work. I know you told me to take longer and I should have but I was ready to get back to yawl. I miss my peeps, you know."

"I know JR. I just wanted to tell you that if you need to talk, you know I'm here for my big brother. You understand?"

"Of course I do Jewel. I'll see you tonight and thanks for the update."

I dropped the rental car off at the airport and I had just cleared security. I called Coach Lawson to check in since he called me.

"Coach Lawson, this is JR. How's it going?"

"What's up JR? I was wondering why I had not heard from you. Did you get my message?"

"I sure did Charlie. I have just been real busy. How is everything?"

"Everything is fine JR. You know Ricky took us to the semifinals right? Well, I just thought I'd let you know how he took over the game once again. Belonte had a good game as well but he was out of his league trying to guard Ricky. I could not believe the coach went man to man in the late stage of the game. Ricky schooled that soon to be Duke freshman, as he erupted for 33 points. The most miraculous nine seconds of basketball came when Ricky stole the ball from Belonte and went coast to coast and finished with a Tommy Hawk slam dunk at the buzzer."

"Coach, this sounded like a very close game?"

"It was JR because everybody got in foul trouble except Ricky. He was really the only one that had a good game. We will need more from the other players if we are going to continue to advance. At one point, Ricky called his own huddle after I called a timeout and he pointed his finger in the chests of seniors, reminding them that if we lose they were done with their high school career and who wants to end it on a game that we gave away. I tell you what. I heard what he said and he pretty much inspired me, as we were behind by about five points with one minute left. As you know..."

I had to interrupt Charlie as time was zooming right on by. "Charlie, I will call you later. I'm at the airport and I got to board now as I head back home."

"Okay JR, I'll talk with you later. Bottom line, another Ricky Lyles show. Let me know how the Jordan deal works out. We were honored to have him in the gym tonight."

I said my goodbye to Charlie as I was walking onto the

aircraft. I was still in a state of worry and concern. I really needed to talk with someone to get this out my system but I really didn't know of anyone I could tell without him or her judging me or without me worrying about them viewing me differently.

I definitely could not talk to Julie about it, for she might nail me for poor judgment. I could not talk to Jewel because she might question my mentoring influence upon her and I sure could not tell Evelyn. She would call off the wedding and probably break up with me for good. The only person I could foresee talking to is Loke. He will be shocked and may even mock me for a minute but I know he will keep it with us. Then again, I need to make for sure he don't intend to tell Julie. I may need to rethink that move.

CHAPTER 27
Back Home Again

I arrived at the airport in Houston to be greeted by my posse (Jewel, Evelyn, and Ricky). Jewel surprised me with a basketball in her hand that she was carrying. Upon further study, I realized that she had gotten Michael Jordan's autograph for me. It was such a nice gesture. I thanked her as I acted like a kid in the candy store.

"JR how was the trip?" Ricky asked.

"It was okay Ricky but very tiresome. I think I got tired from the flight over and then the mental drain of interviewing. I was really absent minded regarding the stress that accompanied interviewing so many people within short time periods."

"Well JR, have you devised a short list from the ten folks you interviewed?" Jewel asked.

"Not really Jewel but I got some notes and I figure you and I could sit down and select the best candidate." Jewel looked so surprised as her face lit up.

"JR, you mean you have not already selected the manager and told them they had the job. I thought that, knowing you, the job would already be given to someone but I'm honored that you are considering my inputs more and more. I'm so proud of you," Jewel said.

"Well JR, Jordan was looking good with them nice suits he wore. It was quite an experience listening and conversing with him. I think he assured all of us that he had Ricky's best interest at heart. He seemed to think that Ricky will be big in the NBA one day soon," Evelyn said.

"Yeah JR, I think Michael Jordan is really cool. He shared a lot of things with me on the game. He even shared with me some things he did when he was younger. Guess what JR! He gave me his cell phone number and said I could feel free to call him anytime. He asked me if I had one and I told him I did but mom took it away from me."

"Ricky, first of all, you will not be calling Michael Jordan okay. Get that out yo mind. He was just being nice," Evelyn quickly expressed.

Ricky interjected again, "I don't think so mom. Jewel did you think he was just being nice? You were there when he said that."

"Ricky, I think he was sincere but your mom is just telling you to be cautious. You should not be calling him without going through me or your mom or JR. If he calls you, he has to come through us. That's fair."

I must admit that hearing these voices brought so much joy to my heart. This was my family and this was where I needed to be, surrounded by them and talking about life's basic problems. This is what I missed even over the past two days. God knows I love these people and would hate to do anything to jeopardize their love, if I haven't already secretly done that.

***

I felt good being back but I must admit the greatest battle I experienced of late was the battle of the mind, as I was still trying to comprehend what happened on that dreadful night at the hotel.

"JR, is everything okay?" Evelyn asked, as we were getting ready for bed.

"Sure Evelyn, I'm just trying to resolve the hiring dilemma regarding the trip I just returned on. It will truly be a very tough decision. I asked Jewel to take a hard look at my notes and perhaps we can come to the right choice."

"Wow, I have never seen you so mentally absorbed in work before and you have more dynamic issues going on with your business here than just selecting a manager." Evelyn was truly correct in every respect possible. I could not give her any clue as to what was really bothering me however.

"I guess I was also feeling nervous about the wedding. Its just normal human nature I guess," said I, thinking that the upcoming marriage would be the perfect cover as to why I was so distracted.

"JR, if you are having second thoughts, we really don't have to do this now. I'm serious. I want you to be totally certain of your decision," Evelyn sincerely disclosed.

Okay, that excuse served its purpose but it has perhaps impacted a decision on a much greater scale. I had to rope this ship back in to where it should be.

"Baby, I have no second thoughts about marrying you nor about the time. I'm just mentally involved in a lot of things, that's all. Everything is fine baby."

"JR, is there anything I can do to assist you?"

"Evelyn," I kissed her on the cheeks and said, "everything is fine baby. It is all good in the hood."

"JR, I keep telling you to lose that phrase. You got Ricky saying that too. We don't live in the hood any more. I'm not sure if you ever did, but we did and I don't acknowledge that as anything to brag about."

We embraced one another in bed and fell asleep all wrapped up in each other's arms.

CHAPTER 28
Loke - My Boy?

Loke, it's not that simple man. I'm just trying to figure out whether or not I am really ready for marriage." I stopped by Loke's house after calling to have a face-to-face and man-to-man talk. I had to see somebody and Loke had scheduled himself a day off. He was somewhat cranky after screwing some honey all night.

"JR, you can just stop even thinking about whether or not you are ready for marriage. You are more ready than anybody. That's a done deal so stop contemplating unless I'm not hearing the full picture."

The only subject I mentioned to Loke was that I was having second thoughts about marriage. He initially started laughing as one of his honeys left the room and we got heavy into conversation.

"Well Loke, I need to be more straight with you."

"JR, you are as straight as any guy I know so what exactly are you trying to say?"

"Well, before I say anything, can you tell me what you doing with a woman up in here if you are so much in love with Julie?" Loke busted out laughing and then he sipped on his drink.

"JR, Julie has not returned not one, not two, not any of my many phone calls. She is obviously not interested. Besides, I had to reevaluate my interests in her."

"You mean in relation to your interests in everybody else right?" I made that comment with much sarcasm.

"No good buddy, good shoes! Have a seat and let me give you my story. Bottom line, I lost my wife to a white man. I caught them in the parking lot of her job. I thought it was all business but later on that night she asked me for a divorce."

I was very shocked beyond my years and I did not have the words for Loke.

"Get out! Loke, you have got to be kidding me!"

"Nope JR, it went down like that. I bet you thought she left me because I was cheating on her but that was not the case. I was loyal to my wife and as faithful as any saint could have been. Case and point, I never, ever cheated on my wife. Her sending me packing like that hit right at my male ego and psyche. I'm certain I have not recovered from that yet as I tend to seek comfort in sleeping with a lot of women. Just pursuing the comfort alone is like being in a bottomless pit."

"Wow Loke, that had to be really tough for you. I see what you are saying but I am still trying to understand the relationship of this conversation to Julie."

"JR, you think about it. Black woman, white man in my wife's case and in my case with Julie it would be black man, white woman."

"Loke, are you trying to pay your wife back?" He sipped on his drink again.

"JR, I don't know. Sometimes I feel like I'm trying to pay my wife back and the rest of society that enslaved our ancestors years ago as well. I don't know."

"I feel ya Loke but Julie ain't one to treat that way. She is very special and her roots link back to us so I beg you to please don't even go there unless your heart is truly in it."

Loke just stared out into space and then he said, "look,

you didn't come here to talk to me about Julie did you? You have nothing to worry about because as I said, she has not responded to me and I've practically given up. Now, enough of my single life drama, what's your problem?"

"Well Loke, can I get a drink first?" He looked at me as shocked as I felt deep within.

"Sure, excuse my manners but I figured it was way too early for you be drinking especially since you are not a true drinker. You kind of hitting it early aren't you?"

"Yeah, I guess I am but I'm not doing too much work today. I just have to sit down with Jewel and go over some resumes to select for this management position. That's what I was doing in Georgia, interviewing candidates. Besides, it's Friday and I'm tired. I don't plan to even leave the housing complex today. I just want to chill and reflect."

"Well in that case, try some of this stuff." I looked at the bottle and I could not read the words as they were written in another language. Thus, I had to ask Loke, "what is this stuff?"

"Its called BOONYOWH! I need to caution you though; this drink is not for people like you. It is terribly strong. Just try it and let me know what you think."

He poured out some in a glass and handed it to me. I sipped it and then I took another sip.

"MMMMM! This is some nice stuff Loke."

He sat back down across from me in his living room area. Loke looked at me as though he could tell something was wrong, but he did not ask. I knocked that drink down real fast and that got an illicit response from Loke.

"Whoa playa! That's some strong stuff now. It has a delayed kick that will knock you up side yo head. You want to drink this next glass nice and slow. It will seethe into your personality like an invited guest if you drink it right."

Loke poured me another glass. I followed his advice and slowly drank it this time.

"Okay playa, what's going on? You are drinking before 10 in da moan? Something is wrong with you. Are you really this tripped up over getting married or what? Once again, if you really feel like it's not your time JR, call it off man. Don't rush into nothing."

"Loke, I went to Georgia and had an affair with another woman," I rushed the words right out of my mouth and invited his response like a sinner inviting a preacher to lay hands on him.

He had a very shocked look on his face but Loke was a soldier and he knew that overreacting would shut me down from confessing.

"You serious! Well, treat it like it was your bachelor's party and press on. Don't dwell on it," he calmly replied.

"Loke, I can't seem to stop thinking about it. I mean, Doralee was fine as a mutha f.....! I tried so hard to resist her but it was as though she took control of my body. My head was hurting so hard because my mind said don't do it but my body was following her every command. I have never experienced that before in my life." I was looking towards the floor as I sipped on my drink.

"I take it that Doralee was the woman you slept with?" Loke asked.

I started sipping on that drink with more intensity and the more I drank the more I wanted to drink. I wanted to feel different than the way I felt and this hook was helping a nigga out, as I was feeling bad within. I was hating myself in the worst way.

"Yeah! Doralee is her name," I slowly exchanged while posing a highly distracted look on my face.

Suddenly my phone rang and at first I did not want to answer it but I knew it was probably Jewel. She was supposed to meet me at the house but I told her to call me for the exact time. I picked up the phone without checking the caller ID.

"Hello."

"Hello JR, how is my man doing?"

My body shook at the sound of her voice. Loke was staring at me as though I was in a coma and to some degree a coma would have felt better.

"Look here, I don't want you to ever call me again. Do you hear me? I have nothing to say to you and I don't want you calling me," I said harshly to that other voice on the phone.

Loke, had the most puzzled look on his face as to say who is that?

"Hold your heels now JR! I am merely calling you for one reason and one reason alone. You see, I figured that by now you would have made your decision on the management position and to my understanding, my phone should have already been ringing off the hook by now with your job offer," the other voice on the phone replied.

"Look here Doralee! I appreciate your interest in the management position but I have chosen to hire someone of a greater qualification for the job. Therefore, you do not have to worry about me calling you. Now, I have to go and I don't want you calling me ever again! Do you hear me?"

"I hear you JR but now you had better hear me. Did this other so-called highly qualified candidate suck your cock as well as I did? Did she screw you four times in one night and have you eating her coochie like a starving slave. Did she do all those things JR?"

I was in complete silence and she raised her voice and shouted, "Answer me dammit! Did she do those thangs? I want an answer now," she demanded.

"The other candidate who will get the job is not a she but a he. This conversation is over. I refuse to revisit your manipulative behavior."

She raised her voice again!

"Manipulative? Manipulative? You wanted me the moment you saw me and you know it. I just made it easy for you and gave you what you wanted. You listen here JR Carter! You got 24 hours to make me an offer for that job or else."

I quickly responded in anger and disgust, "or else what hoe? Or else what? You don't tell me what to do, you stupid Italian!"

She smoothly and calmly responded with words that made me sit down.

"JR, if I don't get an offer within 24 hours, Evelyn will have known Doralee Mayberry on a personal level," then she raised her voice and said, "do you understand what I am saying. Your wedding will never happen. If that's the way you want it, then that's the way it will be. You got 24 hours, punkass!"

Click! She hung up the phone.

I immediately drank the rest of my drink and Loke grabbed me and said, "JR, be careful man. That drink is much stronger than you currently realize. Now who in the hell was that and what did they have to say?"

I sat there looking towards the floor with my eyes staring straight out into the air.

"I'm screwed!"

Loke intervened, "talk to me man. What in the world is going on?"

"Loke, she set me up."

I got up and poured some more of that drink into my glass and Loke tried to stop me but I turned my back to him and walked away long enough to throw down another shot.

"JR, give me that bottle. You are about to be stupid drunk dude. Sit down and tell me what's going on. You can drink that whole bottle if you so desire but it will not change anything."

He tried to take the bottle away from me and I sat down while I was still in a trans.

"Loke, she said that if I did not offer her the management position, Evelyn would know her on a personal level and that my wedding would not take place."

Loke looked at me with his mouth wide open. Then, he fiercely grabbed the bottle of alcohol away from me and just started drinking it from the bottle. Then, he stood up and said, "Wait a minute. You mean to tell me that you screwed one of the interviewees for the management position. JR, please tell me you did not do that!"

Loke stood over me and I just looked straight out into the air.

"JR, do you know how many fine honeys I work with on my job. Do you know how many gorgeous women I have as customers to take care of their teeth? I have always told you that you never mix business with pleasure. I can't believe this. You screwed one of the interviewees."

He sat down beside me and started drinking from the bottle again and then he said, "you right, you are screwed. Naw, you worst than screwed. You are tow da fuck up!"

I sat there like I couldn't even move. Loke continued.

"JR, she set yo ass up. I mean, from the very start, she set you up. Then, on top of that, I heard you call her Italian. Nigga, does the word mafia mean anything to you in relation to her being Italian? You right nigga, you are totally screwed!"

I lost myself as the alcohol was starting to take its effect on me. I plunged out at Loke, while standing up and shouting, "will you please find another way to be helpful. Damn! I know

I fucked up, I said I did and I don't need you repeating the same thang to me over and over again. Besides, you supposed to be this boss playa, tell me what to do dammit and stop telling me that I'm screwed!"

Loke stood up in disgust and anger and pointed his finger at me.

"Now JR, don't even bring it here like that! I have told yo ass time after time to always keep business apart from pleasure. As much as you ran around with me, you mean yo ass didn't at least learn that lesson? I'm not the one who fucked up, you did. So don't you even come at me like I'm yo fucking problem. Yo problem is that Italian hoe that you screwed. Now tell me nigga, was the coochie that damn good to be worth all this? Hell naw! Of all the coochie out there that's drama free, yo ass had to go out there and hook up with helter skelter."

I totally lost it as the alcohol was changing me by the minute. Loke's overnight friend came running into the room but before she had a chance to separate us I had already released my right hand and it hit Loke right upside his left corner chin and he fell to the floor helplessly.

While I was quickly losing my faculties, I somehow realized that I did something that was not right. I was on the floor trying to wake Loke up when all of a sudden I did not seem to exist anymore.

***

I woke up coughing as Loke used something to run across my nose that caused me to inhale it and cough. I was in his guest bedroom while he and his lady friend were tending to my care. I was not certain as to what had happened but all I know was that my head was hurting like someone had beat me down.

"JR, say something man. Can you hear me?"

I opened my eyes and said, "what happened and where am I? Lord God, is it time for me to die or have I died already?"

Loke chuckled and so did his friend.

"You are going be fine JR. You are in my guest bedroom. Nigga you know you caught me off guard with that right hook? You tilted my chin like a mutha."

I listened to Loke but I had no clue as to what he was talking about.

"What day is it and what time is it?" I said, as I had no recollection of anything that had occurred over the past nine hours.

"Its still Friday and its about 5:30pm. Everything is fine JR. I have taken care of everything."

I really did not know what Loke was talking about so I asked him to tell me exactly what occurred so I would know what happened.

"JR, you knocked me out for a minute or so but Laurie ran to my rescue and before you had a chance to say anything to her, she clocked you good and knocked you out. Now, most of the pain you feel now is not from her punch to your chin but from that BOONYOWH that you were drinking and I cautioned you about drinking."

I had to interrupt Loke as I had several questions.

"Loke, why would I hit you? What was I drinking again?"

"You hit me because we were shouting at each other and that alcohol had gradually taken control of your mind and that's why you hit me. I didn't even see it coming because you, like me, are a lover and not a fighter. At least that was what I thought. Anyway, you got that phone call from the lady in Georgia and she had threatened to reveal your secret to your wife to be and that's when you really starting drinking and feeling the effects of that alcohol."

I laid in Loke's bed like a zombie but my senses were gradually beginning to work. I know that because I started stressing again over Doralee.

"Loke, can I get some Tylenol for the headache?"

"Sure partna!" He signaled to Laura. "Laura, can you go and get him some extra strength Tylenol and water." Laura left and got the medicine.

"Loke, I'm still in trouble man. I can't have that woman calling Evelyn."

Loke waved his hands and replied, "JR, don't even worry about it because I already took matters in my own hands."

"What?" I replied.

"JR, I got your cell phone and brought up your caller ID and I called that number to Georgia. She answered the phone and I told her in a professional manner that I was calling on your behalf and I informed her that she had the job and that we would be contacting her with an official offer in writing within the next week."

"Loke, why in the hell did you do that man? I can't hire that hoe."

"JR, you have no choice okay. Now, worst case, all I did was buy you some time. You need to go ahead, hire this hoe, press on with your wedding and inform Evelyn at a later time. Now, you tell me a better way to fix this mess."

"What am I going to tell Jewel as my reason for hiring her?"

"JR, that's small fish playa. You got bigger problems to be concerned with than to worry about justifying your reason for hiring someone to Jewel."

I looked up into the ceiling again and as I saw it, Loke was right on point. I had to quiet that woman down and pacify her temporarily and figure out a way to deal with her in the future. As I was looking straight up into the ceiling, Loke informed me that he called my house and told Jewel and Evelyn that I had left my cell phone in my car at his house, as we were supposedly shopping for the wedding. I'm sure they bought that because I always leave my cell phone in the car. Also, the alibi for coming home with nothing will be the car that I have already purchased for Evelyn.

"Ahhhhhh! Now JR, there is a tidbit of information that I forget to tell you. When I informed that Georgia woman about the job, she emphasized to me that she could only take the job at a salary of $150K. I told her we would present that in writing and call it a deal. I hope that was okay by you."

"Hell naw it ain't okay by me Loke. The job called for $100K and she knew that before she interviewed."

"Well guess what playa? When you decided to Tai datass up, you just increased the salary of the job. I suggest you live with it and press on until this wedding is over with and then re-engage. You do not want this hoe messing up your wedding plans. Trust me! She was ready to engage."

All of a sudden I felt like I needed two more Tylenol tablets as my head was killing me. Then, on top of all that, Loke had to hit me one more time with the most depressing thought that had yet to cross my mind.

"Now JR, I just want to make certain we circle the wagons on this hoe. I heard her say that you screwed her four times throughout the night. Playa, please tell me you had on protection?" I immediately thought to myself, *Damn, I'm screwed. Lights Out! Game Ova!*

CHAPTER 29
Happy People

The wedding stage was set. Loke had just entered the guest bedroom where he and I were getting dressed for the wedding. He was running late as usual.

"JR, it took me forever to get in here. Do you know you got a serious crowd of folks out there for this wedding? Hey man, I didn't know you knew R Kelly?"

I looked at him and said, "what?"

"Dude, R Kelly is out there putting on a concert. He just finished singing his hit song *Marry Me*. He got the women crying and everything."

I was completely surprised and had no clue who the entertainment was.

"Loke, that is news to me. R Kelly is one of my favorite male singers, of course next to Luther, but Jewel is responsible for all this."

We talked and got dressed at the same time. I could not have been more excited.

"Loke, you got the ring?"

He looked at me like I offended him.

"JR, ain't nobody gave me no ring."

I panicked, "Oh shoot! I don't remember what I did with the ring. Oh my goodness!"

I started looking all over for the ring and I even went into my bedroom as Evelyn and the ladies were in a guest room on the other side of the house. Ricky and Jewel saw me but I did not see them.

"There you are," said Jewel.

I immediately confessed to Jewel in a state of urgency.

"Jewel, I think I lost the ring. I last remember it in my room but I cannot find it. We got to get another one fast."

She put her hands on her hips and said, "JR, I got the ring. You go back and continue getting dressed and chill out. When I come and get you and Loke, I will give him the ring."

Phew! I felt so relieved. I was so scared that I had lost it and I was panicking like crazy.

"Thank You Lord! Jewel, what would I do without you?" I kissed her on the cheek and she pushed me away.

"JR, I do not have time for your affection. I'm trying to marry your butt off. Back up and let me do my job. Come on Ricky, I need you to post yourself with the others so you can escort folks into the seating area."

She turned and walked off and I said, "Jewel, was that R Kelly I heard out there?"

She turned around and smiled with a high thumbs up. I could not believe it. I returned to the room with Loke and he was almost dressed and I filled him in on the plan regarding the ring.

***

Here I am standing at the designated altar in the courtyard of my house. The runway ran parallel with the length of the swimming pool and the entire place was decorated with bright white and gold colors. It was so beautiful. I was so glad that this day had finally come. I was so nervous and scared too but anxious to get this formality out the way.

My mom, sister, and other family members were present.

Even my dad made it. Mom and I never spoke again after that last telephone conversation but Jewel informed me that she did reply back to the invitation. Julie's brother Corey made it in town and he and Jewel had been spending some time together. They just hit off from the moment they met.

Julie seemed so happy. She wanted to give me a gift and I said, "No, you have given me more than you can ever know." Julie and her brother looked so much alike. Although she was white and he was light skinned black, they could pose as identical twins. He had a sort of Will Smith swagger about him. Both he and Julie acted just like siblings too and both were blessed with business minds. Her father sat right beside them and I could also tell that Julie was not about to allow anyone to separate her from her family again.

Julie and Loke had been casually and privately dating. I hope its nothing serious but Loke was very conservative at his pool party. He had about thirty-five women there shaking it up like a saltshaker. It was truly a jamming affair but we were both under good behavior. I never thought Loke could be so tamed.

Now, my bachelor's party, well let's just say we were both cautious, due to my ATL drama. I was more and more sold on Julie's idea of Ricky stepping up to the NBA. His team was now 29-0, about to finish the state playoff run and he was packing the stands wherever he played. He was averaging 33 points and 14 boards, 4 assists, and 5 steals per game. Here I am at the altar, waiting for my bride to make that walk down the isle to holy matrimony.

Instead of a traditional wedding song, she marched in on Alicia Keys' song: "If I Ain't Got You Baby" and guess who sang the song? I was shocked when from the back of me a piano came out on a parade float adorned with white and gold wedding attire. Alicia Keys was adorned in a pink ball gown and she played that piano with a glowing smile. I could not believe it. This must be a dream. I got R Kelly and Alicia Keys at my wedding. I don't know how I'm going to afford this. Who knows, I might be broke after this wedding. Anyway, as soon as she started singing, my bride made that proverbial walk, bouncing to the rhythm of Keys' piano and she was stroking them keys hard.

I could not stop the tears from falling down my cheeks. I had to be the happiest man alive. How in the world did Jewel get Alecia Keys and R Kelly to sing at my wedding? I did about ten double takes just to make sure it was Alicia Keys although her voice made it powerfully obvious. Hell, I should be crying because the bill alone for them two would probably send me into bankruptcy. That's truly why I should be crying but I was dropping tears of joy. I looked at my mom in the audience and I thought about all those talks. I looked at her staring me down as though she was doubtful of this event. Then I would look at Evelyn as she was walking, it seemed, in slow motion down the aisle towards me. When she arrived, she just looked so angelical, so beautiful...heaven must have been missing an angel!

"Do you Evelyn Sherree Lyles take Jamie Randell Carter to be your loftily wedded husband, to love and cherish, for better and for worse, until death do you part?" the minister asked.

"I do," said Evelyn.

"I now pronounce you man and wife. You may now kiss the bride," were the popular marital words resounding from the minister's mouth.

I kissed Evelyn as though it was the kiss of life. She was so beautifully adorned. Her hair was flowing like a smooth river of never ending life. As soon as we kissed, the sounds of some thumping horns and band like music was played and on another float came Kirk Franklin and his choir singing, "We Gonna Be Just Like Jesus When We Get There." We marched down the runway to Kirk and his group tearing the crowd up. He was a showpiece too, jumping on tables and he had that choir rocking.

***

It was a glorious affair. After we took it seemed like a thousand photos we went to the reception, which was on the other side of my house where the tennis court was. It was created so nicely with the sunlight shining and everything. We arrived to R Kelly singing his chart topping hit "Happy People." It was so funny because the crowd was out on the dance floor stepping. Even Ricky got out there with Julie, her brother, and father and tried to step.

This day was truly like being in heaven for me. As the formalities ended and R Kelly, Alicia, and Kirk and company practically put on a concert, I had to ask Jewel how the heck could I afford all this. She looked at me and said, "JR, these are all compliments of Julie. She asked if she could do this because she said she knew some people who knew some people who ripped some people off."

Jewel, Evelyn, Ricky, and I all laughed at the same time. I turned around to find Julie and she stared and then winked at me. After bum rushing her and slobbing her down with kisses, I went to meet R Kelly, Alicia Keys, and Kirk Franklin. They were some great performers and I just wanted to shake their hands for making this the event of a lifetime.

***

P.S. Evelyn and I have been married for one year now.

Jewel and Corey were dating seriously. Julie and Loke were still seeing each other. I think they were getting serious, as Loke has ended all his player activity. Ricky took his team to a first time ever record of 32-0, as they met their number one archrival in the state championship.

It had to be the first time that high school teams one and two in the nation met in a state championship. Ricky's team, although undefeated were ranked second to Belmont High. Ricky exploded for 31 points on the dual McDonald's All American starting team, ripping their team to a 100—86 victory.

He also went on to become the MVP of the McDonald's All American All Star game where he blitzed his opponents for 42 points. The tougher the competition, the better Ricky played. This year, his team is again undefeated at 28-0 and about to finalize another state playoff run. Word has it that the Houston Rockets were postured to make Ricky their number one pick in the draft during this upcoming NBA draft, if he was not picked up earlier by another team. However, all communications have been addressed only to the Houston Rockets' management.

Ricky grew another two inches and was clearly the most popular high school athlete in the country as ESPN followed his every game. At 6'4" and as quick as a cat, he was not only packing the high school gymnasiums but he was getting local television coverage, radio coverages from other surrounding stations and he was handling his success like a walk in the park.

OH Yeah! Evelyn is seven months pregnant with our baby girl. Jewel still stayed at our house, as we were becoming a very strong family together. Sidney tried to come back into Jewel's life by relocating to the area. It appears that he came too late but I guess time will tell. Doralee has made her presence known and the future is still clouded with our past. The SAGA continues!

You will have to get the rest of the story in the sequel to Lights Out, Game Ova which will be entitled The Carterchronic. Stay on the lookout because it won't be long.

In addition, I will be dropping another book entitled "Sistas," all to be followed by "When Too Many Women Ain't Enough." Then, stand by for my nonfiction book, which is based on a true story and the title, is yet to be determined. Thanks for supporting my work and I promise you will not be disappointed in the future.